Praise for America's

MARY HIGGINS CLARK

and

REMEMBER ME

"Clark takes the reader on a mysterious and suspenseful ride, twisting plot after plot. . . . A fascinating climax."

—*Nashville Banner*

"Mary Higgins Clark . . . gets better with every book. . . . Her writing is so effortless that you don't realize until you race to the last sentence just how carefully she's plotted this page-turner."

—*Pioneer Press* (St. Paul)

"Like a sleek golden spider weaving an intricate, stunningly beautiful web, master storyteller Mary Higgins Clark tells a tale of murder and love, treachery and innocence, ghosts and ghouls in *Remember Me*. . . . The level of suspense is unrelenting. . . . Whether one's destination is Cape Cod, Tibet, or a hammock in the backyard, *Remember Me* is worth taking along."

—*Lexington Herald-Leader* (KY)

MARY HIGGINS CLARK

REMEMBER ME

POCKET BOOKS

New York   London   Toronto   Sydney

This book is a work of fiction. Names, characters, places and
incidents are products of the author's imagination or are used
fictitiously. Any resemblance to actual events or locales or per-
sons, living or dead, is entirely coincidental.

 POCKET BOOKS, a division of Simon & Schuster, Inc.
1230 Avenue of the Americas, New York, NY 10020

Copyright © 1994 by Mary Higgins Clark

ISBN: 0-7434-9964-6

This Pocket Books printing June 2004

10 9 8 7 6 5 4 3 2 1

POCKET and colophon are registered trademarks of
Simon & Schuster, Inc.

Front cover illustration by Tom Hallman

Manufactured in the United States of America

For information regarding special discounts for bulk purchases,
please contact Simon & Schuster Special Sales at 1-800-456-6798
or business@simonandschuster.com.

Acknowledgments

Twenty years ago I came across a book called *The Narrow Land* by Elizabeth Reynard. The myths and legends and folk chronicles I found in there are the reason this book exists. My gratitude for background material also belongs to these writers of the past: Henry C. Kittredge for his *Cape Codders: People and Their History* and *Mooncussers of Cape Cod;* Doris Doane for *A Book of Cape Cod Houses* with drawings by Howard L. Rich; Frederick Freeman for *The History of Cape Cod;* and William C. Smith for his *History of Chatham.*

Profound and heartfelt thanks to Michael V. Korda, my longtime editor, and his associate, senior editor Chuck Adams. As always, guys, sine qua non.

Garlands to Frank and Eve Metz for consistently terrific jacket design and interior design. Sainthood to Gypsy da Silva for her magnificent copy supervision.

Blessings on Eugene H. Winick, my agent, and Lisl Cade, my publicist, valued companions of this journey called writing a book.

Kudos to Ina Winick for the professional guidance

ACKNOWLEDGMENTS

to understanding post-traumatic stress disorder. Special thanks to the Eldredge Library, Sam Pinkus, Dr. Marina Stajic, the Coast Guard Group at Woods Hole, the Chatham Police Department, the Barnstable County District Attorney's office, Ron Aires of Aires Jewelers. If I didn't get any of the technicalities straight, it certainly wasn't your fault.

A tip of the hat to my daughter Carol Higgins Clark for her insight and suggestions.

And now, dear family and friends. If you Remember Me, give me a call. I'm available for dinner.

IN JOYFUL MEMORY OF
MAUREEN HIGGINS DOWLING, "MO,"
SISTER-IN-LAW AND FRIEND
WITH LOVE

*B*y 9 P.M. *the storm had broken with full force, and a stiff wind was sending powerful waves crashing against the eastern shore of Cape Cod. We're going to get more than a touch of the nor'easter, Menley thought as she reached over the sink to close the window. It might actually be fun, she thought, in an effort to reassure herself. The Cape airports were closed, so Adam had rented a car to drive from Boston. He should be home soon. There was plenty of food on hand. She had stocked up on candles, just in case the electricity went out, although if she was right about what she was beginning to suspect, the thought of being in this house with only candlelight was frightening.*

She switched on the radio, twisted the dial and found the Chatham station that played forties music. She raised an eyebrow in surprise as the Benny Goodman orchestra went into the opening notes of "Remember."

A particularly appropriate song when you're living in a place called Remember House, she thought.

1

Pushing aside the inclination to flip the dial again, she picked up a serrated knife and began to slice tomatoes for a salad. When he phoned, Adam told her he hadn't had time to eat. "But you forgot to remember," the vocalist warbled.

The unique sound that the wind made when it rushed past the house was starting again. Perched high on the embankment over the churning water, the house became a kind of bellows in a wind storm, and the whooshing sound it emitted had the effect of a distant voice calling out "Remember, Remember . . ." The legend was that over the decades that peculiarity had given the house its name.

Menley shivered as she reached for the celery. Adam will be here soon, she promised herself. He'd have a glass of wine while she made some pasta.

There was a sudden noise. What was that? Had a door blown open? Or a window? Something was wrong.

She snapped off the radio. The baby! Was she crying? Was that a cry or a muffled, gagging sound? Menley hurried to the counter, grabbed the monitor and held it to her ear. Another choking gasp and then nothing. The baby was choking!

She rushed from the kitchen into the foyer, toward the staircase. The delicate fan-shaped window over the front door sent gray and purple shadows along the wide-plank floor.

Her feet barely touched the stairs as she raced to the second floor and down the hall. An instant later she was at the door of the nursery. There was no sound coming from the crib. "Hannah, Hannah," she cried.

Hannah was lying on her stomach, her arms outstretched, her body motionless. Frantically, Menley

2

leaned down, turning the baby as she picked her up. Then her eyes widened in horror.

The china head of an antique doll rested against her hand. A painted face stared back at her.

Menley tried to scream, but no sound came from her lips. And then from behind her a voice whispered, "I'm sorry, Menley. It's all over."

1

*A*fterwards, steadfastly through the questioning, Scott Covey tried to make everyone understand just how it had happened.

He and Vivian had been napping on a quilt spread on the boat's deck, the hazy sun and gentle lapping of the water lulling them into sleepy contentment.

He had opened one eye and yawned. "I'm hot," he said. "Want to check out the ocean floor?"

Vivian had brushed her lips against his chin. "I don't think I'm in the mood." Her soft voice was lazy, a contented murmur.

"I am." He sprang up decisively and looked over the side. "It's perfect down there. Water's clear as a bell."

It was nearly four o'clock. They were about a mile off Monomoy Island. The haze of humidity lay like shimmering chiffon, but a faint breeze had begun to stir.

"I'll get my gear," Scott told her. He crossed the deck and reached down into the small cabin they used as a storage area.

Vivian had gotten up, shaking off her drowsiness. "Get my stuff too."

He had turned. "Are you sure, honey? I'm just going in for a few minutes. Why don't you just nap?"

"No way." She'd rushed to him and put her arms around his neck. "When we go to Hawaii next month I want to be able to explore those coral reefs with you. Might as well get some practice."

Later he tearfully pleaded that he hadn't noticed all the other boats had disappeared while they napped. No, he hadn't turned on the radio to check the weather.

They had been down twenty minutes when the squall hit. The water became violent. They struggled to reach the anchored boat. Just as they surfaced, a five-foot wave hit them. Vivian disappeared. He had searched and searched, diving into the water again and again, until his own air was running out.

They knew the rest. The emergency call was received by the Coast Guard as the full force of the fast-moving squall was at its peak. "My wife is missing!" Scott Covey had shouted. "My wife is missing!"

July 28th

2

*E*laine Atkins sat across the table from Adam Nichols. They were at Chillingsworth, the restaurant in Brewster where Elaine took all her important real estate clients. Now, at the peak of the Cape Cod season, every table was filled.

"I don't think you have to eavesdrop to know what they're talking about," she said quietly. Her hand moved slightly in a gesture that encompassed the room. "A young woman, Vivian Carpenter, disappeared scuba diving a couple of weeks ago. She bought her house in Chatham from me, and we became very friendly. While you were on the phone I was told that her body was washed ashore an hour ago."

"I was on a fishing boat once when someone hooked a body that had been in the water for a couple of weeks," Adam said quietly. "It wasn't a pretty sight. How did it happen?"

"Vivian was a good swimmer but not an experienced diver. Scott was teaching her. They hadn't listened to the warning on the radio about the storm. The poor guy is devastated. They'd only been married three months."

Adam raised an eyebrow. "Sounds as though it was pretty careless, to go diving just before a storm."

"Pretty tragic," Elaine said firmly. "Viv and Scott were very happy. She's the one who knew these waters. Like you, growing up she spent every summer on the Cape. It's such a damn shame. Till she met Scott, Viv was kind of a lost soul. She's one of the Carpenters from Boston. Youngest in a family of achievers. Dropped out of college. Pretty much on the outs with the family. Worked at a variety of jobs. Then three years ago, when she turned twenty-one, she came into the trust her grandmother left her. That's when she bought the house. She worshipped Scott, wanted to do everything with him."

"Including scuba diving in bad weather? What does this guy do?"

"Scott? He was assistant business manager for the

7

Cape Playhouse last year. That's when he met Viv. I guess she visited him over the winter. Then he came back for good in May, and the next thing anyone knew they were married.''

"What's his last name?"

"Covey. Scott Covey. He's from the Midwest somewhere.''

"A stranger who marries a rich girl and the rich girl dies three months later. If I were the cops I'd want to read her will fast.''

"Oh, stop," Elaine protested. "You're supposed to be a defense attorney, not a prosecutor. I saw a lot of those two. I was showing them houses. They were looking for something bigger. They were planning to start a family and wanted more room. Trust me. It was a horrible accident.''

"Probably." Adam shrugged. "Maybe I'm getting to be too much of a skeptic.''

They were sipping wine. Elaine sighed. "Let's change the subject," she said. "This is supposed to be a festive occasion. *You* look great, Adam. More than that—you look happy, content, pleased with life. Everything really is okay, isn't it? With Menley, I mean. I'm so eager to meet her.''

"Menley's a trooper. She'll be fine. Incidentally, when she gets up here, don't mention that I told you about those anxiety attacks. She doesn't like to talk about them.''

"I can understand that." Elaine studied him. Adam's dark brown hair was beginning to show flecks of gray. Like her, he'd be thirty-nine on his next birthday. Long and lean, he'd always had a quicksilver quality. She'd known him from the time they were both sixteen, when his family hired a summer housekeeper from the employment service her mother managed.

Nothing ever changes, Elaine thought. She'd noticed the glances other women had given him when he joined her at the table.

The waiter brought over menus. Adam studied his. "Steak tartare, well done," he suggested with a laugh.

She made a face at him. "Don't be mean. I was a kid when I pulled that."

"I'll never let you forget it. 'Laine, I'm awfully glad you made me come up to see Remember House. When the other place fell through I didn't think we'd hit on a desirable rental for August."

She shrugged. "These things happen. I'm just glad it worked out. I can't believe that rental I found for you in Eastham turned out to have all those plumbing problems. But this one is a real gem. As I told you, it wasn't occupied for thirty-five years. The Paleys saw the place, realized it had possibilities and picked it up for a song a couple of years ago. They'd finished the worst of the renovating when Tom had the heart attack. He'd put in twelve hours on a hot day when it happened. Jan Paley finally decided it was too much house for one person, and that's why it's on the market. There aren't that many authentic captain's houses available, so it won't last long, you know. I'm hoping you two will decide to buy it."

"We'll see. I'd like to have a place up here again. If we're going to continue to live in the city, it makes sense. Those old sailors knew how to build a home."

"This one even has a story attached to it. It seems that Captain Andrew Freeman built it for his bride in 1703 and ended up deserting her when he found she'd been engaged in hanky-panky with some guy from town while he was at sea."

Adam grinned. "My grandmother told me the early settlers were Puritans. Anyhow I won't be doing any renovating. This is vacation for us, although it's inevitable that I'll be going back and forth to the city for a few days at a time. I've got to do some work on the retrial of the Potter case. Maybe you read about it. The wife got a bum rap. I wish I'd defended her in the first place."

"I'd like to see you in action in court someday."

"Come to New York. Tell John to bring you down. When are you getting married?"

"We haven't quite set the date, but sometime in the fall. Predictably, John's daughter is less than thrilled about the engagement. She's had John to herself for a long time. Amy starts college in September, so we figure around Thanksgiving would be about right."

"You look happy, 'Laine. And you also look great. Very attractive and very successful. You're skinnier than I've ever seen you. Also your hair's blonder, which I like."

"Compliments from you? Don't ruin our relationship." Elaine laughed. "But I thank you. I am very happy indeed. John's the Mr. Right I've been waiting for. And I thank the gods that you look like yourself again. Believe me, Adam, last year when you came up after you and Menley separated, I was worried about you."

"It was a pretty rough period."

Elaine studied the menu. "This one is on Atkins Real Estate. No arguments, please. Remember House is for sale, and if you decide after renting it that it would be a great buy I get the commission."

After they'd ordered, Adam said, "The phone was busy when I tried Menley before. I'll give a quick call now."

He returned a minute later, looking troubled. "Still busy."

"Don't you have Call Waiting?"

"Menley hates it. She says it's so rude to keep telling people 'wait a minute' and going off the line."

"She has a point, but it still is mighty handy."

Elaine hesitated. "All of a sudden you seem worried. Is she really okay now?"

"She seems to be fine," Adam said slowly. "But when those anxiety attacks come, they're hell. She's practically a basket case when she relives the accident. I'll try her again in a minute, but in the meantime, did I show you a picture of the baby?"

"Have you got a picture with you?"

"Is the Pope Catholic?" He reached in his pocket. "Here's the most recent. Her name is Hannah. She was three months old last week. Isn't she a knockout?"

Elaine studied the picture carefully. "She's absolutely beautiful," she said sincerely.

"She looks like Menley, so she's going to stay gorgeous," Adam said decisively. He returned the snapshot to his wallet and pushed back his chair. "If the line's still busy I'm going to ask the operator to interrupt."

Elaine watched him wend his way through the room. He's nervous about her being alone with the baby, she thought.

"Elaine."

She looked up. It was Carolyn March, a fiftyish New York advertising executive to whom she'd sold a house. March did not wait to be greeted. "Have you heard how much Vivian Carpenter's trust fund was? *Five million dollars!* The Carpenters never talk money, but one of the cousins' wives let that slip. And Viv told people that she'd left everything to her husband. Don't you think that much money should dry Scott Covey's tears?"

3

*T*hat must be Adam. He said he'd call around now. Menley juggled the baby on her shoulder as she reached for the phone. "Come on, Hannah," she murmured. "You've finished half the second bottle. At this rate you'll be the only three-month-old in Weight Watchers."

She held the receiver between her ear and shoulder as she patted the baby's back. Instead of Adam, it was Jane Pierce, editor-in-chief of *Travel Times* magazine. As usual, Jane did not waste words. "Menley, you *are* going to the Cape in August, aren't you?"

"Keep your fingers crossed about that," Menley said. "We heard last night that the house we were supposed to rent has major plumbing problems. I never thought chamber pots were cute, so Adam drove up this morning to see what else we could get."

"It's pretty late to get anything, isn't it?" Jane asked.

"We have one ace in the hole. An old friend of Adam's owns a real estate agency. Elaine found the first place for us and swears she has a terrific replacement. Let's hope Adam agrees."

"In that case, if you do go up . . ."

"Jane, if we do go up I'm going to research another

book for the David series. I've heard so much about the Cape from Adam that I may want to set the next one there." David was the ten-year-old continuing character in a series of novels that had made Menley a well-known children's book author.

"I know this is begging a favor, Menley, but it's that special way you weave in historical background that I need for this piece," the editor pleaded.

When Menley hung up the phone fifteen minutes later, she had been talked into doing an article about Cape Cod for *Travel Times*.

"Oh well, Hannah," she said as she gave one final pat to the baby's back, "Jane did give me my first break ten years ago. Right? It's the least I can do."

But Hannah was contentedly asleep on her shoulder. Menley strolled over to the window. The twenty-eighth-floor apartment on East End Avenue afforded a stunning view of the East River and the bridges that spanned it.

Moving back to Manhattan from Rye after they lost Bobby had saved her sanity. But it would be good to get away for August. After the first terrible anxiety attack, her obstetrician had encouraged her to see a psychiatrist. "You're having what is called delayed post-traumatic stress disorder, which is not uncommon after a frightful experience, but there is treatment available, and I'd recommend it."

She'd been seeing the psychiatrist, Dr. Kaufman, weekly, and Kaufman wholeheartedly endorsed the idea of a vacation. "The episodes are understandable and in the long run beneficial," she said. "For nearly two years after Bobby's death, you were in denial. Now that you have Hannah, you're finally dealing with it. Take this vacation. Get away. Enjoy yourself. Just take your medication. And, of course, call me at any time if you need me. Otherwise, I'll see you in September."

We will enjoy ourselves, Menley thought. She carried the sleeping baby into the nursery, laid her down and quickly changed and covered her. "Now be a love and take a nice long nap," she whispered, looking down into the crib.

Her shoulders and neck felt tight, and she stretched out her arms and rotated her head. The brown hair that Adam described as being the color of maple syrup bounced around the collar of her sweat suit. For as long as she could remember, Menley had wished to grow taller. But at thirty-one she'd reconciled herself to a permanent height of five feet four. At least I can be strong, she'd consoled herself, and her sturdy, slender body was testimony to her daily trips to the exercise room on the second floor of the building.

Before she turned out the light she studied the baby. Miracle, miracle, she thought. She'd been raised with an older brother who had turned her into a tomboy. As a result she'd always scorned dolls and preferred tossing a football to playing house. She was always comfortable with boys and in her teens became the favorite confidante and willing baby-sitter of her two nephews.

But nothing had prepared her for the torrents of love she'd felt when Bobby was born and that were evoked now by this perfectly formed, roundfaced, sometimes cranky infant girl.

The phone rang as she reached the living room. I bet it's Adam and he was trying to get me while I was talking to Jane, she thought as she rushed to answer.

It was Adam. "Hi, love," she said joyously. "Have you found us a house?"

He ignored the question. "Hi, sweetheart. How do you feel? How's the baby?"

Menley paused for a moment. She knew she really couldn't blame him for worrying, still she couldn't resist taking a little jab. "I'm fine, but I really haven't

14

checked on Hannah since you left this morning," she told him. "Wait a minute and I'll give a look."

"Menley!"

"I'm sorry," she said, "but Adam, it's the way you ask; it's as though you're expecting bad news."

"Mea culpa," he said contritely. "I just love you both so much. I want everything to be right. I'm with Elaine. We've got a terrific place. A nearly three-hundred-year-old captain's house on Morris Island in Chatham. The location is magnificent, a bluff overlooking the ocean. You'll be crazy about it. It even has a name, Remember House. I'll tell you all about it when I get home. I'll start back after dinner."

"That's a five-hour drive," Menley protested, "and you've already done it once today. Why don't you stay over and get an early start in the morning?"

"I don't care how late it is. I want to be with you and Hannah tonight. I love you."

"I love you too," Menley said fervently.

After they said good-bye, she replaced the receiver and whispered to herself, "I only hope the real reason for rushing home isn't that you're afraid to trust me alone with the baby."

July 31st

4

*H*enry Sprague held his wife's hand as they walked along the beach. The late afternoon sun was slipping in and out of clouds, and he was glad he had fastened the warm scarf around Phoebe's head. He mused that the approaching evening brought a different look to the landscape. Without the bathers, the vistas of sand and cooling ocean waters seemed to return to a primal harmony with nature.

He watched as seagulls hopped about at the edge of the waves. Clam shells in subtle tones of gray and pink and white were clustered on the damp sand. An occasional piece of flotsam caught his eye. Years ago he had spotted a life preserver from the *Andrea Doria* that had washed ashore here.

It was the time of day he and Phoebe had always enjoyed most. It was on this beach four years ago that Henry had first noticed the signs of forgetfulness in her. Now, with a heavy heart, he acknowledged that he wouldn't be able to keep her at home much longer. The drug tacrine had been prescribed, and sometimes she seemed to be making genuine improvement, but several times recently she had slipped out of the house while his back was turned. Just the other day at dusk he'd found her on this beach, waist-deep in the ocean.

Even as he ran toward her, a wave had knocked her over. Totally disoriented, she'd been within seconds of drowning.

We've had forty-six good years, he told himself. I can visit her at the home every day. It will be for the best. He knew all this was true, still it was so difficult. She was trudging along at his side, quiet, lost in a world of her own. Dr. Phoebe Cummings Sprague, full professor of history at Harvard, who no longer remembered how to tie a scarf or whether she'd just had breakfast.

He realized where they were and looked up. Beyond the dune, on the high ground, the house was silhouetted against the horizon. It had always reminded him of an eagle, perched as it was on the embankment, aloof and watchful. "Phoebe," he said.

She turned and stared at him, frowning. The frown had become automatic. It had begun when she still was trying desperately not to give the appearance of being forgetful.

He pointed to the house above them. "I told you that Adam Nichols is renting there for August, with his wife, Menley, and their new baby. I'll ask them to visit us soon. You always liked Adam."

Adam Nichols. For an instant the murky fog that had invaded Phoebe's mind, forcing her to grope for understanding, parted. That house, she thought. Its original name was Nickquenum.

Nickquenum, the solemn Indian word that meant "I am going home." I was walking around, Phoebe told herself. I was in that house. Someone I know—who was it?—doing something strange . . . Adam's wife must *not* live there . . . the fog rushed back into her brain and enveloped it. She looked at her husband. "Adam Nichols," she murmured slowly. "Who is that?"

August 1st

5

Scott Covey had not gone to bed until midnight. Even so he was still awake when the first hints of dawn began to cast shadows through the bedroom. After that he fell into an uneasy doze and woke up with a sensation of tightness in his forehead, the beginning of a headache.

Grimacing, he threw back the covers. The night had turned sharply cooler, but he knew the drop in temperature was temporary. By noon it would be a fine Cape day, sunny with the midsummer heat tempered by salt-filled ocean breezes. But it was still cool now, and if Vivian were here he'd have closed the windows before she got out of bed.

Today Vivian was being buried.

As he got up, Scott glanced down at the bed and thought of how often in the three months they'd been married he'd brought coffee to her when she woke up. Then they would snuggle in bed and drink it together.

He could see her still, her scrunched up knees supporting the saucer, her back against a pile of pillows, remember her joking about the brass headboard.

"Mother redecorated my room when I was sixteen," she'd told him in that breathy voice she had. "I wanted one of these so much, but Mother said I didn't have any flair for interior decoration and brass beds were getting too common. The first thing I did when I got my hands on my own money was to buy the most ornate one I could find." Then she'd laughed. "I have to admit that an upholstered headboard is a lot more comfortable to lean against."

He'd taken the cup and saucer from her hand that morning and placed it on the floor. "Lean against me," he'd suggested.

Funny that particular memory hitting him now. Scott went into the kitchen, made coffee and toast, and sat at the counter. The front of the house faced the street, the back overlooked Oyster Pond. From the side window through the foliage he could see the corner of the Spragues' place.

Vivian had told him that Mrs. Sprague would be put in a nursing home soon. "Henry doesn't like me to visit her anymore, but we'll have to invite him over to dinner when he's alone," she had said.

"It's fun to have company when we do it together," she'd added. Then she had wrapped her arms around his neck and hugged him fiercely. "You *do* really love me, don't you, Scott?"

How many times had he reassured her, held her, stroked her hair, comforted her until, once again cheerful, she'd switched to listing reasons why she loved him. "I always hoped my husband would be over six feet tall, and you are. I always hoped he'd be blond and handsome so that everyone would envy me. Well, you are, and they do. But most important of all, I wanted him to be crazy about me."

"And I am." Over and over again he had told her that.

Scott stared out the window, thinking over the last two weeks, reminding himself that some of the Carpenter family cousins, and many of Viv's friends, had rushed to console him from the minute she was reported missing. But a significant number of people had not. Her parents had been especially aloof. He knew that in the eyes of many he was nothing more than a fortune hunter, an opportunist. Some of the news accounts in the Boston and Cape papers had printed interviews with people who were openly skeptical of the circumstances of the accident.

The Carpenter family had been prominent in Massachusetts for generations. Along the way they had produced senators and governors. Anything that happened to them was news.

He got up and crossed to the stove for more coffee. Suddenly the thought of the hours ahead, of the memorial service and the burial, of the inevitable presence of the media was overwhelming. Everyone would be watching him.

"Damn you all, we were in love!" he said fiercely, slamming the percolator down on the stove.

He took a quick gulp of coffee. It was boiling hot. His mouth burning, he rushed to the sink and spat it out.

6

*T*hey stopped in Buzzards Bay long enough to pick up coffee, rolls and a copy of the *Boston Globe*. As they drove over the Sagamore Bridge in the packed station wagon, Menley sighed, "Do you think there's coffee in heaven?"

"There'd better be. Otherwise you won't stay awake long enough to enjoy your eternal reward." Adam glanced over at her, a smile in his eyes.

They'd gotten an early start, on the road by seven. Now at eleven-thirty they were crossing Cape Cod Canal. After howling for the first fifteen minutes, an unusually cooperative Hannah had slept the rest of the trip.

The late morning sun gave a silvery sheen to the metal structure of the bridge. In the canal below, a cargo ship was slowly steaming through the gently lapping water. Then they were on Route 6.

"It was at this point every summer that my dad used to shout, 'We're back on the Cape!'" Adam said. "It was always his real home."

"Do you think your mother regrets selling?"

"No. The Cape wasn't the same for her after Dad died. She's happier in North Carolina near her sisters. But I'm like Dad. This place is in my blood; our family has summered here for three centuries."

Menley shifted slightly so that she could watch her husband. She was happy to finally be here with him. They had planned to come up the summer Bobby was born, but the doctor hadn't wanted her to be so far away in late pregnancy. The next year they'd just bought the house in Rye and were settling in, so it didn't make sense to come to the Cape.

The next summer they'd lost Bobby. And after that, Menley thought, all I knew was the awful numbness, the feeling of being detached from every other human being, the inability to respond to Adam.

Last year, Adam had come up here alone. She had asked him for a trial separation. Resigned, he had agreed. "We certainly can't go on like this, Men," he had admitted, "going through the motions of being married."

He had been gone for three weeks when she realized she was pregnant. In all that time he hadn't called her. For days she had agonized about telling him, wondering what his reaction would be. Finally she had phoned. His impersonal greeting had made her heart sink, but when she said, "Adam, maybe this isn't the news you want to hear but I'm pregnant and I'm very happy about it," his whoop of joy had thrilled her.

"I'm on my way home," he had said without a pause.

Now she felt Adam's hand in hers. "I wonder if we're thinking the same thing," he said. "I was up here when I heard her nibs was on the way."

For a moment they were silent; then Menley blinked back tears and began to laugh. "And remember how after she was born Phyllis carried on about naming her Menley Hannah." She mimicked the strident tone of her sister-in-law. "I think it's very nice to keep the family tradition of naming the first daughter Menley, but please don't call her Hannah. That's so old-fashioned. Why not name her Menley Kimberly and then she can be Kim? Wouldn't that be cute?"

Her voice resumed its normal pitch. "Honestly!"

"Don't ever get mad at me, honey," Adam chuckled. "I hope Phyllis doesn't wear out your mother." Menley's mother was traveling in Ireland with her son and daughter-in-law.

"Phyl is determined to research both sides of the family tree. It's a safe bet that if she finds horse thieves among her ancestors we'll never hear about it."

From the backseat they heard a stirring. Menley looked over her shoulder. "Well, it looks like her ladyship is going to be joining us soon, and I bet she'll be one hungry character." Leaning over, she popped the pacifier into Hannah's mouth. "Say a prayer that holds her until we get to the house."

She put the empty coffee container in a bag and reached for the newspaper. "Adam, look. There's a picture of the couple you told me about. She's the one who drowned when they were scuba diving. The funeral is today. The poor guy. What a tragic accident."

Tragic accident. How many times had she heard those words. They triggered such terrible memories. They flooded over her. *Driving on that unfamiliar country road, Bobby in the backseat. A glorious sunny day. Feeling so great. Singing to Bobby at the top of her lungs. Bobby joining in. The unguarded railroad crossing. And then feeling the vibrations. Looking out the window. The conductor's frantic face. The roar and the screech of metal as the braking train bore down on them. Bobby screaming, "Mommy, Mommy." Flooring the accelerator. The crash as the train hit the back door next to Bobby. The train dragging the car. Bobby sobbing, "Mommy, Mommy." Then his eyes closing. Knowing he was dead. Rocking him in her arms. Screaming and screaming, "Bobby, I want Bobby. Bobbbbyyyyyyyy."*

Once again Menley felt the perspiration drenching her body. She began to shiver. She pressed her hands on her legs to control the trembling spasms of her limbs.

Adam glanced at her. "Oh my God." They were approaching a rest stop. He pulled into it, braked the car and turned to wrap his arms around her. "It's okay, sweetheart. It's okay."

In the backseat, Hannah began to wail.

Bobby wailing, "Mommy, Mommy."

Hannah wailing . . .

"Make her stop!" Menley screamed. *"Make her stop!"*

7

*I*t was quarter of twelve, Elaine realized, glancing at the dashboard clock. Adam and Menley should be arriving any minute, and she wanted to check the house before they got there to make sure everything was in order. One of the services she offered her clients was that a rental property would be thoroughly cleaned before and after a tenancy. She pressed her foot more firmly on the accelerator. She was running late because of attending the funeral service for Vivian Carpenter Covey.

Impulsively, she stopped at the supermarket.

I'll pick up some of the smoked salmon that Adam loves, she thought. It would go nicely with the bottle of chilled champagne she always left for high-ticket clients. Then she could just scribble a welcoming note and be out of the house before they arrived.

The overcast morning had evolved into a splendid day, sunny, in the mid-seventies, sparkling clear. Elaine reached up, opened the sunroof and thought about what she had told the television reporter. As the funeral cortege was preparing to leave the church, she had noticed him stopping people at random to ask for comments. Deliberately, she'd gone over to him. "May I say something?"

She'd looked into the camera squarely. "I'm Elaine Atkins. I sold Vivian Carpenter her home in Chatham three years ago, and the day before her death I was showing larger places to her and her husband. They were very happy and planning to start a family. What has happened is a tragedy, not a mystery. I think the people who are spreading ugly rumors about Mr. Covey should just check to see how many people there were in boats that day who hadn't heard the Coast Guard warning and were nearly swamped when the squall hit."

The memory brought a satisfied smile. She was sure Scott Covey had been watching from inside the limo.

She drove past the lighthouse to the Quitnesset section of Morris Island, down past the Monomoy National Wildlife Refuge; she turned onto Awarks Trail, then veered onto the private road that led to Remember House. When she rounded the bend, and the place came into view, she tried to imagine Menley's reaction upon seeing it for the first time.

Larger and more graceful than much of the architecture of the early eighteenth century, it stood as a tribute to the love Captain Andrew Freeman had initially felt for his young bride. With its starkly beautiful lines, and perched as it was on the bluff, it made a majestic silhouette against the background of sky and sea. Morning glories and holly berries vied with wild roses to splash color throughout the property. Locust trees and oaks, heavy with age, offered oases of shade from the brilliant sunshine.

The paved driveway led from the side of the house to the parking area behind the kitchen. Elaine frowned as Carrie Bell's van came into view. Carrie was an excellent cleaning woman, but she was always late. She should have been out of there by now.

Elaine found Carrie in the kitchen, her purse under her arm. Her thin, strong-featured face was pale. When she spoke, her voice, always a shade too loud, was rushed and subdued. "Oh, Miss Atkins. I know I'm a little behind, but I had to drop Tommy off at my mother's. Everything's shipshape, but let me tell you I'm glad to be getting out of here."

"What's wrong?" Elaine asked quickly.

"I got the fright of my life," Carrie said, her voice still tremulous. "I was in the dining room when I was sure I heard footsteps upstairs. I thought you might have come in so I called out to you. When nobody answered, I went up to take a look. Miss Atkins, you know that antique cradle that's in the bedroom with the single bed and crib?"

"Of course I know it."

Carrie's face went a shade paler. She clutched Elaine's arm. "Miss Atkins, the windows were closed. There was absolutely no breeze. But the spread on the bed was a little wrinkled, the way it would be if someone was sitting on it. And the cradle was moving. *Someone I couldn't see was sitting on the side of that bed, rocking the cradle!*"

"Now, Carrie, you've just heard those silly stories people made up about this house when it was abandoned," Elaine told her. "Those old floors are uneven. If that cradle was moving, it's because you're so heavy footed and probably stepped on a loose board."

From behind she could hear the sound of a car coming up the driveway. Adam and his family were here. "The whole idea is ridiculous," she said sternly. "Don't you dare say a word about that to the Nicholses," she warned, turning to watch as Adam and

Menley got out of the station wagon. She knew her warning was pointless, however—Carrie Bell would share that story with everyone she met.

8

Nathaniel Coogan had been on the Chatham police force for eighteen years. A Brooklyn native, Nat had been attending John Jay College in Manhattan, working toward a degree in criminal science, when he met his wife, a lifelong resident of Hyannis. Deb had no interest in living in New York, so after graduation he had willingly applied for a job in police work on the Cape. Now a detective and the forty-year-old father of two teenage sons, he was one of those rare birds, an easygoing, happy man, content with his family and job, his only major concern being the unwanted fifteen or so pounds his wife's excellent cooking had added to his already ample frame.

Earlier that day, however, another concern had surfaced. Actually it had been bothering him for some time. Nat knew that his boss, Chief of Police Frank Shea, firmly believed that Vivian Carpenter Covey's death had been an accident. "We had two other near-drownings that day," Frank pointed out. "It was Vivian Carpenter's boat. She knew those waters better than her husband did. If anyone should have thought

27

to turn on the radio, she was the one.'' Still it bothered Nat, and like a dog worrying a bone, he was unwilling to let go until his suspicions were justified or put to rest.

That morning, Nat had gotten into the office early and studied the autopsy pictures the ME had sent from Boston. Even though he had long ago taught himself to be clinically objective about the photographs of victims, the sight of the slender body—or what was left of it—swollen with water, mangled by fish bites, hit him like a dentist's drill on an exposed nerve. Murder victim or accident victim? Which was it?

At nine o'clock he went into Frank's office and asked to be assigned to the case. "I really want to stay on it. It's important.''

"One of your hunches?'' Shea asked.

"Yep.''

"I think you're wrong, but it won't hurt to be thorough. Go ahead.''

At ten Nat was at the memorial service. No eulogy for the poor kid, he thought. What did the stony faces of Vivian Carpenter's parents and sisters hide? Grief that it was noblesse oblige to conceal from prying eyes? Anger at a senseless tragedy? Guilt? The media had written plenty about Vivian Carpenter's forlorn history. It was nothing like that of her older sisters, one of them a surgeon, one a diplomat, both suitably married, whereas Vivian, thrown out of boarding school for smoking pot, later became a college dropout. Although she didn't need the money, when she moved to the Cape she took a job, then gave it up, something she would do a half-dozen times.

Scott Covey sat alone in the first pew, weeping through the service. He looks the way I'd feel if something happened to Deb, Nat Coogan thought. Almost convinced that he was barking up the wrong tree, he left the church at the end of the service, then hung around outside to pick up the remarks people were making.

They made good listening. "Poor Vivian. I'm so sorry for her, but she kind of wore you out, didn't she?"

The middle-aged woman who had been addressed sighed. "I know. She could never just relax."

Nat remembered that Covey had said that he had unsuccessfully urged his wife to keep napping while he went scuba diving.

A television reporter was rounding up people to tape. Nat watched as an attractive blond woman went to the reporter on her own. He recognized her, Elaine Atkins, the real estate agent. He sidled over to hear her comments.

When she was finished, Nat jotted down a note. Elaine Atkins said that the Coveys had been looking for a new house and were planning to start a family. She seemed to know them reasonably well. He decided he would have to talk to Miss Atkins himself.

When he got back to the office, he took out the autopsy pictures again, trying to figure out what it was that bothered him about them.

9

Menley wiggled from under Adam's arm and moved quietly to her side of the bed. He half murmured her name but did not awaken. She got up, slipped on her robe and looked down at him, a smile tugging at her lips.

The dynamic criminal lawyer who could sway juries with his rhetoric looked utterly defenseless in sleep. He was lying on his side, his head pillowed on one arm. His hair was tousled, the patches of gray more apparent, the faint beginning of a tonsure clearly visible.

The room was chilly, so Menley leaned down and drew the blanket over his shoulders, brushing her lips against his forehead. On her twenty-fifth birthday she'd decided that she'd probably never find anyone she wanted to marry. Two weeks later, she'd met Adam on an ocean liner, the *Sagafjord*. The ship was making a round-the-world tour, and because she had written extensively about the Far East, Menley had been invited to lecture on the leg between Bali and Singapore.

On the second day out, Adam had stopped by her deck chair to chat. He'd been taking depositions in Australia and impulsively signed up for the same leg of the voyage. "Great stops along the way, and I can use a week's vacation," he'd explained. By the end of that day, she had realized that Adam was the reason she'd broken her engagement three years earlier.

It had been different for him. He'd fallen in love with her gradually, over the course of the next year. Menley sometimes wondered whether she would ever have heard from him again if they hadn't lived three blocks apart in Manhattan.

It helped that they had some important things in common. Both were active New Yorkers and each was passionate about Manhattan, although they had been raised in distinctly different worlds. Adam's family had a Park Avenue duplex, and he'd gone to Collegiate. She had been brought up in Stuyvesant Town, on Fourteenth Street, where her mother still lived, and she had attended the local parochial schools. But by coincidence they both had graduated from Georgetown University, although eight years apart. They both loved the ocean, and Adam had spent his summers on Cape Cod, while she had gone swimming on day trips to Jones Beach.

When they started dating it was obvious to Menley that at thirty-two Adam was very content with his bachelor life. And why not? He was a successful defense attorney. He had a handsome apartment; a string of girlfriends. Sometimes weeks would go by between his calls.

When he had proposed, Menley suspected that it had something to do with his approaching thirty-third birthday. She didn't care. When they were married something her grandmother had told her years before echoed in her ears: "In marriage, one often is more in love than the other. It's better if the woman is the one who doesn't love as deeply."

Why is it better? Menley had wondered, and asked herself again as she looked at him sleeping so peacefully. What's *wrong* with being the one who loves the most?

It was seven o'clock. The strong sunlight was forcing its way into the room around the edges of the drawn shades. The spacious room was simply furnished with a four-poster, a two-on-three dresser, an armoire, a night table and a straight-backed chair. All the pieces were obviously authentic. Elaine had told her that just before Mr. Paley died, he and his wife had been going to auctions to collect early-eighteenth-century furniture.

Menley loved the fact that each of the bedrooms had a fireplace, although they were unlikely to need them in August. The room next to theirs was small, but it seemed perfect for the baby. Menley wrapped the robe around her more tightly as she stepped into the hall.

When she opened the door to Hannah's room, a brisk breeze greeted her. I should have covered her with a quilt, Menley thought, dismayed at her omission. They'd looked in on the baby at eleven when they went to bed, debated about the quilt, then decided it wasn't necessary. Obviously it had gotten much cooler than expected during the night.

Menley hurried over to the crib. Hannah was sleeping soundly; the quilt was tucked securely around her. Surely I couldn't have forgotten coming in during the night, Menley thought. Who covered her?

Then she felt foolish. Adam must have gotten up and looked in on the baby, although it was something that rarely happened, since he was a heavy sleeper. Or I might have come in myself, she realized. The doctors had prescribed a bedtime sedative that made her terribly groggy.

She wanted to kiss Hannah but knew if she did she risked instant awakening. "See you later, babe," she whispered. "I need a peaceful cup of coffee first."

At the bottom of the staircase she paused, suddenly

aware of the rapid beating of her heart, of a sensation of overwhelming sadness. The thought leaped into her head: *I'm going to lose Hannah too.* No! No! That's ridiculous, she told herself fiercely. Why even *think* like that?

She went into the kitchen and put the coffee on to perk. Ten minutes later, a steaming cup in her hand, she stood in the front parlor, looking out at the Atlantic Ocean as the sun rose higher in the sky.

The house faced Monomoy Strip, the narrow sandbar between ocean and bay that Menley had been told was the scene of countless shipwrecks. A few years ago the ocean had broken through the sandbar; Adam had pointed out where houses had tumbled into the sea. But Remember House, he assured her, was set far enough back so that it would always be safe.

Menley watched as the ocean charged against the sandbar, spraying fountains of salt-filled mist into the air. Sunbeams danced on the whitecaps. The horizon was already dotted with fishing boats. She opened the window and listened to the hawking of the gulls, the thin, noisy chirping of the sparrows.

Smiling, she turned from the window. After three days she felt comfortably settled here. She walked from room to room, planning what she would do if she were decorating them. The master bedroom contained the only authentic furniture. Most of the furnishings in the other rooms were the kind people put in homes that they are planning to rent—inexpensive couches, Formica tables, lamps that looked like they might have been purchased at a garage sale. But the deacon's bench, now painted a garish green, could be sanded down and refinished. She ran her hand over it, imagining the velvety walnut grain.

The Paleys had done massive structural repairs to the building. There was a new roof, new plumbing, new wiring, a new heating system. A lot of cosmetic work remained to be done—faded wallpaper in a jarring modern design was an eyesore in the dining room; dropped acoustical ceilings destroyed the noble height of the parlors and library—but none of those things mattered. The house itself was the important thing. It would be a joy to complete the restoration. There was a double parlor, for example—if she owned the house, she'd use one of them as a den. Later on Hannah and her friends would enjoy having a gathering place.

She ran her fingers over the minister's cabinet that was built into the wall next to the fireplace. She'd heard the stories of the early settlers and how a little glass of spirits was offered to the minister when he came to call. The poor man probably needed it, she thought. In those days there was rarely a fire laid in parlors. The ordained must have been blue with cold.

Early Cape families lived in the keeping room, as the kitchen was called, the room where the great fireplace gave warmth, where the air was inviting with the aroma of cooking, where children did their schoolwork by candlelight on the refectory table, where the family passed the long winter evenings together. She wondered about the generations of families who had replaced the original ill-fated owners here.

She heard footsteps on the stairs and went into the foyer. Adam was coming down, Hannah in his arms. "Who says I don't hear her when she cries?" He sounded very pleased with himself. "She's changed and hungry."

Menley reached for the baby. "Give her to me. Isn't it wonderful to have her to ourselves with only a part-time baby-sitter? If Elaine's future stepdaughter is half as good a sitter as she's supposed to be, we'll have a terrific summer."

"What time is she coming?"

"Around ten, I think."

* * *

At exactly ten o'clock, a small, blue car pulled into the driveway. Menley watched Amy as she came up the walk, noting her slim figure, her long ash blond hair clipped into a ponytail. It struck Menley that there was something aggressive about the girl's posture, the way her hands were jammed into the pockets of her cutoffs, the belligerent thrust of her shoulders.

"I don't know," Menley murmured as she went to open the door.

Adam looked up from the office work he had spread out on the table. "You don't know what?"

"Ssh," Menley cautioned.

Once in the house, however, the girl gave a different impression. She introduced herself, then went right over to the baby, who was in the small daytime crib they'd set up for her in the kitchen. "Hi, Hannah." She moved her hand gently until Hannah grabbed at her finger. "Good girl. You've got some grip. Are you going to be my buddy?"

Menley and Adam exchanged glances. The affection seemed genuine. After a few minutes of talking with Amy, Menley felt that, if anything, Elaine had understated the girl's expertise. She'd been baby-sitting since she was thirteen and most recently had stayed with a family with year-old twins. She was planning to be a nursery school teacher.

They agreed that she would come in for several afternoons a week, to help out while Menley was doing research for her writing projects, and occasionally would stay for the evening if they wanted to go out for dinner.

As the girl was leaving, Menley said, "I'm so glad Elaine suggested you, Amy. Now do you have any questions for me?"

"Yes . . . I . . . no, never mind."

"What is it?"

"Nothing, honest, nothing."

When she was well out of earshot, Adam said quietly, "That kid is afraid of something."

10

*H*enry Sprague sat on the couch in the sunroom, the photo album on his lap. Phoebe was beside him, seemingly attentive. He was pointing out pictures to her. "This is the day we took the kids to see the Plymouth Rock for the first time. At the rock you told them the story of the pilgrims landing. They were only six and eight then, but they were fascinated. You always made history sound like an adventure story."

He glanced at her. There was no hint of recognition in her eyes, but she nodded, anxious to please him. It had been a rough night. He'd awakened at two to find Phoebe's side of the bed empty. Heartsick, he'd rushed to see if she'd gotten out of the house again. Even though he'd put special locks on the doors, she had somehow managed to leave through the kitchen window last week. He'd reached her just as she was about to start the car.

Last night she'd been in the kitchen with the kettle on and one of the gas jets open.

Yesterday he had heard from the nursing home. There would be an opening on September first.

"Please reserve it for my wife," he had told them miserably.

"What nice children," Phoebe said. "What are their names?"

"Richard and Joan."

"Are they all grown up?"

"Yes. Richard is forty-three. He lives in Seattle with his wife and boys. Joan is forty-one, and she lives in Maine with her husband and daughter. You have three grandchildren, dear."

"I don't want to see any more pictures. I'm hungry."

One of the effects of the disease was that her brain sent false signals to her senses. "You had breakfast just a few minutes ago, Phoebe."

"No, I didn't." Her voice became stubborn.

"All right. Let's go in and fix something for you." As they got up, he put his arm around her. He'd always been proud of her tall, elegant body, the way she held her head, the poised warmth that emanated from her. *I wish we could have just one more day the way it used to be,* he thought.

As Phoebe hungrily ate a roll and gulped milk, he told her that they were having company. "A man named Nat Coogan. It's business."

There was no use trying to explain to Phoebe that Coogan was a detective who was coming to talk to him about Vivian Carpenter Covey.

As Nat drove past Vivian Carpenter's house, he studied it carefully. It was vintage Cape, the kind of house that had been added to and expanded over the years so that now it rambled agreeably along the property. Surrounded by blue and purple hydrangeas, impatiens spilling from the window boxes, it was a postcard-perfect residence, although he knew that in all likelihood the rooms were fairly small. Still, it was obviously well kept and on valuable property. According to the real estate agent, Elaine Atkins, Vivian and Scott Covey had been looking for a larger home for the family they planned to start.

How much would this place go for, Nat wondered? Situated on Oyster Pond, maybe an acre of property? Half a million? Since Vivian's will left everything to her husband, this would be another asset Scott Covey had inherited.

The Sprague residence was the next house. Another very attractive place. This one was an authentic saltbox, probably built in the late eighteenth century. Nat had never met the Spragues but used to enjoy the articles Professor Phoebe Sprague wrote for the *Cape Cod Times*. They all had to do with legends from the early Cape. He hadn't seen any new ones in recent years, however.

When Henry Sprague answered the bell, invited him in and introduced him to his wife, Nat understood immediately why Phoebe Sprague was no longer contributing articles. Alzheimer's, he thought, and with compassion became aware of the tired creases etched around Henry Sprague's mouth, of the quiet pain in his eyes.

He refused the offer for coffee. "I won't be long. Just a few questions, sir. How well did you know Vivian Carpenter Covey?"

Henry Sprague wanted to be kind. Painfully honest, he also did not want to dissemble. "As you probably know, Vivian bought that house three years ago. We introduced ourselves to her. You can see my wife is not well. Her problem was just beginning to become obvious at that time. Unfortunately, Vivian began to drop in on us constantly. She was taking a course in cooking and kept bringing over samples of food she had prepared. It got to the point where my wife was becoming very nervous. Vivian meant to be kind, but

I finally had to ask her to stop visiting unless we specifically had plans to get together.''

He paused and added, "Emotionally, Vivian was an extremely needy young woman.''

Nat nodded. It fit in with what he had heard from others. "How well do you know Scott Covey?''

"I've met him, of course. He and poor Vivian were married very quietly, I gather, but she did have a reception at home that we attended. That was in early May. Her family was there and so were a smattering of friends and other neighbors.''

"What did you think of Scott Covey?''

Henry Sprague avoided a direct answer. "Vivian was radiantly happy. I was pleased for her. Scott seemed very devoted.''

"Have you seen much of them since then?''

"Only from a distance. They seemed to go out on the boat quite a bit. Sometimes when we were all barbecuing in the back we'd exchange pleasantries.''

"I see.'' Nat sensed that Henry Sprague was holding something back. "Mr. Sprague, you've said that Covey seemed very devoted to his wife. Did you get the feeling he was honestly in love with her?''

Sprague did not have a problem answering that question. "He certainly acted as though he was.''

But there was more, and again Henry Sprague hesitated. He felt he might be guilty of simple gossip if he told the detective something that had happened in late June. He'd dropped Phoebe off at the hairdresser, and Vivian had been there as well, having her hair done. To kill time, he'd gone across the street to the Cheshire Pub, to have a beer and watch the Red Sox and Yankees game.

Scott Covey had been sitting on a stool in the bar. Their eyes met, and Henry went over to greet him. He didn't know why, but he had the impression that Covey was nervous. A moment later a flashy brunette in her late twenties came in. Covey had jumped up. "For heaven's sake, Tina, what are *you* doing here?" he'd said. "I thought you had a run-through Tuesday afternoons."

She had looked at him dumbfounded but recovered quickly. "Scott, how *nice* to bump into you. No rehearsal today. I was supposed to meet some of the other kids from the show either here or at the Impudent Oyster. I'm late, so if they're not here I'll rush over there."

When she left, Scott told Henry that Tina was in the chorus of the musical currently at the Cape Playhouse. "Vivian and I went to opening night and started talking to her at the cast party in the Playhouse Restaurant," he had explained carefully.

Henry had ended up having a sandwich and beer with Scott while they watched the game. At two-thirty Covey left. "Viv should be finished now," he had said.

But when Henry picked up Phoebe a half hour later, Covey was still in the reception area of the salon, waiting for his wife. When she finally came out, tremulously proud of the blond highlights in her hair, he had overheard Covey reassure her that he hadn't minded waiting at all, that he and Henry had watched the game together over lunch. At the time Henry had wondered if Scott's omission of the meeting with Tina had been deliberate.

Maybe not, Henry thought now. Maybe he forgot because it simply wasn't important to him. Maybe it had all been Henry's imagination that Covey had seemed nervous that day. Don't be a meddlesome gossip, he told himself as he sat with the detective. There's no point in bringing this up.

What aren't you telling me? Nat wondered as he gave Henry Sprague his card.

11

Menley drove Adam to the Barnstable Airport. "You're very grumpy," she teased as she stopped at the drop-off area.

A smile quickly cleared the frown from his face. "I admit it. I don't want to have to go back and forth to New York. I don't want to leave you and Hannah. I don't want to leave the Cape." He paused, "Let's see, what else?"

"Poor baby," Menley said mockingly, taking his face between her hands. "We'll miss you." She hesitated, then added, "It's really been a great couple of days, hasn't it?"

"Spectacular."

She straightened his tie. "I think I like you better in cutoffs and sandals."

"I like myself better. Men, are you sure you don't want to have Amy stay overnight with you?"

"Positive. Adam, please . . ."

"Okay, sweetheart. I'll call you tonight." He leaned into the backseat and touched Hannah's foot. "Stay out of trouble, Toots," he told her.

Hannah's sunny if toothless grin followed him as with a final wave he disappeared into the terminal.

After lunch, Adam had received an urgent call from

his office. There was an emergency hearing scheduled to revoke the Potter woman's bail. The prosecution claimed that she had made threats against her mother-in-law. Adam had expected to have at least ten days at the Cape before having to go back to New York overnight, but this seemed like a genuine emergency, and he decided it was necessary to handle it personally.

Menley steered the car out of the airport, turned onto the rotary and followed the sign to Route 28. She came to the railroad crossing and felt icy perspiration form on her forehead. She stopped, then glanced fearfully both ways. A freight train was far down the tracks. It was not moving. The warning lights weren't flashing. The gates were up. Even so for a moment she sat paralyzed, unable to move.

The impatient beep of car horns behind her forced her to take action. She jammed her foot on the accelerator. The car leapt across the tracks. Then she had to hit the brake to avoid slamming into the car ahead. Oh God, she thought, help me, please. Hannah bounced in the car seat and began to cry.

Menley pulled the car into the parking lot of a restaurant and drove to the most distant spot. There she stopped, got in the back and took Hannah from the car seat.

She cradled the baby against her and they cried together.

12

Graham Carpenter could not sleep. He tried to lie quietly in the king-sized bed that had long ago replaced the double bed he and Anne had shared in the early days of their marriage. As they were approaching their twentieth anniversary they had both admitted that they wanted more room and made the change. More room to stretch out, more free time, more travel. With their second daughter in college it was all possible.

The night this bed had arrived, they had toasted each other with champagne. Vivian was conceived shortly after that. Sometimes he wondered if from the very beginning she had known that she was unwanted. Was her lifelong hostility to them and insecurity with others triggered in the womb?

A fanciful notion. Vivian had been a demanding, malcontent child who became a problem teenager and a difficult adult. An underachiever at school, self-pitying, her motto had been, "I do my best."

To which his angry response was, "No, damn it, you *don't* do your best. You don't know the meaning of the word."

At the boarding school where the older girls had excelled, Vivian was suspended twice, then finally dismissed. For a while she had flirted with drugs, fortunately something she hadn't continued. And then there was the apparent constant need to annoy Anne. She'd ask her to go shopping for clothes, then refuse to follow any of Anne's suggestions.

She didn't finish college, didn't ever stay longer than six months on any job. Years ago he had begged his mother not to let her have access to her trust fund until she was thirty. But she'd come into it all at twenty-one, bought that house and afterwards rarely contacted them. It was an absolute shock when in May she had phoned to invite them to her house to a reception. She had gotten married.

What could he say about Scott Covey? Good looking, well mannered, bright enough, certainly devoted to Vivian. She had literally glowed with happiness. The only sour note had come when one of her friends joked about a prenuptial agreement. She had flared, "No, we *don't* have one. In fact, we're making wills in favor of each other."

Graham had wondered what Scott Covey had to leave anyone. Vivian insinuated he had a private income. Maybe.

About one thing, for once, Vivian had been telling the unvarnished truth. She had changed her will the same day she was married, and now Scott would inherit all the money from her trust fund, along with her house in Chatham. And they had been married twelve week. *Twelve weeks.*

"Graham." Anne's voice was soft.

He reached for her hand. "I'm awake."

"Graham, I know Vivy's body was in very bad shape. What about her right hand?"

"I don't know, dear. Why?"

"Because, nobody has said anything about her emerald ring. Maybe her hand was gone. But if it wasn't, Scott may have the ring, and I'd like to have it back.

It's always been in our family, and I can't imagine some other woman wearing it."

"I'll find out, dear."

"Graham, why couldn't I ever reach Vivian? What did I do wrong?"

He grasped her hand more tightly. There was no answer he could give her.

That day he and Anne played golf. It was physical and emotional therapy for both of them. They got home around five, showered, and he fixed them cocktails. Then he said. "Anne, while you were dressing I tried to reach Scott. There's a message on the machine. He's on the boat and will be back around six. Let's swing by and ask him about the ring. Then we'll go out to dinner." He paused. "I mean you and I will go out for dinner."

"If he has the ring, he doesn't have to part with it. It was Vivian's to leave to him."

"If he has the ring we'll offer to buy it at fair market value. If that doesn't work, we'll pay him whatever he asks for it."

Graham Carpenter's mouth set in a grim line. Scott's reaction to this request would allay or verify the suspicion and doubt that was choking his soul.

13

*I*t was five-thirty when Menley and Hannah finally got back to Chatham. When they left the parking lot, she had forced herself to drive over the railroad crossing again. Then she had circled the rotary and driven over it a third time. No more panicky driving for me, she vowed. Not when it means I'm jeopardizing Hannah.

The sun was still high over the ocean, and to Menley it seemed as though the house had a contented air about it as it basked in the warm rays that enveloped it. Inside, the sun streaming through the stained glass of the fan-shaped window over the door cast a rainbow of colors onto the bare oak floor.

Holding Hannah tightly, Menley walked to the front window and looked out over the ocean. She wondered if, when this house was first built, the young bride had ever watched to see the mast of her husband's ship as he returned from a voyage. Or had she been too busy dallying with her lover?

Hannah stirred restlessly. "Okay, chow time," Menley said, wishing once again that she had been able to nurse Hannah. When the post-traumatic stress symptoms began, the doctor had ordered tranquilizers and discontinued the nursing. "You need tranquilizers, but she doesn't," he had explained.

Oh well, you're certainly thriving anyway, Menley thought as she poured formula into the bottle and warmed it in a saucepan.

At seven o'clock she tucked Hannah into the crib, this time snug in a sleeping bag. A glance about the room confirmed that the quilt was folded on the bed where it belonged. Menley stared at it uneasily. She had casually asked Adam if he had covered the baby during the night. No, he had replied, obviously wondering why she asked.

She had thought quickly and said, "Then she isn't as much a kicker up here as she was at home. Probably the sea air keeps her sleeping quietly."

He hadn't realized there had been a far different reason for the question.

She hesitated outside the baby's room. It was silly to leave the hall light on. It was much too bright. But for some reason Menley felt uneasy about the prospect of coming upstairs later with only a tiny night-light to guide her footsteps.

She had her evening mapped out. There were fresh tomatoes in the refrigerator. She'd fix a quick pomodoro sauce, pour it over linguine and make a watercress salad. There was a half loaf of Italian bread in the freezer.

That will be perfect, Menley thought. And while I eat, I'll make some notes for the book.

The few days in Chatham had already given her ideas on what she would do with the story line. With Adam away, she would spend the long, calm evening fleshing them out.

14

He had spent the whole day on *Viv's Toy*. The twenty-two-foot inboard/outboard motorboat was in excellent shape. Vivian had been talking about replacing it with a sailboat. "Now that I've got a captain for it, should we get one big enough to do serious sailing?"

So many plans! So many dreams! Scott hadn't been scuba diving since that last day with Vivian. Today he fished for a while, checked his lobster pots and was rewarded with four two-pounders, then put on his scuba gear and went down for a while.

He docked the boat at the marina and reached home at five-thirty, then immediately went next door to the Sprague house with two of the lobsters. Henry Sprague answered the door.

"Mr. Sprague, I know at our reception your wife seemed to enjoy the lobster. I caught some today and hoped you might like to have a couple of them."

"That's very kind," Henry said sincerely. "Won't you come in?"

"No, that's fine. Just enjoy them. How is Mrs. Sprague?"

"About the same. Would you like to say hello? Wait, here she is."

He turned as his wife came down the hall. "Phoebe, dear, Scott has brought lobster for you. Isn't that nice of him?"

Phoebe Sprague looked at Scott Covey, her eyes widening. "Why was she crying so hard?" she asked. "Is she all right now?"

"Nobody was crying, dear," Henry Sprague said soothingly. He put an arm across her shoulders.

Phoebe Sprague pulled away from him. "Listen to me," she shrieked. "I keep telling you there's a woman living in my house and you won't believe me. Here, you." She grabbed Scott's arm and pointed to the mirror over the foyer table. The three of them were reflected in it. "See that woman." She reached over and touched her own image. "She's living in my house and he won't believe me."

Somewhat troubled by Phoebe Sprague's ramblings, Scott went home, deep in thought. He had planned to steam one of the remaining lobsters for himself, but he found he had no taste for food. He made a drink and checked the answering machine. There were two messages: Elaine Atkins had phoned. Did he want to leave the house on the market? She had a prospective buyer. The other was from Vivian's father. He and his wife had an urgent matter to discuss. They would stop by around six-thirty. It would take only a few minutes.

What's *that* about? Scott wondered. He checked his watch; it was ten after six already. He set down the drink and hurried in for a quick shower. He dressed in a dark blue knit shirt, chinos and Docksiders. He was just combing his hair when the bell rang.

It was the first time Anne Carpenter had been in her daughter's home since the body was found. Not knowing what she was looking for, she searched the living room with her eyes. In the three years Vivian had owned the house, Anne had only been in it a few times, and it looked about the same as she remembered. Vivian had replaced the bedroom furniture but left this room pretty much as she had found it. On her first visit Anne had suggested that her daughter get rid of the loveseat and some of the cheap prints, but Vivian had flared up at her, despite the fact that she *had* asked for suggestions.

Scott insisted they have a drink. "I just made one. Please join me. I haven't wanted people around, but it's awfully good to see you."

Reluctantly, Anne admitted to herself that his demeanor seemed genuinely sad. He was so strikingly good looking with his blond hair and tanned skin and hazel eyes, it was easy to see how Vivian had fallen in love with him. But what did he see in her except her money? Anne asked herself, then recoiled at her own question. What a horrible thought for a mother, she scolded herself.

"What are your plans, Scott?" Graham Carpenter asked.

"I don't have any. I still have the feeling that this is all a bad dream. I don't think I've come to grips with reality yet. You know Viv and I had been looking for a bigger house. The upstairs bedrooms are really small, and when we had a baby we'd have wanted a place where live-in help wouldn't be under our feet all the time. We even had names picked out. Graham for a boy, Anne for a girl. She told me that she always felt she was a big disappointment to the two of you and she wanted to make it up to you. She felt it was her fault, not yours."

Anne felt a lump in her throat. She watched the convulsive tightening of her husband's mouth. "We always seemed to be at cross-purposes," she said quietly. "Sometimes it happens like that, and as a parent you hope it will change. I'm glad if Vivy truly wanted it to change. We certainly did."

The phone rang. Scott jumped up. "Whoever it is, I'll call back." He hurried into the kitchen.

A moment later Anne watched with curiosity as her husband picked up his drink and walked down the hall to the bathroom. He returned just as Scott came back.

"I just wanted to put a dash more water in the scotch," Graham explained.

"You should have gotten some ice water from the kitchen. There was nothing private about the phone conversation. That was the real estate agent wanting to know if it was all right to bring a prospective buyer around tomorrow," Scott said. "I told her to take the house off the market."

"Scott, there is something we need to ask." Graham Carpenter clearly was trying to keep his emotions under control. "The emerald ring Vivian always wore. It's been in her mother's family for generations. Do you have it?"

"No, I don't."

"You identified the body. She never took it off her finger. She wasn't wearing it when she was found?"

Scott looked away. "Mr. Carpenter, I'm grateful you and Mrs. Carpenter didn't see the body. It had been so badly attacked by marine life that there was very little left to identify. But if I had that ring I would have given it to you immediately. I knew it was a family treasure. Is there anything else of Vivian's that you want? Would her clothes fit her sisters?"

Anne winced. "No . . . no."

The Carpenters got up together. "We'll call you for dinner soon, Scott," Anne said.

"Please do. I only wish we'd gotten to know each other better."

"Unless you can't part with them, perhaps you'll assemble some pictures of Vivian for us," Graham Carpenter said.

"Of course."

When they reached the car and started to drive away, Anne turned to her husband. "Graham, you never put water in your scotch. What were you doing?"

"I wanted to get a look at the bedroom. Anne, didn't you notice that there wasn't a single picture of Vivian in the living room? Well, I have news. There isn't a picture of her in the bedroom either. I'll bet you there isn't a trace of our daughter anywhere in that house. I don't like Covey and I don't trust him. He's a phony. He knows more than he's telling, and I'm going to get to the bottom of it."

15

*T*hey had set up a computer, printer and fax machine on the desk in the library. The computer and printer took up most of the surface, but it would suffice, especially since Menley didn't intend to devote all that much time to working. Adam had his portable type-writer, which Menley was always trying to get him to discard but which could be set up anywhere.

Adam had so far successfully resisted Menley's efforts to get him to learn how to use a computer. But then Menley had been equally stubborn about learning to play golf.

"You're well coordinated. You'd be good at it," Adam insisted.

The memory made Menley smile as she worked at the long refectory table in the kitchen. No, not the kitchen, the keeping room, she reminded herself. Let's get the jargon right, especially if I'm going to set a book here. Alone in the house with just the baby, it seemed cozier to work in this wonderfully shabby room, with its huge fireplace and side oven, and the smell of the garlic bread lingering in the air. And she was only going to make notes tonight. She always did them in a loose-leaf notebook. "Here we go again," she murmured aloud as she wrote *David's Adventures in the Narrow Land*. It's so crazy how all this had worked out, she thought.

After college she had managed to get the job at *Travel Times*. She knew that she wanted to be a writer but what kind of a writer she wasn't sure. Her mother had always hoped she would concentrate on art, but she knew that wasn't right for her.

Her break at the magazine came when the editor in chief asked her to cover the opening of a new hotel in Hong Kong. The article had been accepted almost without editing. Then hesitantly she had shown the watercolor paintings she'd made of the hotel and its surrounding area. The magazine had illustrated the article with the paintings, and at twenty-two Menley became a senior travel editor.

The idea for doing a series of children's books using a "yesterday and today" theme, in which David, a contemporary child, goes back into the past and follows the life of a child from another century, evolved gradually. But now she had completed four of them, doing both the text and artwork. One was set in New York, one in London, one in Paris and one in San Francisco. They had become popular immediately.

Listening to all Adam's stories about the Cape had

made her interested in setting the next book here. It would be about a boy in Pilgrim times growing up on the Cape, the Narrow Land as the Indians had called it.

Like all the other ideas that had eventually ended up as a book, once hatched, it would not go away. The other day they had gone to the library in Chatham and she had borrowed books on the early history of the Cape. Then she'd found some dusty old books in a cabinet in the library at Remember House. So tonight she sat down to read; soon she was happily lost in her research.

At eight o'clock the phone rang. "Mrs. Nichols?"

She did not recognize the voice. "Yes," she said cautiously.

"Mrs. Nichols, I'm Scott Covey. Elaine Atkins gave me your number. Is Mr. Nichols there?"

Scott Covey! Menley recognized the name. "I'm afraid my husband isn't here," she said. "He'll be back tomorrow. You can reach him by late afternoon."

"Thank you. I'm sorry to have bothered you."

"No bother. And I'm so sorry about your wife."

"It's been pretty awful. I'm only praying that your husband can help me. It's bad enough to have lost Viv, but now the police are acting as though they think it wasn't an accident."

Adam called a few minutes later, sounding weary. "Kurt Potter's family is determined to see that Susan goes back to prison. They know she killed him in self-defense, but to admit it also means admitting that they'd ignored the warning signs."

Menley could tell he was exhausted. After only three days of vacation he was already back in the office. She did not have the heart to bring up Scott

Covey's request now. When he got back tomorrow, she'd ask him to meet with Covey. Of all people, she understood what it was like to have the police question a tragic accident.

She assured Adam that she and Hannah were fine, that they both missed him and that she was keeping busy doing research for the new book.

The talk with Scott Covey and then with Adam had broken her concentration, however, and at nine o'clock she turned out the lights and went upstairs.

She checked the peacefully sleeping Hannah, then sniffed the air. There was a musty smell in the room. Where was it coming from? she wondered. She opened the window a few inches more. A strong, salty sea breeze quickly swept through the room. That's better, she thought.

Sleep did not come easily. The railroad crossing today had brought back vivid memories of the terrible accident. This time she thought about the signal light that day. She was sure she had glanced at it—it was something she did automatically—but the sun was so strong that she hadn't realized it was flashing. The first indication of what was happening was the vibrations caused by the train rushing toward them. Then she heard the frantic, shrill scream of its whistle.

Her throat went dry, her lips felt bloodless. But at least this time she did not begin to perspire or tremble. At last she fell into an uneasy sleep.

At two o'clock she sat bolt upright. The baby was screaming, and the sound of an oncoming train was echoing through the house.

August 5th

16

Adam Nichols could not overcome the sense that something was wrong. He slept fitfully, and each time he awoke it was with the knowledge that he'd just had a vague, troublesome dream and could not remember what it was.

At six o'clock, as dawn broke over the East River, he threw back the sheet and got up. He made coffee and brought it out on the terrace, wishing that it were seven-thirty and he could call Menley. He would wait till then, since the baby was usually sleeping past seven now.

A smile flickered on his lips as he thought of Menley and Hannah. His family. The miracle of Hannah's birth three months ago. The grief of losing Bobby finally beginning to ease for both of them. A year ago at this time he'd been at the Cape alone and wouldn't have bet a nickel that their marriage would survive. He'd spoken to a counselor about it and had been told that the death of a child frequently caused the end of the marriage. The counselor had said there was so much pain the parents sometimes couldn't exist under the same roof.

Adam had begun to think that maybe it would be better for both of them to start over separately. Then

Menley had phoned and Adam knew he desperately wanted their marriage to work.

Menley's pregnancy had been uneventful. He had been with her in the labor room. She'd been in a lot of pain but doing great. Then from down the hall they could hear a woman screaming. The change in Menley had been dramatic. Her face went ashen. Those enormous blue eyes grew even larger, then she had covered them with her hands. "No . . . no . . . help me, please," she had cried, as she trembled and sobbed. The tension in her body dramatically increased the strength of the contractions, the difficulty of the birth.

And when Hannah was finally born, and the doctor had laid her in Menley's arms in the delivery room, incredibly she had pushed her away. "I want Bobby," she had sobbed. "I want Bobby."

Adam had taken the baby and held her against his neck, whispering, "It's all right, Hannah. We love you, Hannah," as though he was afraid she could understand Menley's words.

Later Menley had told him, "At the moment they gave her to me, I was reliving holding Bobby after the accident. It was the first time I really knew what I'd felt at that moment."

That was the beginning of what the doctors called the post-traumatic stress disorder. The first month had been very difficult. Hannah had started out as a colicky infant who screamed for hours. They'd had a live-in nurse, but one afternoon when the nurse was on an errand, the baby had started shrieking. Adam came home to find Menley sitting on the floor by the crib, pale and trembling, her fingers in her ears. But miraculously a formula change turned Hannah into a sunny baby, and Menley's anxiety attacks for the most part passed.

I still shouldn't have left her alone so soon, Adam

thought. I should have insisted that at least the baby-sitter stay over.

At seven o'clock he couldn't wait any longer. He phoned the Cape.

The sound of Menley's voice brought a rush of relief. "Her nibs get you up early, honey?"

"Just a bit. We like the morning."

There was something in Menley's voice. Adam bit back the question that came too easily to his lips. *You okay?* Menley resented his hovering over her.

"I'll be up on the four o'clock flight. Want to get Amy to mind Hannah and we'll go out to dinner?"

Hesitation. What was wrong? But then Menley said, "That sounds great. Adam . . ."

"What is it, honey?"

"Nothing. Just that we miss you."

When he hung up, Adam called the airline. "Is there any earlier flight I can get on?" he asked. He would be out of court by noon. There was a one-thirty flight he might be able to make.

Something was wrong, and the worst part of it was that Menley wasn't going to tell him what it was.

17

*E*laine Atkins' real estate office was on Main Street in Chatham. Location, location, location, she thought as a passerby stopped to look at the pictures that she had taken of available homes. Since she'd moved to Main Street, the drop-in traffic had improved dramatically, and more and more she'd been able to convert these expressions of preliminary interest into an excellent percentage of sales.

This summer she'd tried a new gimmick. She'd had aerial photographs taken of houses with particularly good locations. One of them was Remember House. When she'd arrived at work this morning at ten, Marge Salem, her assistant, told her there had already been two inquiries about it.

"That aerial photo really does the trick. Do you think it was wise to rent it to the Nicholses without asking for the right to show it?" Marge asked.

"It was necessary," Elaine said briskly. "Adam Nichols isn't the type who's going to want people trooping through a house he's renting, and he did pay top dollar for it. But we're not losing a sale. My hunch is that the Nicholses will decide to buy that place."

"I would have thought that he'd look in Harwich Port. That's where his family came from and always summered."

"Yes, but Adam always liked Chatham. And he knows a good buy when he sees it. He also likes to own, not rent. I think he regrets not buying the family home when his mother sold it. If his wife is happy here, we've got a customer. Watch and see." She smiled at Marge. "And if by chance he doesn't, well, Scott Covey loves that place. When things settle down for him he'll be in the market again. He won't want to keep Vivian's house."

Marge's pleasant face became serious. The fifty-year-old housewife had started working for Elaine at the beginning of the summer and found that she thoroughly enjoyed the real estate business. She also loved gossip and, as Elaine joked, could pick it out of the air. "There are a lot of rumors floating around about Scott Covey."

Elaine made a quick gesture with her hand, always a sign of impatience. "Why don't they leave that poor guy alone? If Vivian hadn't come into that trust fund, everyone would be keening with him. That's the trouble with people in these parts. On principle, they don't like to see family money go to an outsider."

Marge nodded. "God knows that's true."

They were interrupted by the tingling of the bell over the front door, signaling the arrival of a potential client. After that they were busy all morning. At one o'clock, Elaine got up, went into the bathroom and came out wearing fresh lipstick and with her hair recombed.

Marge studied her. Elaine was wearing a white linen dress and sandals, making an attractive contrast to her deeply tanned arms and legs. Her dark blond hair streaked with highlights was pulled back by a band. "If I hadn't mentioned it before, you look terrific," Marge said. "Obviously being engaged suits you."

Elaine wiggled her ring finger, and the large solitaire on it glittered. "I agree. I'm meeting John for lunch at the Impudent Oyster. Hold the fort."

When she returned an hour later, Marge said, "There've been a bunch of calls. The top one is the most interesting."

It was from Detective Nat Coogan. It was imperative that he speak with Miss Atkins at her earliest convenience.

18

*B*y mid-morning, Menley had begun to convince herself that the terror that had awakened her had been simply a vivid dream. With Hannah held tightly in her arms she walked outside to the edge of the embankment. The sky was vividly blue and reflected in the water that broke gently against the shoreline. It was low tide, and the long expanse of sandy beach was tranquil.

Even without the ocean it's a wonderful piece of property, she thought as she studied the grounds. In the many years the house had been abandoned, the locust and oak trees had grown unchecked. Now heavily laden with leaves, they were in natural harmony with the velvety fullness of the pines.

The lush midsummer look, Menley thought. Then she noticed an occasional leaf already tinged with rust. Autumn would be beautiful here as well, she reflected.

Her father had died when her brother Jack was eleven and she was only three. Education was more important than a house, her mother had decided, and had used whatever she could save from her salary as a nurse supervisor at Bellevue Hospital to send them both to Georgetown. She still lived in that same four-room apartment where Menley and Jack had grown up.

Menley had always wanted to live in a house. As a little girl she drew pictures of the one she would have someday. And it was pretty much like this place, she thought. She'd had so many plans for the house she and Adam had bought in Rye. But after Bobby was gone it held too many memories. "Living in Manhattan is right for us," she said aloud to Hannah. "Daddy can be home from work in ten minutes. Grandma enjoys baby-sitting and I'm a city slicker. But Daddy's family has always been on the Cape. They were among the first settlers. It might be kind of wonderful to have this house for the summer and holidays and long weekends. What do you think?"

The baby turned her head and together they looked at the house behind them. "There's still a load of work to do," Menley said. "But it would be fun to really restore it to the way it used to be. I guess it was just the two of us being here alone that made the dream seem so real when I was waking up. Don't you agree?"

Hannah wriggled impatiently, and her lip drooped. "Okay, you're getting tired," Menley said. "God, you're a crabby kid." She started back toward the house, then paused and studied it again. "It has a wonderful sheltering look, doesn't it?" she murmured.

She felt suddenly lighthearted, hopeful. Adam would be home this afternoon and their vacation could get back on track. Except . . .

Except if Adam decides to represent Scott Covey, she thought. Adam never does anything halfheartedly. It would take a lot of his time. Even so I hope he does represent him. She remembered the horror when, two weeks after Bobby's funeral, Adam had received a phone call. The assistant district attorney was considering prosecuting Menley for reckless manslaughter.

"He said that you've had a couple of speeding tickets. He thinks he can prove that you ignored the warning signal at the crossing because you were racing to beat the train." Then Adam's face had become grim. "Don't worry, honey. He won't get to first base." The D.A. had backed off when Adam produced a formidable list of other fatal accidents at that crossing.

Elaine had told them that one of the reasons Scott Covey was being judged harshly was because some people said he should have known about the squall.

Menley thought, I don't care if it does cut into our vacation. Covey needs help just as I did.

19

The Carpenter summer home in Osterville was not visible from the road. As Detective Nat Coogan drove through the gates and along the wide driveway, he observed the manicured lawn and flower beds. I'm suitably impressed, he thought. Big, big bucks, but old money. Nothing flamboyant.

He stopped in front of the house. It was an old Victorian mansion with a wide porch and gingerbread latticework. The unpainted shakes had weathered to a mellow gray, but the shutters and window frames gleamed snowy white in the afternoon sun.

When he had phoned this morning asking for an

MARY HIGGINS CLARK

interview, he had been somewhat surprised at how readily Vivian Carpenter's father had agreed to see him.

"Do you want to come today, Detective Coogan? We were planning to play golf this afternoon but there's plenty of time for that."

It was not the reaction Nat had expected. The Carpenters did not have the reputation of being accessible people. He had anticipated a frosty response, a demand to know why he wanted to see them.

Interesting, he thought.

A maid led him to the sunporch at the back of the house where Graham and Anne Carpenter were seated on brightly cushioned wicker chairs, sipping iced tea. At the funeral service, Nat had gotten the impression that these were cold people. The only tears he had seen shed for Vivian Carpenter Covey had been her husband's. Looking at the couple in front of him, he was embarrassed to realize how wrong he'd been. Both her parents' patrician faces were visibly strained, their expressions filled with sadness.

They greeted him quietly, offered iced tea or whatever beverage he preferred. On his refusal, Graham Carpenter came directly to the point. "You're not here to offer condolences, Mr. Coogan."

Nat had chosen a straight-backed chair. He leaned forward, his hands linked, a habit his colleagues would have recognized as his unconscious posture when he felt he was onto something. "I do offer condolences, but you're right, Mr. Carpenter. That is not the reason I'm here. I'm going to be very blunt. I'm not satisfied that your daughter's death was an accident, and until I am satisfied I'm going to be seeing a lot of people and asking a lot of questions."

It was as though he had jolted them with a live wire. The lethargy disappeared from their expressions. Graham Carpenter looked at his wife, "Anne, I told you . . ."

She nodded. "I didn't want to believe . . ."

"What didn't you want to believe, Mrs. Carpenter?" Nat asked quickly.

They described for him their reasons for being suspicious of their son-in-law, but Coogan found them disappointing. "I understand your feelings about not finding a picture of your daughter anywhere in her home," he told them, "but it's been my experience that after this kind of tragedy, people react differently. Some will bring out every picture they can find of the person they've lost, while others will immediately store or even destroy pictures and mementos, give away the clothes, sell the car of the deceased, even change homes. It's almost as though they believe removing any reminder will make it easier to get over the pain."

He tried a new tack. "You met Scott Covey after your daughter married him. Since he was a stranger, you must have been concerned. By any chance did you investigate his background?"

Graham Carpenter nodded. "Yes, I did. Not a very in-depth investigation, but everything he told us was true. He was born and raised in Columbus, Ohio. His father and stepmother retired to California. He attended but did not graduate from the University of Kansas. He tried acting but didn't get far and worked as a business manager for a couple of small theatrical companies. That's how Vivian met him last year." He smiled mirthlessly. "Vivian insinuated that he had a private income. I think that was a fabrication for our benefit."

"I see." Nat stood up. "I'll be honest. So far everything I've been told checks out. Your daughter was crazy about Covey, and he certainly acted as though he was in love with her. They were planning to go to

Hawaii, and she'd told a number of people that she was determined to be a good scuba diver by the time they got there. She wanted to do everything with him. He's an excellent swimmer but had never handled a boat before he met her. The squall wasn't supposed to come in until midnight. Frankly, *she's* the one who was experienced and should have known to turn on the radio in order to monitor the weather.''

"Does that mean you're giving up the investigation?" Carpenter asked.

"No. But it *does* mean that except for the obvious factors that Vivian was a wealthy young woman and they had been married only a brief time, there's really nothing to go on."

"I see. Well, I thank you for sharing this with us. I'll walk you out."

They had reached the door of the sunporch when Anne Carpenter called after them. "Mr. Coogan."

Both Nat and Graham Carpenter turned.

"Just one thing. I know my daughter's body was in terrible condition because of the length of time it was in the water and the marine life attacking it . . ."

"I'm afraid that's true," Nat agreed.

"Anne, dear, why torture yourself," her husband protested.

"No, hear me out. Mr. Coogan, were the fingers of my daughter's right hand intact, or missing?"

Nat hesitated. "One hand was badly mutilated. The other was not. I believe it was the right hand that was in bad shape, but I'd want to check the autopsy pictures. Why do you ask?"

"Because my daughter always wore a very valuable emerald on the ring finger of her right hand. From the day my mother gave it to her, Vivian never took it off. We asked Scott about it because it was a family piece and we wanted it back if it had been found. But he told us in so many words that her hand was mutilated and the ring missing."

"I'll call you within the hour," Nat said.

Back in his office, Nat studied the autopsy pictures for long minutes before he called the Carpenters.

All ten fingertips were missing. On the left hand the wedding band was on the ring finger. But it was the ring finger of the right hand that was a mess. Between the knuckle and hand it had been eaten to the bone. What had attracted the scavengers to it? Nat wondered.

There was no sign of the emerald ring.

When he called the Carpenters, Nat was careful not to jump to conclusions. He told Graham Carpenter that his daughter's right hand had suffered massive trauma and the ring was missing.

"Do you know if it was a loose or tight fit?" he asked.

"It had become tight," Carpenter said. Then he paused before asking, "What are you saying?"

"I'm not saying anything, Mr. Carpenter. It is simply one more circumstance to consider. I'll stay in touch."

As he hung up, Nat thought about what he had just learned. Could this be the smoking gun? he wondered. I'd bet the ranch that Covey ripped the ring off and then swam away from that poor kid. If the finger was bruised, there was blood near the surface, and that drew the scavengers.

August 6th

20

"*E*laine owes me one," Adam muttered as he looked through the window of the keeping room and watched a car turn in from the driveway. They'd taken a picnic basket to the beach while Hildy, the cleaning woman Elaine had sent, went through the house. At two o'clock they went up for the appointment Adam had made with Scott Covey.

Adam showered and changed to shorts and a tee shirt. Menley was still in her bathing suit and cover-up when they heard Covey's car drive up.

"I'm glad he's here," she told Adam. "While you're busy, I'll grab a nap with Hannah. I want to be sharp when I meet all your old buddies."

Elaine was having a buffet supper in their honor at her home and had invited some of the people Adam had grown up with during summers at the Cape.

He caught her around the waist. "When they tell you how fortunate you are, be sure to agree."

"Puh . . . leeze."

The doorbell rang. Menley glanced at the stove. There was no way she could grab Hannah's bottle and be out of the kitchen before Scott Covey came in. She was curious about meeting the man with whom she felt so much empathy, but she also wanted to stay out of the way in case Adam for any reason decided not to represent him. Curiosity won out, however; she decided to wait.

Adam strode to the door. His greeting for Scott Covey was cordial but reserved.

Menley stared at the visitor. No wonder Vivian Carpenter fell for him, she thought immediately.

Scott Covey was stunningly good looking, with even but strong features, a deep tan and dark blond hair that waved and curled even though he wore it short. He was lean as well, but broad shoulders added a hint of strength. When Adam introduced him to Menley, however, it was his eyes she found most compelling. They were a rich, deep hazel, but it wasn't just the color that fascinated her. Rather, she saw in them the same anguish she'd seen in her own eyes when she looked in the mirror after Bobby had died.

He's innocent, she decided. I'd stake my life on it. She was holding Hannah in her right arm. With a smile she shifted the baby and held out her hand. "I'm glad to meet you . . ." she said, then hesitated. He was about her age, she reasoned, and he was a good friend of one of Adam's best friends. So what should she call him? Mr. Covey sounded stilted. ". . . Scott," she finished. She reached for the baby's bottle. "And now Hannah and I will let you two have a chance to talk."

Again she hesitated. It was impossible to ignore the reason he was there. "I know I told you on the phone the other night, but I'm very sorry about your wife."

"Thank you." His voice was low, deep and musical. The kind of voice you could trust, she thought.

Hannah had no intention of going to sleep. When Menley put her down, she howled, pushed away the bottle and kicked off the blankets. "I may list you with an adoption agency," Menley threatened with a smile. She looked at the antique cradle. "I wonder."

The small single bed in the room had two pillows on it. She put one in the cradle, laid a still-fussing Hannah on top of it and covered her with the light quilt. Then she sat on the edge of the bed and began to rock the cradle. Hannah's fussing tapered off. In a few minutes her eyes began to close.

Menley's eyes were heavy too. I should get out of this bathing suit before I nap, she thought. But it's bone dry now, so what's the difference? She lay down and pulled up the folded afghan at the foot of the bed. Hannah whimpered. "Okay, okay," she murmured, reaching out her hand and rocking the cradle gently.

She didn't know how long it was before the sound of light footsteps awakened her. Opening her eyes, she realized she must have dreamed them, since no one was there. But there was a chill in the room. The window was open, and the breeze must have gotten sharper. She blinked and looked over the edge of the bed. Hannah was blissfully asleep.

Boy, the service you get, kid, she thought. Even in my sleep I wait on you!

The cradle was moving from side to side.

21

"*T*his is a wonderful house," Scott Covey said as he followed Adam into the library. "My wife and I were looking at it just a few days before she died. She intended to make an offer on it, but like a true New Englander she had no intention of looking eager to have it."

"Elaine told me about that." Adam indicated one of the battered club chairs by the windows and settled in the other one. "I don't have to point out that the furnishings are garage-sale rejects."

Covey smiled briefly. "Viv was filled with ideas about going to antique shops and really giving the rooms the look they had in the early seventeen hundreds. Last summer she'd worked for a short time for an interior designer. She was like a kid in a candy store at the prospect of doing this big house herself."

Adam waited.

"I'd better get down to business," Covey said. "First, thank you for seeing me. I know it's your vacation and I know you wouldn't have done it if Elaine hadn't asked you."

"That's true. Elaine is an old friend, and she obviously believes you need help."

Covey lifted his hands in a gesture of futility. "Mr. Nichols—"

"Adam."

"Adam, I understand why there's so much talk. I'm a stranger. Vivian was wealthy. But on the Bible, I swear I had no idea she had so much money. Viv was desperately insecure and could be secretive. She loved me, but she was just beginning to understand how much I loved her. Her self-image was terrible. She was so afraid people only bothered with her because of her family background and her money."

"Why was her self-image that bad?"

Covey's expression became bitter. "Her whole damn family. They always put her down. In the first place, her parents didn't want to have her, and when she was born, they tried to make her a carbon copy of her sisters. Her grandmother was the one exception.

She understood Viv, but unfortunately she was an invalid who spent most of her time in Florida. Viv told me her grandmother had left her a million-dollar trust and that three years ago, at twenty-one, she came into it. She told me she had paid six hundred thousand for the house, was living on the rest and wouldn't come into another dime until she was thirty-five. By anybody's standards she was well off, but I understood that the balance of the trust reverted to her grandmother's estate if anything happened to her. Yes, because of her death I received the house, but I never thought her estate went beyond a couple hundred thousand dollars more. I had absolutely no idea she'd already received five million dollars."

Adam linked his fingers and looked up at the ceiling, thinking aloud. "Even if she was only worth the amount of money she told you, people could justifiably say that for a marriage of three months, you did mighty well."

He looked back at Covey and shot the next question. "Was anyone else aware that your wife had not shared her true financial status with you?"

"I don't know."

"No close friend who was a confidante?"

"No. Vivian didn't have what I would call close friends."

"Did her father and mother approve of the marriage?"

"They never knew about it until it was over. That was Vivian's decision. She wanted a quiet wedding at city hall, a honeymoon in Canada and then a home reception when we got back. I know her parents were shocked and I don't blame them. It's possible she did tell them that I didn't know the extent of the inheritance. In a way, as much as she defied them, Vivian desperately wanted their approval."

Adam nodded. "On the phone you said that a detective has been asking you about a family ring."

Scott Covey looked directly at Adam. "Yes, it was an emerald, a family heirloom, I believe. I absolutely remember that Viv was wearing the ring on the boat. The only thing that makes sense is she must have changed it to her left hand that morning. When I was going through her things I found her engagement ring in the drawer at home. Her wedding ring was a narrow gold band. She always wore the engagement and wedding rings together."

He bit his lip. "The emerald ring had been getting tight to the point it was cutting off circulation. That last morning Viv was tugging at it and twisting it. When I was leaving for the store I told her if she was determined to get it off to soap or grease her finger first. She bruised very easily. When I got back we took off for the boat and I didn't think to ask about it and she never mentioned it. But Viv was superstitious about that ring. She never went anywhere without it. I think when I identified her body and didn't see the ring I assumed it was because her right hand was mutilated."

His face suddenly became contorted. He pushed his knuckles against his mouth to stifle the dry sobs that shook his shoulders. "You just can't understand. No one can. One minute we're down there, swimming next to each other, watching a school of striped bass go by, the water so clear and calm. Her eyes were so happy, like a little kid in an amusement park. And then, in a second, it all changed." He buried his face in his hands.

Adam studied Scott Covey intently. "Go on," he said.

"The water went gray, got so rough. I could see Viv was panicking. I grabbed her hand and put it on my belt. She knew I meant that she should hang on to me.

I started to swim for the boat, but it was so far away. The anchor must have been dragging, because the current was fierce. We weren't making progress, so Viv let go of my belt and started to swim next to me again. I could tell that she thought we'd make better time if we both swam. Then, just as we were surfacing, a huge wave came and she was gone. She was gone.''

He dropped his hands from his face and blurted, ''Christ, how can anyone think I'd deliberately allow my wife to die? I'm haunted thinking I should have been able to save her. It was my fault for not being able to find her, but before God, I tried.''

Adam straightened up. He remembered the night of Bobby's death, with Menley sedated, barely conscious, sobbing over and over, ''It was my fault, my fault . . .'' He reached over and squeezed Scott Covey's shoulder. ''I'll represent you, Scott,'' he said, ''and try to relax. You'll get through this. Everything will be all right.''

22

*A*my arrived at seven o'clock to baby-sit Hannah. She greeted Menley, then immediately knelt in front of the baby swing Adam had set up in the keeping room.

"Hi, Hannah," Amy said softly. "Did you go swimming today?"

Hannah looked at her visitor complacently.

"You should have seen her splashing in a puddle in the sand," Menley said. "She yelled when I took her out of it. You'll find that Hannah lets you know when she isn't happy."

Amy smiled briefly. "That's what my mother used to say about me."

Menley knew that Elaine was engaged to Amy's father, but she didn't know whether he was divorced or a widower. It seemed to her that Amy was inviting the question. "Tell me about your mother," she suggested. "I can see she raised a nice daughter."

"She died when I was twelve." The girl's voice was flat, emotionless.

"That's rough." It was on the tip of Menley's tongue to suggest that it was so nice that Elaine would be Amy's new mother, but she suspected that wasn't the way Amy saw it. She remembered how her brother Jack had objected to their mother dating. One man, a doctor, liked her a lot. Whenever he phoned, Jack would call out, "Stanley Beamish for you, Ma." Stanley Beamish was a nerdy character in a mercifully brief TV series that had aired when they were kids.

Her mother would hiss, "His name is Roger!" but her lips would be twitching with a smile when she reached for the phone. Then Jack would flap his arms in imitation of Stanley Beamish, who had the ability to fly.

Roger hadn't lasted long as a potential stepfather. He was a nice guy, Menley thought now, and who knows? Mother might have been much happier if she'd toughed it out, instead of telling Roger that it wouldn't work. Maybe I'll have a chance to talk to Amy a bit this month, she thought. It might make it easier for her.

"It's time to put the crown princess away for the night," she said. "I've made a list of the emergency telephone numbers: police, fire, ambulance. And Elaine's number."

"That one I know." Amy straightened up. "Is it okay if I hold Hannah?"

"Sure. I think it's a good idea."

With the baby in her arms, Amy seemed more confident. "You look awfully pretty, Mrs. Nichols," she said.

"Thank you." Menley felt inordinately pleased by the compliment. She realized she'd been a bit nervous about meeting Adam's friends. She didn't have the knockout looks of the models he used to date, and she knew that over the years he had brought some of them to the Cape. Far more important than that, however, she was sure she must be the object of speculation. Everyone knew her history. Adam's wife who had driven the car over the railroad track and lost his son. Adam's wife who wasn't with him last year in the month he spent at the Cape.

Oh, they'll be eyeing me all right, she thought. After several false starts, she'd chosen to wear a peacock blue raw silk jumpsuit with a blue-and-white corded belt and white sandals.

"Why don't we try to get Hannah settled before I go?" She led the way to the stairs. "The television is in this parlor. But I'd like you to leave the baby monitor on high volume and look in on Hannah every half hour or so. She's great for kicking off the blankets, and the cleaning woman put both sleepers in the wash. The dryer isn't hooked up yet."

"Carrie Bell. She was here?" Amy's voice sounded incredulous.

"Well, no, this woman's name is Hildy. She'll be coming in once a week. Why?"

They were at the top of the stairs. Menley stopped and turned to look at Amy.

Amy blushed. "Oh, nothing. I'm sorry. I knew Elaine was going to suggest someone else to you."

Menley took Hannah from Amy. "Her dad will want to say good night." She went into the master bedroom. Adam was just putting on his navy linen sports jacket. "One of your younger admirers to pay homage," she told him.

He kissed Hannah. "No late dates, Toots, and don't give Amy a hard time." The tenderness in his face belied his flippant tone. Menley felt her heart twist. Adam had been crazy about Bobby. If anything happened to Hannah . . .

Why do you keep thinking that? she asked herself fiercely. She forced her own voice to sound bantering. "Your daughter thinks you look terrific. She wants to know if you're getting gussied up for all your old girlfriends?"

"Nope." Adam leered at her. "I've just got one girl. No," he corrected, "two girls." He addressed the baby. "Hannah, tell your mommy that she looks very sexy and I wouldn't throw her out of bed for anybody."

Laughing, Menley brought the baby back to the nursery. Amy was standing by the side of the crib, her head tilted as though she was listening for something. "Do you get a funny feeling in this room, Mrs. Nichols?" she asked.

"What do you mean?"

"I'm sorry. I don't know what I mean." Amy looked embarrassed. "Please don't mind me. I'm just being silly. Have a great time. I promise you Hannah will be fine and I'll be on the phone in a shot if there's any kind of problem. Besides, Elaine's house is less than two miles away."

Menley paused for a moment. Was there something

odd about the baby's room? Hadn't she felt it herself? Then shaking her head at her own silliness, Menley settled Hannah in the crib and popped the pacifier in her mouth before she could launch a protest.

23

*E*laine lived near the Chatham Bars Inn in a small Cape that had started its existence in 1780 as a half house. Over the years it had been enlarged and renovated so that now it blended handsomely with its more impressive neighbors.

At seven o'clock she made a quick final inspection. The house gleamed. The guest towels were in the powder room, the wine was chilled, the table attractively set. She had made the lobster salad herself, a long, tiresome job; the rest of the buffet was prepared by the caterer. She was expecting twenty people in all and had hired one man to serve, another to tend the bar.

John had offered to handle the bar, but she'd declined. "You're my host, aren't you?"

"If that's what you want."

Whatever Elaine wants, Elaine gets, she thought, knowing just what he would say before he said it.

"Whatever Elaine wants, Elaine gets," John said with a rumble of laughter. He was a big, solid man with a deliberate manner. At fifty-three his thinning hair was completely gray. His full face was open and pleasant. "Come here, sweetie."

"John, don't muss my hair."

"I like it mussed, but I won't. I just want to give you a little hostess gift."

Elaine took the small package. "John, how sweet. What is it?"

"A bottle of olives, what else? Open it."

It was an olive bottle but inside there appeared to be only a wad of blue tissue.

"Now what's this about?" Elaine asked as she unscrewed the top of the jar and reached into it. She began to pull out the tissue.

"Go easy," he cautioned. "Those olives are expensive."

She held the tissue in her hand and opened it. Inside were crescent-shaped onyx earrings edged with diamonds. "John!"

"You said you were wearing a black and silver skirt, so I thought you ought to have earrings to match."

She put her arms around his neck. "You are too nice to be true. I'm not used to being pampered."

"It's going to be my pleasure to pamper you. You've worked hard enough, long enough, and you deserve it."

She held his face between her hands and drew his lips to hers. "Thank you."

The bell rang. Someone was standing at the screen door. "Will you two stop necking and let your company in?"

The first guests had arrived.

It's a very nice party, Menley told herself as she came back from the buffet table and reclaimed her seat on the couch. Six of the couples were lifelong summer Capeys, and some of them were into reminiscing.

79

"Adam, remember the time we took your dad's boat to Nantucket. He was seriously unhappy."

"I forgot to mention our plans to him," Adam said with a grin.

"It was my mother who went on the warpath," Elaine said. "She went on and on about my being the only girl with five young men. 'What will people think?' "

"The rest of us were furious we weren't invited," the quiet brunette from Eastham drawled. "We all had a crush on Adam."

"You didn't have a crush on me?" her husband protested.

"That started the next year."

"The time we dug the pit for the clam bake . . . I nearly broke my neck collecting seaweed . . . That stupid kid who ran down the beach and almost fell into the pit . . . The year we . . ."

Menley smiled and tried to listen, but her mind was elsewhere.

Elaine's fiancé, John Nelson, was sitting on the chair next to the couch. He turned to Menley. "What were you doing as a teenager when these people were cavorting at the Cape?"

Menley turned to him with relief. "I was doing the same thing Amy is doing right now, baby-sitting. I went down to the Jersey shore three years straight with a family with five kids."

"Not much of a vacation."

"It was okay. They were nice kids. Incidentally, I do want to tell you that Amy is a lovely girl. She's terrific with my baby."

"Thank you. I don't mind telling you it's a problem that she resents Elaine."

"Don't you think that going to college and meeting new friends will change that?"

"I hope so. She used to worry that I'd be lonesome

when she went to college. Now she seems to be afraid that after Elaine and I are married, she won't have a home anymore. Ridiculous, but my fault because I made her feel like the lady of the house, and now she doesn't want to be bumped." He shrugged. "Oh well. She'll get over it. Now I just hope, young lady, that you learn to enjoy the Cape the way I did. We came here from Pennsylvania on a vacation twenty years ago, and my wife liked it so much we pulled up stakes. Fortunately I was able to sell my insurance business and buy into one in Chatham. Whenever you're ready to purchase a house, I'll take good care of you. Lots of people don't really understand insurance. It's a fascinating business."

Ten minutes later Menley excused herself to get another cup of coffee. Insurance is not *that* fascinating, she thought, then felt guilty for thinking it. John Nelson was a very nice man, even if he was a little dull.

Adam joined her as she refilled her cup. "Having fun, honey? You were in such a deep discussion with John that I couldn't catch your eye. How do you like my friends?"

"They're great." She tried to sound enthusiastic. The fact was she'd much rather be home alone with Adam. This first week of their vacation was almost over, and he'd spent two days of it in New York. Then this afternoon they had come up from the beach for his appointment with Scott Covey, and tonight they were with all these people who were strangers to her.

Adam was looking past her. "I haven't had a chance to talk to Elaine privately," he said. "I want to tell her about the meeting with Covey."

Menley reminded herself that she'd been delighted when Adam told her he'd decided to take Scott's case.

The bell rang and without waiting for a response a woman in her sixties opened the screen door and came in. Elaine jumped up. "Jan, I'm so glad you made it."

Adam said, "Elaine told me she was inviting Jan Paley, the woman who owns Remember House."

"Oh, that's interesting. I'd love to get a chance to talk to her." Menley studied Mrs. Paley as she embraced Elaine. Attractive, she thought. Jan Paley wore no makeup. Her gray-white hair had a natural wave. Her skin was finely wrinkled, with the look of someone who was indifferent about exposure to the sun. Her smile was warm and generous.

Elaine brought her to meet Menley and Adam. "Your new tenants, Jan," she said.

Menley caught the look of sympathy that came into the other woman's eyes. Clearly Elaine had told her about Bobby. "The house is wonderful, Mrs. Paley," she said sincerely.

"I'm so glad you like it." Paley refused Elaine's offer to prepare a plate for her. "No thanks. I left a dinner party at the club. Coffee will be fine."

It was a good time to let Adam talk to Elaine about Scott Covey. People had begun to drift around the room. "Mrs. Paley, why don't we?" Menley nodded toward the empty loveseat.

"Perfect."

As they settled, Menley could hear the beginning of another story about a long-ago summer adventure.

"I went with my husband to his fiftieth high school reunion a couple of years ago," Jan Paley said. "The first evening I thought I'd go out of my mind hearing about the good old days. But after they got it out of their systems, I had a lovely time."

"I'm sure it's like that."

"I must apologize," Paley said. "Most of the furniture in the house is really dreadful. We hadn't completed the renovation and simply used what was there when we bought it until we were ready to decorate."

"The master bedroom pieces are beautiful."

"Yes. I'd seen them at an auction and couldn't pass

them up. The cradle, however, I found under a load of junk in the basement. It's authentic early seventeenth century, I believe. It may even have been part of the original furnishings. The house has quite a history you know.''

''The version I heard is that a ship captain built it for his bride and then left her when he learned she was involved with someone else.''

''There's more to it than that. Supposedly the wife, Mehitabel, swore she was innocent and on her death-bed vowed to stay in the house until her baby was returned to her. But of course half the old houses on the Cape have developed legends. Some perfectly sensible people swear they live in haunted houses.''

''Haunted!''

''Yes. In fact one of my good friends bought an old place that had really been ruined by do-it-yourselfers. After the house was completely restored and authentically decorated, early one morning, when she and her husband were asleep, she awakened when she heard footsteps coming up the stairs. Then her bedroom door opened and she swears she could see the impression of footsteps on the carpet.''

''I think I'd have died of fright.''

''No, Sarah said she experienced the most benevolent feeling, the kind you have as a child when you wake up and your mother is tucking the blankets around you. Then she felt a pat on her shoulder, and in her head she could hear a voice saying, 'I'm so pleased with the care you have taken of my house.' She was sure it was the lady for whom it had been built letting her know how happy she was to have it restored.''

''Did she ever see a ghost?''

''No. Sarah is a widow now and quite elderly. She says she sometimes senses a benevolent presence and feels they're two old girls enjoying their home together.''

"Do you believe that?"

"I don't disbelieve it," Jan Paley said slowly.

Menley sipped coffee and then found the courage to ask a question. "Did you experience any sense of something odd about the baby's room in Remember House, the small front room next to the master bedroom?"

"No, but we never used it. Frankly for a while after my husband died last year I really thought I'd keep Remember House. But then I sometimes felt such overwhelming sadness that I knew it would be better to let it go. I should never have let Tom do so much of the heavy restoration himself, even though he thoroughly enjoyed every minute of it."

Do we all feel guilty when we lose someone we love? Menley wondered. She glanced across the room. Adam was standing in a group with three other men. She smiled ruefully as she watched Margaret, the thin brunette from Eastham, join them and smile brilliantly up at Adam. A little leftover crush? she thought. I can't say I blame you.

Jan Paley said, "I bought your four David books for my grandson. They're simply wonderful. Are you working on one now?"

"I've decided to set the next one on the Cape in the late sixteen hundreds. I'm just starting to do some research."

"The pity is that the one to have talked to a few years ago would have been Phoebe Sprague. She was a great historian and was preparing notes for a book on Remember House. Perhaps Henry would let you see some of her material."

The party broke up at ten-thirty. On the way home Menley told Adam about Jan Paley's suggestion. "Do you think it would be too pushy to ask Mr. Sprague about his wife's notes or at least ask where she found the best source material?''

"I've known the Spragues all my life," Adam said. "I intended to call them anyway. Who knows? Henry might enjoy sharing Phoebe's research with you."

Amy was watching television in the parlor when they arrived. "Hannah never woke up," she said. "I checked her every half hour."

As Menley walked the girl to the door, Amy said shyly, "I feel so dumb about what I said earlier, that there was something funny about Hannah's room. I guess it's because of that story Carrie Bell was telling people, about the cradle rocking by itself and the spread mussed the way it would be if someone was sitting on the bed."

Menley felt her throat go dry. "I didn't know about that, but it's ridiculous," she said.

"I guess so. Good night, Mrs. Nichols."

Menley went directly to the baby's room. Adam was already there. Hannah was blissfully asleep in her favorite position, her arms over her head. "We can't call her 'her crabbiness' anymore," Adam murmured.

"How many names do we have for this poor kid?" Menley asked as she slipped into bed a few minutes later.

"I can't count that high. Good night, honey." Adam held her tightly. "I hope you had a good time."

"I did." Later she murmured, "I'm not sleepy. Will it bother you if I read for a while?"

"You know I can sleep through a festival of lights." He scrunched his pillow. "Listen, when Hannah wakes up, shake me alive. I'll take care of her. You've been getting up with her all week."

"Great." Menley reached for her reading glasses and began to read one of the books about early Cape history that she had found in the library. It was heavy, and the watersoaked cover was curling. Inside, the pages were flaking and dusty. Even so it made fascinating reading.

She was intrigued to learn that boys went to sea when they were only ten years old and that some of them became captains of their own ships when they were still in their early twenties. She decided that in the new David book it would be interesting to have a seventeenth-century boy who had made seafaring his career.

She came to a chapter that gave brief biographies of some of the most prominent seafarers. One name caught her eye. Captain Andrew Freeman, born in 1663 in Brewster, went to sea as a child and became master of his own ship, the *Godspeed,* at twenty-three. Pilot and skipper, he had the reputation of being absolutely fearless, and even pirates learned to give a wide berth to the *Godspeed.* He drowned in 1707, when against all reason he set sail knowing a nor'easter was coming. The masts broke, and the ship foundered and sank with its entire crew. The wreckage was strewn for miles along the Monomoy sandbar.

I've got to find out more about him, Menley thought. When she finally laid the book on the night table and turned out the light at two o'clock she felt the exhilaration that always came when a story line was firmly rooted in her mind.

Hannah started fussing at quarter of seven. As she had promised, Menley shook Adam awake and settled back with her eyes closed. In a few minutes he returned, the baby leaning against his shoulder, still half asleep. "Menley, why did you switch Hannah to the cradle last night?"

Menley sat up with a start and stared at him.

Confused and slightly alarmed, she thought, I don't remember going in to her. But if I say that, Adam will think I'm crazy. Instead she yawned and murmured, "When Hannah woke up, she wouldn't settle down, so I rocked her for a while."

"That's what I thought," Adam agreed.

Hannah lifted her head from his shoulder and turned. The shades were down, and the light that peeked around their edges was muted. Hannah yawned elaborately and fluttered her eyelids, then smiled and stretched.

In the shadowy room, the contours of her face were so like Bobby's, Menley thought. That was the way Bobby had awakened, too, yawning and smiling and stretching.

Menley looked up at Adam. She did not want him to see that she was on the verge of panicking. She rubbed her eyes. "I read so late. I'm still sleepy."

"Sleep as long as you want. Here, give the morning star a kiss and I'll take her downstairs. I'll take good care of her."

He handed her the baby. "I know you will," Menley said. She held Hannah so that the little face was only inches from her own. "Hi, angel," she whispered as she thought, Your daddy can take good care of you and I promise you this: if the day ever comes when I think I can't, I'll be history.

August 7th

24

Henry and Phoebe Sprague sat at a table outside the Wayside Inn. For the first time this season Henry had brought Phoebe out for Sunday brunch, and a pleased smile was playing on her lips. She had always been a people watcher, and the main street of Chatham was lively today. Tourists and residents were window-shopping, drifting in and out of the specialty shops or heading for one of the many restaurants.

Henry glanced down at the menu the hostess had given him. We'll order eggs Benedict, he thought. Phoebe always enjoys them here.

"Good morning. Are you ready to order, sir?"

Henry looked up and then stared at the boldly pretty waitress. It was Tina, the young woman whom he'd seen in the pub across the street from the hairdresser in early July, the one whom Scott Covey had explained was an actress appearing at the Cape Playhouse.

There was no hint of recognition on her face, but then she'd barely glanced at him before she rushed out of the pub that day. "Yes, we can order," he said.

Throughout breakfast, Henry Sprague kept up a running commentary on the passersby. "Look,

Phoebe, there are Jim Snow's grandchildren. Remember how we used to go to the theater with the Snows?"

"Stop asking me if I remember," Phoebe snapped. "Of course I do." She went back to sipping coffee. A moment later she hunched forward and looked around, her eyes darting from table to table. "So many people," she murmured. "I don't want to be here."

Henry sighed. He'd hoped that the outburst had been a good sign. For some people, tacrine was a remarkably helpful drug, temporarily stopping, even reversing, deterioration in Alzheimer's patients. Since it had been prescribed for Phoebe, he thought he had seen occasional flashes of clarity. Or was he grasping at straws?

Their waitress came with the bill. When Henry laid the money down, he glanced up at her. The young woman's expression was worried and subdued, the exuberant smile singularly absent. She's recognized me, Henry thought, and wonders if I've put her together with Scott Covey.

He enjoyed the realization and was not about to tip his hand. With an impersonal smile he got up and pulled back Phoebe's chair. "Ready, dear?"

Phoebe got up and looked at the waitress. "How are you, Tina?" she asked.

25

Nat Coogan and his wife, Debbie, owned a twenty-foot outboard. They'd bought it secondhand when the boys were little, but because of the care Nat had lavished on it, it was still in excellent condition. Since the boys were spending the afternoon with friends in Fenway Park at the Red Sox game, Nat had suggested to Debbie that they go for a picnic on the boat.

She raised an eyebrow. "You don't like picnics."

"I don't like sitting in fields with ants crawling all over everything."

"I thought you were going to check the lobster pots and then come back and watch the game." She shrugged. "There's something else going on here that I'm not getting, but okay. I'll make some sandwiches."

Nat looked at his wife affectionately. Can't put anything over on Deb, he thought. "No, you just relax for a few minutes. I'll take care of everything."

He went to the delicatessen where he bought salmon, pâté, crackers and grapes. Might as well do everything they did, he thought.

"Pretty fancy," Deb observed as she put the food in a hamper. "Were they out of liverwurst?"

"No. This is what I wanted." From the refrigerator he plucked the chilled bottle of wine.

Debbie read the label. "Are you guilt-complexed for some reason? That's expensive stuff."

"I know it is. Come on. The weather's going to change later."

They dropped anchor exactly one and a half miles from Monomoy Island. Nat did not tell his wife that this was the spot where Vivian Covey had spent her last hours. It might unsettle her.

"This actually is fun," Debbie admitted. "But what have you suddenly got against the deck chairs?"

"Just thought a change of pace would be interesting." He spread an old beach blanket on the deck and laid out the food. He had brought cushions for them to sit on. Finally he poured wine into their glasses.

"Hey, take it easy," Debbie protested. "I don't want to get a buzz on."

"Why not?" Nat asked. "We can nap when we're finished."

The sun was warm. The boat rocked gently. They sipped the wine, nibbled on the cheese and pâté, picked at the grapes. An hour later, Debbie looked drowsily at the empty bottle. "I can't believe we drank all that," she said.

Nat wrapped up the leftover food and put it in the picnic hamper. "Want to stretch out?" he asked as he arranged the cushions side by side on the blanket. He knew she was not a daytime drinker.

"Great idea." Debbie settled down and immediately closed her eyes.

Nat stretched out beside her and began to review some of what he had learned the past few days. Friday after he'd studied the autopsy pictures he'd dropped in on Scott Covey. Covey's explanation that his wife had probably switched the emerald ring to her other hand seemed to him a little glib and perhaps rehearsed.

He glanced at the empty wine bottle warming in the sun. The autopsy report showed that Vivian Carpenter had consumed several glasses of wine shortly before her death. But when he queried her parents about her drinking habits, they'd both told him that she was not a daytime drinker. A single glass of wine made her sleepy, especially in the sun, the same reaction Deb was having.

Would anyone who was sleepy from drinking wine, and who was just learning to scuba dive, have insisted on joining her husband when he said he was going to take a brief underwater swim?

Nat didn't think so.

At three o'clock he sensed a subtle change in the motion of the boat. Heavy rain showers had been predicted for about three-thirty.

Nat stood up. This spot was on line with the entrance to the harbor, and as he watched, from all directions small craft were heading in.

Covey claimed he and Vivian had been down about twenty minutes when the squall hit. That meant that when he got up from the nap that afternoon, he *must* have noticed small craft going in toward shore. There must have been some sense of the current getting stronger.

At that point anyone with half a brain would have turned on the radio and checked the weather report, Nat reasoned.

Deb stirred and sat up. "What are you doing?"

"Thinking." He looked down at her as she stretched. "Want to go for a quick swim, honey?"

Debbie lay back and closed her eyes.

"Forget it," she murmured. "I'm too sleepy."

26

*S*cott Covey spent Sunday in the house. Relieved that Adam Nichols had agreed to represent him, he still was uneasy about one of the specific warnings Adam had given him. "When a rich wife dies in an accident shortly after her marriage to a man no one knows well, and that man is the only one present at her death, there's bound to be talk. You've cooperated with the police, and that was all to the good. Now stop cooperating. Refuse to answer any more questions."

That admonition was fine with Scott.

Nichols' second piece of advice was easy to follow too. "Don't change your lifestyle. Don't start throwing money around."

He had no intention of being that much of a fool.

Finally Adam had said, "And very important— don't be seen with another woman while the police are openly suspicious."

Tina. Should he explain to Adam that before he met Viv, he'd been involved with her? That the relationship had started last year when he was working at the playhouse? Would Adam understand that he'd had nothing to do with her after he met Viv?

He could explain that Tina hadn't realized he'd

come back to the Cape. Then of all the damn luck she quit her job in Sandwich and started working at the Wayside Inn. After she saw him and Viv having dinner there she started calling him. The one time he'd agreed to meet her in person, Henry Sprague, of all people, had to be sitting beside him in the pub! Sprague was nobody's fool. Should he explain to Adam that Tina only stopped by the house one time after Viv was missing, to offer sympathy?

At four o'clock the phone rang. Grimly, Scott went to answer it. It had better not be that detective, he thought.

It was Elaine Atkins, inviting him to a barbecue at her fiancé's place. "Some of John's friends will be here," she said. "Important people, the kind you should be seen with. I saw Adam last night, by the way. He told me he's going to represent you."

"I can't thank you enough for that, Elaine. And of course I'll be happy to join you."

As he drove down the street an hour later, he noticed Nat Coogan's eight-year-old Chevy parked in front of the Sprague house.

27

Nat Coogan had dropped in on the Spragues without phoning in advance. It was not something he did without calculation, however. He knew there was something Henry Sprague had not told him about Scott Covey, and he hoped that the element of surprise might encourage Sprague to answer the question he planned to ask him.

Sprague's cool greeting gave Nat the message he expected. A phone call ahead of time would have been appreciated. They were expecting guests.

"It will just take a minute."

"In that case, please come in."

Henry Sprague hastily led the way through the house to the deck. Once there, Nat realized the reason he was hurrying. Sprague had left his wife alone outside, and in the minute he was gone she had started to walk across the lawn to the Carpenter/Covey house.

Sprague quickly caught up with her and guided her back to the deck. "Sit down, dear. Adam and his wife are going to visit us." He did not invite Nat to be seated.

Nat decided to lay all his cards on the table. "Mr. Sprague, I believe that Scott Covey deliberately abandoned his wife when they were scuba diving, and I'm going to do everything in my power to prove it. The other day I had the very strong sense that there was something you were debating about telling me. I know you're the kind of man who minds his own business, but this *is* your business. Picture how terrified Vivian was when she knew she was going to drown. Imagine how *you'd* feel if someone deliberately led your wife into danger and then abandoned her."

For some time, Henry Sprague had been valiantly trying to give up smoking. Now he found himself reaching into the breast pocket of his sports shirt for the pipe he had left in his desk drawer. He promised himself that he would get it when he let this detective out. "Yes, you're right, there was one thing. Three weeks before Vivian's death I happened to be in the Cheshire Pub at the same time Scott Covey was there," he said reluctantly. "A young woman named Tina came in. I'm sure they were planning to meet. He made a pretense of being surprised to see her, and she took the cue and ran off. She was not someone I knew. But then I saw her again this morning. She's a waitress at the Wayside Inn."

"Thank you," Nat said quietly.

"There's one thing more. My wife knew her by name. I don't know when they could have met except . . ."

He looked over at Vivian Carpenter Covey's home. "Several times lately when I've turned my back, Phoebe has walked over to the Carpenter place. The house isn't air-conditioned, and the windows are usually open. She may have seen Tina there. It's the only explanation I can come up with."

28

"*I* think it was a good idea to get Amy to mind Hannah for a couple of hours," Adam said as they drove past the lighthouse and through the center of Chatham. "From what I understand, Phoebe can't handle much distraction. I gather also that she probably won't be able to discuss her notes, but I'm really glad that Henry was receptive to the idea of sharing them with you."

"I am too." Menley tried to sound enthusiastic, but it was a struggle. It should have been a perfect day, she thought. They'd spent a couple of hours on the beach, then read the Sunday papers while Hannah napped. Around three-thirty, when the thunderstorm broke, they stood at the window and watched the rain lash at the ocean and the angry surge of the waves. An easy, comfortable day, time spent together, sharing things, the kind of day they used to know.

Except that now always in Menley's mind was the specter of a breakdown. What was happening to her? she wondered. She had not told Adam about the panic attack at the railroad crossing, even though he would have understood. But to tell him that the night he was in New York she had awakened to the sound of a train, thundering as though it were roaring through the house! What would any rational human being think about a story like that? Likewise, could she tell him that she had no memory of being in the baby's room last night? No, never!

It would have seemed like whining to let him know that at Elaine's party she felt isolated by the camaraderie she witnessed but could not share. I have plenty of friends, Menley reassured herself. It's just that here I'm an outsider. If we *do* decide to buy Remember House I'll get to know everyone really well. And I'll bring my own friends up to visit.

"You're very quiet suddenly," Adam said.

"Just daydreaming."

The Sunday afternoon traffic was heavy and they inched their way down Main Street. At the rotary they turned left and drove a mile to the Sprague home on Oyster Pond.

As Adam braked in front of the house, a blue Chevy pulled away. Henry Sprague was standing in the doorway. His greeting to them was cordial, but it was clear that he was preoccupied.

"I hope Phoebe's okay," Adam murmured to Menley as they followed him to the deck.

Henry had told his wife they were coming. Mrs. Sprague pretended to recognize Adam and smiled absently at Menley.

Alzheimer's, Menley thought. How awful to lose touch with reality. At Bellevue, her mother had sometimes had patients with Alzheimer's on the floor she supervised. Menley tried to remember some of the stories her mother had told her about helping them to retrieve memory.

"You've researched a great deal about the early history of the Cape," she said. "I'm going to write a children's story about the Cape in the sixteen hundreds."

Mrs. Sprague nodded but did not answer.

Henry Sprague was describing Nat Coogan's visit to Adam. "I felt like a damn gossip," he said, "but there's something about that Covey fellow that doesn't ring true. If there's any chance he let that poor girl drown . . ."

"Elaine doesn't think so, Henry. She sent Scott Covey to me last week. I agreed to represent him."

"You! I thought you were on vacation, Adam."

"I'm supposed to be, but it's obvious that Covey is right to be concerned. The police are on a fishing expedition. He needs representation."

"Then I'm talking out of turn."

"No. If it comes to an indictment, the defense has the right to know which witnesses will be called. I'll want to talk to this Tina myself."

"Then I feel better." Henry Sprague gave a relieved sigh and turned to Menley. "This morning I collected what I could find of Phoebe's files on the early Cape days. I always told her that her research notes were an awful hodgepodge for someone who turned out polished articles and essays." He chuckled. "Her answer was to tell me that she worked in orderly chaos. I'll get them for you."

He went into the house and returned in a few minutes with an armful of thickly packed expandable manila files.

"I'll take good care of them and get them back to you before we go home," Menley promised. She looked at the material longingly. "It will be a treat to dig into this."

"Henry, we're giving some serious thought to buying Remember House," Adam said. "Have you been in it since it was renovated?"

Phoebe Sprague's expression changed suddenly, became fearful. "I don't want to go to Remember House," she said. "They made me go in the ocean. That's what they're going to do to Adam's wife."

"Dear, you're confused. You haven't been in Remember House," Henry said patiently.

She looked uncertain. "I thought I was."

"No, you were on the beach near it. This is Adam's wife you're with now."

"Is it?"

"Yes, dear."

He lowered his voice. "A few weeks ago Phoebe wandered out about eight o'clock at night. Everyone was searching for her. We always enjoyed walking on your beach, and I decided to drive over there. I found her in the ocean not far from your house. Another few minutes and it would have been too late."

"I couldn't see their faces but I know them," Phoebe Sprague said sadly. "They wanted to hurt me."

August 8th

29

*O*n Monday morning, Adam called the Wayside Inn, established that a waitress named Tina was scheduled to work there that day, then called Scott Covey and made an appointment to meet him at the inn.

Menley had arranged for Amy to come and mind Hannah while she delved into Phoebe Sprague's files, something it was obvious she was looking forward to. "You won't miss me," Adam laughed. "You've got a look in your eye like a pirate chasing a ship full of gold."

"Being in this house helps so much to capture the sense of the early days," Menley said eagerly. "Did you know that the door of the main parlor is so large because it was made wide enough to get a casket through it?"

"That's cheerful," Adam said. "My grandmother used to tell me stories about the old house she lived in. I've forgotten most of them." He paused, wistful for a moment. "Well, I'm off to begin the defense of my new client." Menley was feeding Hannah cereal. Adam kissed the top of Menley's head and gave a friendly pat to Hannah's foot. "You're too messy to kiss, Toots," he told her.

He hesitated, trying to decide whether or not to mention that he planned to walk past Elaine's real estate agency and drop in on her if she was there. He decided not to say anything about it. He did not want Menley to know the reason for that visit.

Adam arrived at the Wayside Inn fifteen minutes before Covey was due. It was easy to spot Tina from Henry Sprague's description. As he walked in, she was clearing a small table near the window. He asked the hostess to seat him there.

Very attractive in a showy way, he thought as he took the menu from her. Tina had shiny dark hair, lively brown eyes, a pink-and-white complexion and perfect teeth that were displayed in a radiant smile. An unnecessarily tight uniform displayed every line of her rounded figure. Late twenties, he decided, and she's been around.

Her cheery "Good morning, sir," was followed by a frankly admiring stare. A phrase from the song "Paper Doll," which his mother used to sing, popped into his mind: "flirty, flirty eyes . . ." Tina *definitely* had flirty, flirty eyes, he decided.

"Just coffee for now," he said. "I'm waiting for someone."

Scott Covey came in exactly at nine. From across the room, Adam watched his expression change when he realized Tina would be their waitress. But when he sat down and she came over with the menu, he accepted it without acknowledging her, and she likewise gave no outward sign of recognition, saying merely, "Good morning, sir."

They both ordered juice, coffee and a Danish. "I don't have much appetite these days," Covey said quietly.

"You'll have even less if you play games with me," Adam warned.

Covey looked startled. "What's that supposed to mean?"

Tina was clearing a nearby table. Adam nodded toward her. "It means that the police know that you met that lovely young lady in the Cheshire Pub before your wife died, and that she may have been in your house."

"Henry Sprague." Covey looked disgusted.

"Henry Sprague knew you hadn't just bumped into her at the pub. But if you hadn't given him a cock-and-bull story about her being in the cast of the play at the Cape Playhouse, he wouldn't have said anything to the detective. And how does Mrs. Sprague know Tina?"

"She doesn't."

"Phoebe knew enough to call her by name. How often has Tina been at your house?"

"Once. She dropped by when Viv was missing. That Sprague woman doesn't know what she's doing. It's pretty spooky to see her staring in the window or opening the door and walking in. Since she got so bad, she gets confused about the houses. She must have been hanging around when Tina came that one time. Don't forget, Adam, a lot of people dropped by in those weeks."

"What was your relationship with Tina before your wife died?"

"Absolutely none from the minute I met Viv. Before that, yes. Last year when I was working in the office at the playhouse I was dating her."

Adam raised an eyebrow. "Dating?"

"I was involved with her." Scott Covey looked anguished. "Adam, I was single. She was single. Look at her. Tina's a party girl. We both knew it was going nowhere, that when the season was over I'd be leaving. She used to work at the Daniel Webster Inn in Sandwich. It's just hard luck that she got a job here and Viv and I ran into her. She called me that one time, to ask me to meet her for a drink. She came to

the house to tell me how sorry she was about Viv.
That's all."

Tina was heading toward them with the coffeepot.
"Another cup, sir?" she asked Scott.

"Tina, this is my attorney, Adam Nichols," Scott
said. "He's going to represent me. You know the rumors."

She looked uncertain and said nothing.

"It's all right, Tina," Scott told her. "Mr. Nichols
knows we're old friends, that we used to date and that
you stopped by the house to offer condolences."

"Why did you want to meet Scott in the Cheshire
Pub that day when Henry Sprague was there?" Adam
asked.

She looked directly at him. "When Scott left the
Cape at the end of the season last year, I never heard
from him again. Then when he came in here with his
wife, I was furious. I thought he'd been seeing her
while we were going together. But that wasn't true.
He met her at the end of the summer. I just needed to
hear that."

"I would suggest you make sure that you tell the
police that story," Adam said, "because you're going
to be questioned by the police. I will have another
coffee and the check, please."

When she left the table, Adam leaned across to
Scott. "Listen as you've never listened before. I have
agreed to represent you but I must tell you there are a
lot of negative factors piling up. At your expense, I'm
going to put an investigator on this."

"An investigator! Why?"

"His job will be to do exactly the same fieldwork
the Chatham police are engaged in. If there's a grand
jury hearing, we can't afford surprises. We need to see
the autopsy pictures, the diving gear your wife was
wearing, know the currents that day, find other boat-

ers to testify about nearly being swamped because the storm came up so fast.''

He paused as Tina laid down the check and left again; then he resumed. ''We need more witnesses like Elaine who can testify to how great your marriage was. And finally my investigator is going to investigate you just as the cops are doing right now. If you've got any blemishes in your background, I need to know them and be able to explain them away.''

He glanced at the bill and pulled out his wallet.

''Here, let me.'' Scott reached for it.

Adam smiled. ''Don't worry. It's on the expense account.''

As they walked down the outside steps of the inn, the blue Chevy Adam had seen leaving the Spragues' pulled up and parked. ''Tina has a visitor,'' Adam said dryly as Detective Coogan got out of the car and walked into the restaurant.

30

*A*my arrived at nine-thirty. After greeting Menley, instead of going immediately to Hannah she lingered by the refectory table, which was now piled with the books and files Menley was planning to sort through.

''Mrs. Nichols, my dad and Elaine had some people

over for a barbecue last night, and Scott Covey was there. He's *gorgeous!*''

So that's the reason for the bright eyes this morning, Menley thought. "He certainly is," she agreed.

"I'm glad Mr. Nichols is going to represent him. He's so nice, and the police are giving him a hard time."

"That's what we understand."

"It's weird to think that he and his wife were looking at this house only a day or two before she died."

"Yes, it is."

"He talked to me for a while. His mother died and he has a stepmother. He told me that at first he wouldn't let himself like her and then afterwards he was sorry he had wasted so much time being mean to her. They're really close."

"I'm glad he told you that, Amy. Does it make you feel a little better about your dad getting married?"

She sighed. "I guess so. Listening to him made me believe it will be okay."

Menley got up from the table and put her hands on the young girl's shoulders. "It will be better than okay. You'll see."

"I guess so," Amy said. "It's just . . . no, it'll be all right. I just want my dad to be happy."

Hannah was in the playpen, examining a rattle. Now she shook it vigorously.

Menley and Amy looked down at her and laughed. "Hannah does not like to be ignored," Menley said. "Why don't you put her in the carriage and sit outside for a while?"

When they left, she opened the Sprague files, stacked the contents on the refectory table and began to try to put the papers and books and clippings in some kind of order. It was a treasure chest of historical research. There were copies of letters that dated back to the sixteen hundreds. There were bills and genealogies and old maps and page upon page of memos Phoebe Sprague had made, noting their sources.

Menley found files marked with dozens of categories, among them SHIPWRECKS; PIRATES; MOONCUSSERS; MEETING ROOMS; HOUSES; SEA CAPTAINS. As Henry Sprague had warned, the papers within the files were far from orderly. They were simply there, some folded, some torn scraps, some with highlighted paragraphs.

Menley decided to glance into each file to get a sense of its contents and try to establish an overall picture. She was also on the alert for any mention of Captain Andrew Freeman, in hopes of learning more about Remember House.

An hour later she came across the first one. In the file marked HOUSES there was a reference to a house being built by Tobias Knight for Captain Andrew Freeman. "A dwelling house of goodly size, so as to house the chatles he has transported." The year was 1703. That must refer to this house, Menley thought.

Further back in that file she found a copy of a letter Captain Freeman had written to Tobias Knight, directing the construction of the house. One sentence stood out: "Mehitabel, my wife, be of gentle size and strength. Let the boards be tightly joined so no unseemly draft penetrate to chill her."

Mehitabel. That was the unfaithful wife. "Of gentle size and strength," Menley thought. ". . . so that no unseemly draft penetrate to chill her." Why would any woman deceive a man who cared for her like that? She pushed back the chair, got up, walked to the front parlor and looked out. Amy had placed the carriage almost at the end of the bluff and was sitting by it, reading.

How long had Mehitabel lived in this house? Menley wondered. Was she ever in love with Captain Freeman? When he was due to return home from a voyage, did she ever go up to the widow's walk to watch for him?

She had asked Adam about the small railed platform that crowned the roofs of many old Cape houses. He'd told her they were called widow's walks because in the early days, when a sea captain was expected home, his wife would keep a vigil there, straining her eyes for the first sight of his ship's masts appearing over the horizon. So many vessels did not return that in time the platforms became known as widow's walks.

She mused that the one on this house must command a sweeping view of the ocean. She could imagine a slender young woman standing on it. It would be one of the sketches she would make to illustrate the book.

Then she smiled as she looked out at the carriage where Hannah was sleeping in the sunshine. She felt suddenly calm and at peace. I'll be fine, she thought. I worry too much. Work always puts me back on balance.

She returned to the kitchen and began to go through more files and compile her own lists—names typical of the times; descriptions of clothing; references to weather.

It was quarter past twelve when she glanced at the clock. I'd better think about lunch, she decided and went out to fetch Amy and Hannah.

Hannah was still fast asleep. "This air is like a sedative, Amy," Menley said, smiling. "When I think of the way this kid wouldn't close an eye for the first six weeks of her life!"

"She was unconscious the minute the carriage started rolling," Amy said. "I should charge you half price."

"Not a bit of it. You being here meant I've had a wonderful couple of hours. The files I've been studying have terrific background material."

Amy looked at her curiously. "Oh, I thought I caught a glimpse of you standing up there." She pointed to the widow's walk.

"Amy, except for a few minutes looking out the downstairs window, I haven't budged until just now." Shading her eyes, Menley looked up at the widow's walk. "There's a strip of metal on the left chimney. The way the sun is hitting it, it looks as though something is moving."

Amy looked unconvinced, but she shook her head and said, "Well, the sun was in my eyes when I looked up, and I had to squint. I guess I just thought I saw you."

Later, while Amy was feeding Hannah, Menley slipped upstairs. A folding staircase in a second-floor closet led to the widow's walk. She opened the closet door and felt a blast of cold air. Where's that draft coming from? she wondered.

She pulled the ladder down, climbed the rungs, unlocked and pushed up the trapdoor, then stepped out. Cautiously, she tapped the flooring. It was secure. She walked a few steps and put her hand on the railing. It was almost as high as her waist. That too was secure.

What did Amy see when she thought I was up here? she asked herself. The walk was about ten feet square and nestled between the two massive chimneys. She crossed it and looked out at the spot more than one hundred feet away where Amy had been sitting. Then she turned to examine the space behind her.

Was the metal strip on the corner of the left chimney what had caught Amy's eye? The sunbeams were dancing off the metal, creating moving shadows.

I still don't know how she could make a mistake like that, Menley thought as she went back down the ladder. God, it's clammy in here. She shivered at the deepening chill within the narrow closet.

At the bottom of the steps she became immobilized

as a sudden thought leapt into her mind. Was it possible that Amy was right? When I was picturing Mehitabel watching for her captain from the widow's walk, was the image so vivid because I came up here myself? Menley wondered.

Could I really be losing touch like that? The possibility filled her with despair.

31

*A*dam left his car at the Wayside Inn and walked the two blocks to Elaine's real estate office. Through the window he could see her sitting at her desk. He was in luck. She was alone.

The window was filled with pictures of available properties. As he turned toward the door the aerial photo of Remember House caught his eye and he studied it. Good picture, he thought. It had captured the panorama of the view from the house; the ocean, sandbar, beach, cliff, a fishing boat, all depicted with remarkable clarity. He read the card attached to the picture: REMEMBER HOUSE. FOR SALE. No way, he thought.

When the door opened, Elaine glanced up, then pushed back her chair and hurried into the reception area. "Adam, what a nice surprise." She kissed him lightly.

He followed her back into her office and settled in a comfortable chair. "Hey, what are you trying to do, sell my house from under me?"

She raised an eyebrow. "I wasn't aware you were buying it."

"Let's call it a definite maybe. I just haven't told you yet. Menley loves it, but I don't want to rush her into making a commitment. We have an option till September, don't we?"

"Yes, and I was sure you'd want it."

"Then why the picture in the window?"

She laughed. "It brings in business. People inquire and I say it's optioned and steer them onto someplace else."

"You always were a smart cookie."

"I had to be. Poor Mother never could hold a job. She always picked a fight with someone and got fired."

Adam's eyes softened. "You didn't have it easy, growing up, 'Laine. I hate to be paying too many compliments, but I have to tell you that you look great all the time these days."

Elaine made a face at him. "You're just getting mellow."

"No, not really," Adam said quietly. "Maybe just a little less dense. I don't know if I ever thanked you for being so terrific when I came up here last year."

"Between losing Bobby and separating from Menley you were in pretty bad shape. I was glad to be around for you."

"I'm going to ask for more help now."

"Is anything wrong?" she asked quickly.

"No, not really. It's just that I'll have to go back and forth to New York more than I expected. I'm not happy about leaving Menley alone so much. I think she's having more episodes of that post-traumatic

110

stress than she's letting on. I think she feels she has to tough it out by herself, and maybe she does."

"Would it help if Amy stayed over?"

"Menley doesn't want that. My thought was that some nights when I'm away, Amy could stay with Hannah, and you, or you and John, might invite Menley out for dinner. When I'm home it's good for us to spend most of the time together. We're still . . . Well, never mind."

"Adam, what is it?"

"Nothing."

Elaine knew enough not to urge Adam to finish whatever he had been about to say. Instead she said, "Let me know when you're going to New York again."

"Tomorrow afternoon."

"I'll call late today, invite both of you to dinner tomorrow, then insist that Menley come alone."

"And I'll insist from my end." Adam smiled. "That's a relief. Incidentally I had breakfast with Scott Covey."

"And?" Elaine's eyes opened wide.

"Nothing I can talk about now. Attorney-client privilege."

"I always end up on the outside," she said, then sighed. "Oh, that reminds me. Big news. Circle your calendar for the Saturday after Thanksgiving. John and I are getting married."

"Terrific. When did you set the date?"

"Last night. We had a barbecue, and Scott Covey was there. He talked with Amy about his stepmother, and later Amy told her father that she was happy for us. John called me at midnight. Scott really made the difference."

"Well you keep telling me Covey's a nice guy." Adam got up. "Walk me to the door."

In the reception area he put his arm over Elaine's

shoulders. "So will John get mad if I come running to you with a problem after you're hitched?"

"Of course not."

At the door he hugged her and kissed her cheek. "You used to do better than that," she laughed. In a sudden move, she turned his face and pressed her lips firmly on his.

Adam stepped back and shook his head. "That's called long-term memory, 'Laine."

32

The breakfast service was virtually over. Only a few stray diners lingered over coffee. The manager had told Tina to sit at one of the tables at the far end of the room and talk to the detective. She brought coffee for both of them. Then she lit a cigarette.

"I'm trying to stop," she told Nat after the first puff. "And I only lapse once in a while."

"Like when you're nervous?" Nat suggested.

Tina's eyes narrowed. "I'm not nervous," she snapped. "Why should I be?"

"You tell me," Nat suggested. "One reason I could give is like maybe if you were running around with a newly married man whose rich wife died suddenly. And if that death turned out to be a homicide, a lot of people might wonder how much you knew about the bereaved husband's plans. Hypothetical case, of course.''

"Listen, Mr. Coogan,'' Tina said, "I dated Scott last year. He always said that at the end of the summer he'd be on his way. I'm sure you've heard of summer romances.''

"And I've heard of some that didn't end when summer was over,'' Nat said.

"This one did. It was only when I saw him with his wife, right in this room, and asked around and found out he'd been seeing her last August that I got mad. I had a guy who was crazy about me, even wanted to get married, and I dumped him for Scott.''

"And that's why a month ago you met Scott in that pub?''

"Like I just told Mr. Nichols—''

"Mr. Nichols?''

"He's Scott's lawyer. He was here with Scott this morning. I explained to him that it was me who called Scott, not the other way around. He didn't want to see me, but I insisted. Then when I got to the pub, some man was talking to Scott and I could tell Scott didn't want it to look like I was meeting him, so I didn't hang around.''

"But you *did* see him another time?''

"I called him. He asked me to say what I had to say over the phone. So I told him off.''

"Told him off?''

"I told him I wished he'd never come around, that if he'd just left me alone I'd have married Fred and I'd be in great shape now. Fred was crazy about me, and he had money.''

"But you said you knew all along that Scott intended to take off after the season at the playhouse was over.''

Tina took a long drag on the cigarette and sighed. "Listen, Mr. Coogan, when a guy like Scott rushes you and tells you he's crazy about you, you think to yourself that maybe you're the one who can hang on to him. Lots of girls have landed guys who swore they'd never get married.''

"I suppose that's true. So your beef with Scott was that he was probably pulling the same line on Vivian at the same time.''

"But he wasn't. She met him the last week he was here. She wrote to him. She visited him when he got a job at the theater in Boca Raton. She chased him. At least that made me feel a little better.''

"Scott told you that?''

"Yeah.''

"And then you paid a consolation call after his wife disappeared. Maybe you hoped he'd turn to you in his hour of need.''

"Well, he didn't.'' Tina pushed back the chair. "And it wouldn't have done him a bit of good if he had. I'm seeing Fred again, so you see, there's no reason for you to be bothering me. It's been nice meeting you, Mr. Coogan. My coffee break's over.''

On his way out, Nat stopped at the business office of the Wayside Inn and asked to see the application Tina had filled out when she applied for the waitressing job. From it he learned that she was from New Bedford, had been on the Cape for five years, and her last job was at the Daniel Webster Inn in Sandwich.

In the references she'd supplied, he found the name he was looking for. Fred Hendin, a carpenter in Barnstable. Barnstable was the next town over from Sandwich. He'd bet anything that Fred Hendin was the big spender Tina had dropped last year and then taken up with again. He hadn't wanted to ask Tina too much about him. He didn't want her to warn him that he'd be questioned.

It would be interesting to talk to Tina's patient

suitor and to her fellow employees at the Daniel Webster Inn.

A brazen young lady, Nat thought as he handed back Tina's job application. And pretty smug. She thinks she's handled me pretty well. We'll see.

33

*A*nne and Graham Carpenter had enjoyed house guests for the weekend; their daughters Emily and Barbara had visited with their families. They all went sailing, then the adults golfed while the three teenage grandchildren were at the beach with friends. Saturday night they had dinner at the club. That there was none of the discord and contention that Vivian had brought to such family gatherings served in a perverse way to make Anne all the more aware of her absence.

None of us loved her the way she needed to be loved, she said to herself. That thought and the question of the emerald ring lurked constantly in the back of her mind. The ring was the one object that Vivian had sincerely treasured. Had it been ripped from her finger by the only person who had made her feel loved? The question plagued Anne Carpenter all weekend.

On Monday morning over breakfast, she brought up

the subject of the ring. "Graham, I think Emily had a good idea about the emerald."

"What's that, dear?"

"She pointed out that it's still on our insurance policy. She feels we should report it as missing. In a situation like this, wouldn't we be covered?"

"We might be. But we'd be giving the money to Scott as Vivian's heir."

"I know. But that ring was valued at $250,000. Don't you think that if we hinted to the insurance company that we question Scott's version of how it got lost, they might put an investigator on him?"

"Detective Coogan is conducting an investigation. You know that, Anne."

"Would it hurt if the insurance company got involved?"

"I suppose not."

Anne nodded as the housekeeper came to the table with the coffeepot. "I will have a little more, Mrs. Dillon, thank you."

She sipped in silence for a few minutes, then said, "Emily reminded me that Vivy had complained about the ring being tight when she took it off to clean it. Remember? She broke that finger when she was little and the knuckle was enlarged. But the ring fit fine once it was in place, so Scott's story about her moving it to her other hand doesn't make sense."

Her eyes glistened with tears as she said, "I remember the stories my grandmother told me about emeralds. One story was that it's very bad luck to lose an emerald. The other is that emeralds have the reputation of finding their way back home."

34

Jan Paley had spent a quiet Sunday. For her it was the most difficult day of the week. There were too many memories of pleasant Sundays when she and her husband, Tom, read the papers, shared the crossword puzzle, walked on the beach.

She lived on Lower Road in Brewster, in the same house they'd bought thirty years ago. They'd planned to sell it when the renovations to Remember House were completed. Now she was extremely grateful that they hadn't already moved when she lost Tom.

Jan was always relieved when Monday came and her weekday activities resumed. Recently she had become a volunteer at the Brewster Ladies Library, working there on Monday afternoons. It was a pleasant and useful pastime, and she enjoyed the company of the other women.

Today as she drove to the library she thought about Menley Nichols. She had taken an instant liking to the young woman, which was gratifying since she admired her books enormously. She was also glad that the next book in the David series was going to be set on the Cape. On Saturday night, when she and Menley had talked about Remember House, Menley had indicated that she might use Captain Andrew Freeman as the model for the story of a young boy growing up and going to sea.

Jan wondered if Menley had acted on her suggestion to ask Henry Sprague about Phoebe's research files, but as she drove down the tree-lined highway, another thought occurred to her. At the beginning of the eighteenth century it was common practice for a sea captain to take his wife and even his children with him on a long voyage. Some of those wives had kept journals that were now in the collection of the Brewster Ladies Library. She hadn't gotten around to reading them yet, but it would be interesting to browse through them now and see if by any chance Captain Freeman's wife had been one of the contributors.

It was a beautiful day, and predictably the only car in the parking lot belonged to Alana Martin, the other Monday volunteer. I'll have plenty of time to read this afternoon, Jan thought.

"Those gals got around," she murmured to Alana an hour later as she sat at one of the long tables with a dozen handwritten journals stacked around her. "One of them wrote that she 'was two years on board.' Went to China and India, had a baby born during an Atlantic storm and came home 'refreshed and tranquil of spirit despite some hardships along the way.' This is the jet age, but I've never been to China."

The journals made fascinating reading, but she could find no reference to Captain Andrew Freeman's wife. Finally she gave up. "I guess Captain Freeman's wife didn't take pen in hand, or if she did, we don't have her memoirs here."

Alana was checking the shelves for out-of-order books. She paused and took off her glasses, a habit she had when she was trying to remember something. "Captain Freeman," she mused. "I remember finding some stuff on him years ago for Phoebe Sprague. It

seems to me we even have a sketch of him somewhere. He grew up in Brewster.''

''I didn't know that,'' Jan said. ''I thought he was
from Chatham.''

Alana put her glasses back on. ''Let me take a
look.''

A few minutes later, Jan was reading through the
annals of Brewster and jotting notes. She culled from
the book the fact that Andrew's mother was Elizabeth
Nickerson, daughter of William Nickerson of Yarmouth, who in 1653 married Samuel Freeman, a
farmer. As a wedding gift, she received from her father
a grant of forty acres of upland and ten acres in Monomoit, as Chatham was then known.

I wonder if the Chatham property was where Remember House was eventually built, Jan thought.

Samuel and Elizabeth Freeman had three sons,
Caleb, Samuel and Andrew. Only Andrew lived past
babyhood, and at age ten he went to sea in the *Mary
Lou*, a sloop under the command of Captain Nathaniel
Baker.

In 1702 Andrew, age thirty-eight, now the captain of
his own ship, the *Godspeed*, married Mehitabel Winslow, age sixteen, daughter of the Reverend Jonathan
Winslow of Boston.

I can't wait to tell Menley Nichols I found all this,
Jan exulted. Of course she may have Phoebe's files
and already have come across it.

''Want to take a peek at Captain Andrew Freeman?''

Jan looked up. Alana was at her elbow, smiling tri-
umphantly. ''I knew I'd seen a sketch of him. It must
have been drawn by someone on his ship. Isn't he
impressive?''

The pen-and-ink drawing depicted Captain Andrew
Freeman at the helm of the *Godspeed*. A large man,
broad and tall, with a short dark beard, strong fea-

tures, a firm mouth, eyes that were narrowed as though he was looking into the sun. There was an air of confidence and command about him.

"He had the reputation of being fearless, and he looks the part, doesn't he?" Alana commented. "I tell you, I wouldn't want to be the wife who cheated on him and got caught."

"Do you think it's all right if I make a copy of this?" Jan asked. "I'll be careful."

"Sure."

When she went home later that afternoon, Jan called Menley and told her that she had some interesting material for her. "One find is really special," she promised. "I'll drop everything off for you tomorrow. Will you be home around four o'clock?"

"That would be fine," Menley agreed. "I've been doing some sketching today for the illustrations, and of course Mrs. Sprague's files are glorious. Thank you for suggesting them." She hesitated, then asked, "Do you think there's any chance there might be a picture of Mehitabel anywhere?"

"I don't know," Jan said. "But I'll certainly keep looking."

When she hung up, Jan was lost in thought. Menley Nichols sounded genuinely glad to hear from her, but there was something in her voice that made Jan uneasy. What was it? And then the unanswered question once again ran through her mind.

Tom had suffered the heart attack at Remember House. He'd come in from working outside, clutching his chest. She'd made him lie down, then ran to phone the doctor. When she came back, he'd grabbed her hand and pointed to the fireplace. "Jan, I just saw . . ."

What had Tom seen? He didn't live long enough to finish the sentence.

35

Menley had sent Amy home at two o'clock, after Hannah had been tucked in for an afternoon nap. Several times she had caught the teenager studying her and was slightly unnerved by the scrutiny. It was the same expression she so often saw on Adam's face, and it made her uncomfortable. She was relieved when she heard Amy's car start down the driveway.

Adam wouldn't be home for another hour or so, she knew. After his meeting with Scott Covey he had a golf date with three of the friends who'd been at Elaine's party. Well, maybe they'll get all the "do-you-remember's" out of their systems, she thought, then felt a little guilty. Adam loves golf and has so little opportunity to play, and it's good that he has friends here.

It's just that I'm so confused, she mused. Hearing the train, not remembering putting Hannah in the cradle, not absolutely sure I wasn't on the widow's walk when Amy thought she saw me. But I'll go mad if Adam insists on having someone here all the time. She hated thinking of that first month after Hannah was born, when she'd been having the frequent anxiety attacks and they'd had a live-in nurse. She could still hear the well-intentioned soothing, but incredibly irritating, voice constantly urging her away from the baby. "Now Mrs. Nichols, why don't you have a nice rest? I'll take care of Hannah."

She couldn't allow that to happen again. She went to the sink and splashed cold water on her face. I've got to get over these flashbacks and lapses, she thought to herself.

Menley settled down at the refectory table and went back to Phoebe Sprague's files. The one marked SHIP-WRECKS made fascinating reading. Sloops and packets and schooners and whaling vessels—during the seventeenth and eighteenth centuries so many of them foundered in vicious ocean storms in this area, even right below this house. In those days the Monomoy strip was known as the White Graveyard of the Atlantic.

There was a reference to the *Godspeed,* which in fierce battle had overcome the "pasel of roughes on a pirate ship," and whose captain, Andrew Freeman, personally hauled down the "bloodie flagg" the pirates had run up to the masthead.

The tough side of the captain, Menley thought. He must have been quite a guy. A mental image of him was forming in her mind. Lean face. Skin creased and roughened by the sun and wind. A close-cropped beard. Strong, irregular features dominated by piercing eyes. She reached for her sketchpad and with quick, sure strokes transferred the mental image to paper.

It was three-fifteen when she looked up again. Adam would be along soon, and Hannah was due to wake up. She had just time enough to glance through one more file. She chose the one marked MEETING ROOMS. On the Cape in the early days, the meeting rooms were the churches.

Phoebe Sprague had copied old records she had obviously found interesting. The pages included stories of fiery ministers who stood in the pulpit expounding the "Appetising of God" and the "Prompt Confusion of the Devil"; timid young ministers who gratefully accepted the salary of fifty pounds per annum and "a house and land and a good supply of firewood cut and brought to the door." Fining a member of the congregation for small violations of the Sabbath had obviously been a common occurrence. There was a long list of minor infractions, like whistling, or allowing a pig to run loose on the Lord's Day.

Then, as she was just about to close the file, Menley came across the name Mehitabel Freeman.

On December 10, 1704, at meeting, several goodwives stood up to testify that in the past month while Captain Andrew Freeman was at sea, they had observed Tobias Knight visiting Mehitabel Freeman "at unseemly hours."

According to the account, Mehitabel, three months pregnant at the time, had jumped up to deny the charge hotly, but Tobias Knight, "humble and contrite, did confess his adultery and welcome the chance to cleanse his soul."

The judgment of the deacons was to commend Tobias Knight for his pious renunciation of his sin and "to refuse to put him to open punishment but sentence him to pay for the said offence the sum of five pounds to the poor of the burough." Mehitabel was given the opportunity to renounce her unchastity. Her furious refusal and scathing denunciation of both Tobias Knight and her accusers sealed her fate.

It was decreed that at the first town meeting six weeks after her delivery, "the adulteress Mehitabel Freeman would be presented to receive forty stripes save one."

My God, Menley thought. How awful. She couldn't have been more than eighteen at the time and, to quote her husband, "of gentle size and strength."

There was a notation in Phoebe Sprague's handwriting: "The *Godspeed* returned from a voyage to England on March 1st and sailed again on March 15th. Was the captain present for the baby's birth? Birth registered as being on June 30th, as child of Andrew and Mehitabel, so no question seems to have been raised that he was the father. He returned mid-August, around which time her sentence would have been carried out. Sailed again immediately, taking baby, and was away nearly two years. Next record of *Godspeed* returning is August 1707."

And all that time she didn't know where her baby was or if it was even alive, Menley thought.

"Hey, you're really into that material."

Menley looked up, startled. "Adam!"

"That's my name."

Clearly relaxed, he was smiling. The visor of his cap shaded his face, but his blue sports shirt was open at the neck and revealed a touch of fresh sunburn, which was also apparent on his arms and legs. He leaned over Menley and put his arms around her. "When you're this deep into research there's no point in asking if you missed me."

Trying to pull herself back into the present, Menley leaned her head against his arm. "I counted every minute you were gone."

"Now that's serious. How's her nibs?"

"Fast asleep."

Menley looked up and saw him glance at the baby monitor. He's making sure it's on, she thought. A cry, passionate and heartbreaking raced through her head. "Oh, love, why can you not trust me?"

36

When Fred Hendin pulled his car into the driveway of his modest Cape Cod home in Barnstable, he quickly learned that the man in the car parked across the street was waiting for him.

Nat Coogan, shield in hand, caught him at the door. "Mr. Hendin?"

Fred glanced at the shield. "I gave at the office." His half smile belied the suggestion of sarcasm.

"I'm not selling tickets for the policemen's ball," Nat said pleasantly, quickly assessing the man in front of him. Late thirties, he thought. Norwegian or Swedish background. The man was barely medium height, with strong arms and neck, faded blondish hair in need of trimming. He was wearing denim overalls and a perspiration-soaked tee shirt.

Hendin inserted his key in the lock. "Come in." He moved and spoke deliberately, as though he thought through everything before speaking or acting.

The room they entered reminded Nat of the first house he'd bought when he and Deb were married. It was made up of essentially small rooms, but there was a compact hominess to the floor plan that always appealed to him.

Fred Hendin's living room might have been furnished from a catalogue. Imitation leather couch and matching recliner, walnut veneer end tables, matching coffee table, artificial flower arrangement, threadbare beige carpet, prim beige curtains that didn't quite reach the windowsills.

The obviously expensive entertainment center housed in a fine cherrywood breakfront seemed out of place. It consisted of a forty-inch television set, VCR and stereo system with CD player. There were shelves of videotapes. Nat unabashedly inspected them, then whistled. "You've got a great collection of classic films," he commented. Then he examined the cassettes and CDs. "You must like forties and fifties music. My wife and I are nuts for it too."

"Jukebox music," Hendin said. "I've been collecting for years."

On the top shelves there were a half-dozen wooden sculptures of sailing vessels. "If I'm being too intrusive just say so," Nat said as he reached up and carefully removed an exquisitely carved schooner. "You did this?"

"Uh-huh. I carve while I'm listening to the music. A good hobby. And relaxing. What do you do when you listen to it?"

Nat replaced the carving and turned to face Hendin. "Sometimes I'll be fixing something around the house or tinkering with the car. If the kids are away and we're in the mood, my wife and I dance."

"You've got me there. I have two left feet. I'm getting myself a beer. Want one? Or a soda?"

"No thanks."

Nat watched Hendin's back as he disappeared through the door frame. Interesting guy, he thought. He looked again at the top shelves of the breakfront, appreciating the finely carved sculptures. He's a real craftsman, he thought. Somehow he could not picture this man and Tina together as a couple.

When Hendin returned he was carrying cans of beer and soda. "It's there if you change your mind," he said as he placed the soda in front of Nat. "All right, what do you want?"

"This is routine. You may have heard or read about Vivian Carpenter Covey's death?"

Hendin's eyes narrowed. "And last year Scott Covey was running around with my girlfriend and you want to know if he's still involved with her."

Nat shrugged. "You don't waste time, Mr. Hendin."

"Fred."

"Okay, Fred."

"Tina and I are going to get married. We started dating early last summer, and then Covey came along. Talk about old smoothie. I warned Tina that she was wasting her time, but listen, you've seen the guy. He fed her a line like you wouldn't believe. Unfortunately, she did."

"How did you feel about it?"

"Sore. And in a funny way, sorry for Tina. She's not as tough as she looks or sounds."

Yes she is, Nat thought.

"It was just as I figured," Hendin said. "Covey did a disappearing act at the end of the summer."

"And Tina came running back to you."

Hendin smiled. "That's what I kind of liked. She's got spunk. I went to see her where she was waitressing and said I knew Covey was gone and I thought he was a louse. She told me not to waste my pity."

"Meaning she was still in touch with him?" Nat asked quickly.

"No way. Meaning she wasn't going to be grateful to me. We only dated once in a while over the winter. She saw a lot of other guys. Then in the spring she finally came around to figuring I'm not so bad."

"Did she tell you she contacted Scott Covey when he moved back here?"

Hendin's forehead became a mass of furrows. "Not right away. She told me a couple of weeks ago. You got to realize Tina isn't the kind to let things go. She was damn sore and had to get it out of her system." He gestured. "See this room, this house? It was my mother's. I moved in a couple of years ago after she died." He took a long swallow of beer.

"When Tina and I started talking about getting married, she told me there was no way she was going to live with all this junk. She's right. I just didn't bother to change anything except for making the breakfront and setting up my films and tapes in it. Tina wants a bigger house. We're looking around for a 'handyman's special.' But what I mean is, Tina says it straight."

Nat consulted his notes. "Tina lives in a rented condo in Yarmouth."

"Uh-huh. Just over the town line, a couple of miles from here. Makes it convenient for the two of us."

"Why did she give up her job at the Daniel Webster Inn and go to work in Chatham? That's a good forty-minute drive from here in summer traffic."

"She liked the Wayside Inn. The hours are better. The tips are good. Listen, Coogan. Stay off Tina's case."

Hendin put his beer down and stood up. There was no mistaking that he was not about to discuss Tina any further.

Nat sank deeper into the chair and became aware of the sharp edges of broken plastic around the worn spot behind his head. "Then of course you totally condoned Tina's visit to Scott Covey when his wife was still missing."

Bull's eye, Nat thought as he watched Hendin's face

128

cloud. A faint flush darkened the skin tone of his face, accentuating the prominent cheekbones. "I think we've talked enough," he said flatly.

37

*I*t had been a remarkably pleasant day. As happened occasionally, for some inexplicable reason, Phoebe had experienced brief moments of lucidity.

At one point she'd asked about the children and Henry had quickly placed a conference call. Listening in on an extension, he'd heard the joy in Richard and Joan's voices as they spoke to their mother. For a few minutes there'd been a real exchange.

Then she asked, "And how are . . ."

Henry understood the pause. Phoebe was groping for the names of the grandchildren. Swiftly he provided them.

"I know." Now Phoebe's voice was irritable. "At least you didn't start by saying 'Remember . . .' " Her sigh was an angry reproach.

"Dad," Joan sounded near tears.

"Everything's fine," he warned her.

A click told him that Phoebe had hung up. The wonderful moments of reprieve apparently were over. Henry stayed on the phone long enough to tell his children that the nursing home had an opening on September first.

"Take it for her," Richard said firmly. "We'll come down and stay through Labor Day."

"So will we," Joan echoed.

"You're good kids," Henry said, trying to push back the huskiness that was enveloping his throat.

"I want to be with someone who thinks of me as a kid," his daughter told him, a catch in her voice.

"See you in a couple of weeks, Dad," Richard promised. "Hang in there."

Henry had been on the bedroom extension, Phoebe in her old office. Now Henry hurried to the foyer, the worry that Phoebe in a split second might wander away always with him. But she had not strayed; he found her sitting at the desk where she had spent so many productive hours.

The bottom drawer, which had held so many files, was open and empty. Phoebe was staring at it. The hair she used to wear in a smooth chignon was slipping from the pins that Henry had used to try to secure it in a bun.

She turned when she heard him come in. "My notes." She pointed to the empty drawer. "Where are they?"

Even now he would not refuse her truth. "I lent them to Adam's wife. She wants to consult them for a book she's writing. She'll credit you, Phoebe."

"Adam's wife." The look of irritation that had crossed her face evolved into a questioning frown.

"She was here yesterday. She and Adam live in Remember House. She's going to write a book about the time when the house was built and use the story of Captain Freeman."

Phoebe Sprague's eyes took on a dreamy quality. "Someone should clear Mehitabel's name," she said.

130

"That's what I wanted to do. Someone should investigate Tobias Knight."

She slammed shut the drawer. "I'm hungry. I'm always hungry."

Then as Henry walked toward her, she looked directly at him. "I love you, Henry. Help me, please."

38

When Hannah woke up Menley and Adam went for a late afternoon swim. The Remember House property granted private beach rights, which meant that, while anyone could walk on their beach, no one could settle on it.

The midday warmth was edged now with a hint of early autumn. The breeze was cool, and there were no more strollers passing by.

Adam sat beside Hannah, comfortably propped up in her stroller while Menley swam. "Your mama certainly loves the water, kiddo," he said as he watched Menley dive into the increasingly turbulent waves. Alarmed, he stood up as he saw her venturing farther out. Finally he walked to the water's edge and waved to her, beckoning her to come in.

Had she not seen him, or pretended not to see him? he wondered as she swam farther out. A strong wave gathered, crested and broke. She rode it in and emerged from the surf, sputtering and smiling, her salt-filled hair hanging around her face.

"Terrific!" she exulted.

"And dangerous. Menley, this is the Atlantic Ocean."

"No kidding. I thought it was a wading pool."

Together they walked across the beach to where Hannah still sat, complacently observing a seagull hopping along the shore.

"Men, I'm not joking. When I'm not here, I don't want you swimming out so far."

She stopped. "And be sure to leave the monitor on when your daughter is asleep. Right? And don't you think it would be nice to have Amy stay overnight? To mind *me*, not Hannah, *me*? Right? And isn't your little weapon the implied threat that we need full-time live-in help because maybe this post-traumatic stress thing is a problem? After all, I was the one who drove the car in front of the train when your son was killed."

Adam grasped her arms. "Menley, stop it. Damn it. You keep blaming me for not forgiving you for Bobby's death, but there's no question of blame here. The only problem is that you can't forgive yourself."

They went back to the house, stiffly aware that each had hurt the other deeply and that they should talk this one through. The phone was ringing as they opened the door, however, and Adam ran for it. Any talk would have to come later. Menley tossed a towel over her damp swimsuit, picked up Hannah and listened.

"Elaine! How are you?"

Menley watched as a look of concern came over his face. What was Elaine saying to him? she wondered. And a moment later, What did he mean when he said, "Thanks for telling me"?

Then his tone changed, becoming cheerful again. "Tomorrow night? I'm sorry but I'm on my way to New York. But listen, maybe Menley . . ."

No, Menley thought.

Adam covered the receiver with one hand. "Men, Elaine and John are having dinner tomorrow night at the Captain's Table in Hyannis. They want you to join them."

"Many thanks, but I want to just stay in and work. Another time." Menley nuzzled Hannah. "You're a terrific kid," she murmured.

"Men, Elaine really wants you to come. I hate to think of you alone in this place. Why don't you go? You can get Amy to sit for a few hours."

The implied threat, Menley thought. Go and show how sociable you are, or Adam will want someone to be with you at all times. She forced herself to smile. "That sounds wonderful."

Adam was back on the phone. " 'Laine, Menley would love to come. Seven should be fine." He covered the receiver with his hand again and said, "Men, they think it would be a good idea if Amy stays over. They don't want her driving home late."

Menley looked at Adam. She knew that even Hannah had felt the tension in her body. The baby stopped smiling and began to whimper. "Tell *'Laine,*" Menley said, emphasizing the name and Adam's personal abbreviation of it, "that I am perfectly capable of being alone in this or any other house, and if Amy can't drive home at ten o'clock on a summer evening, then she is too immature to be minding my child."

The thaw began at dinner. While Menley fed and bathed Hannah, Adam made a quick trip to the market and returned with fresh lobsters, watercress, green beans and a crisp loaf of Italian bread.

They prepared dinner together, sipped a cold chardonnay while the lobsters steamed and at the end of the meal brought their cups of espresso with them while they strolled to the end of the property and watched powerful waves pound the shoreline.

The taste of the salt-filled wind on her lips calmed Menley. If Adam were the one going through these bouts of anxiety and depression, I'd be worried too, she reminded herself.

Later, when they were going to bed, they checked Hannah for the last time that night. She had moved around in the crib so that she was lying from side to side. Adam straightened her, covered her and for a moment rested his hand on her back.

Something else Menley had gleaned from the files flashed through her mind. In the old Cape days the special love between a father and his baby daughter had been acknowledged and even named. The daughter was her father's *tortience*.

Later, their arms around each other, drifting off to sleep, Adam asked the question he could no longer suppress. "Men," he whispered, "why didn't you want Amy to know you'd been on the widow's walk?"

39

When Nat Coogan got to work on Tuesday morning, he found a note on his desk. "See me." It was signed by his boss, Frank Shea, the chief of police.

What's up? he wondered as he headed for his boss's

office. He found Frank on the phone with the district attorney. Shea's fingers were drumming on the desk. His usual amiable expression was missing.

Nat settled in a chair, listening to the half of the conversation he could hear and guessing the rest.

The heat was on. Graham Carpenter's insurance company had gotten in on the act. They were more than happy to subscribe to Carpenter's theory that his daughter had experienced foul play, that her emerald ring had been forced from her finger by Scott Covey and was now in his possession.

Nat raised his eyebrows as he realized that the next part of the discussion had to do with the study of ocean currents. He gathered that Coast Guard experts were willing to testify that if Vivian Carpenter Covey had been scuba diving where her husband claimed they were when they got separated, her body would not have washed ashore in Stage Harbor but instead would have been carried out toward Martha's Vineyard.

When Shea got off the phone, he said, "Nat, I'm glad you listened to that bird-dog hunch of yours. The DA was very pleased to hear that we already have an active investigation going. It's good that we've got a head start, because when the media get wind of this, it'll turn into a circus. Remember what they did with the von Bulow case."

"Yes, of course. And we face some of the same problems the prosecution did in that case. Innocent or guilty, von Bulow got off because he had a good lawyer. I'm convinced Covey is guilty as sin, but proving it is another matter. He has a damn good lawyer too. It's a lousy break for us that Adam Nichols took on Covey's case."

"We may have a chance to find out how good Nichols is soon enough.

"We're about to find more hard evidence. On the

basis of the missing emerald ring and everything else we know, the DA is getting a search warrant for Covey's home and boat. I want you there when his people go in."

Nat got up. "I can hardly wait."

In the privacy of his own office, Nat gave vent to some of the irritation he felt. Now that it was obvious that the media would pick up the scent on the case and start howling for news, the district attorney was going to have the state police take over the investigation. It's not just that I want to break this case myself, Nat thought. It's that I think it's a stupid grandstand play, rushing it to a grand jury before we have something absolutely solid to go on.

He took off his jacket, rolled up his sleeves and loosened his tie. Now he was comfortable. Deb was always after him not to loosen his tie when they went out to dinner. She'd say, "Nat, you look so nice, but when you pull your tie down and open the top button of your shirt you spoil it. I swear you must have been hanged in a previous incarnation. They say that's the reason some people can't wear anything tight around the neck."

Nat sat at his desk a few moments longer, thinking about Deb, about how lucky he was to have her, thinking about the bond between them, the love and the trust.

He picked up the coffee mug, went out to the machine in the hall, absentmindedly poured a cup and carried it back to the office.

Trust. A good word. How much had Vivian Carpenter trusted her husband? If you could believe Scott Covey, she didn't trust him enough to tell him the full extent of her inheritance.

Seated at his desk again, Nat leaned back and sipped the coffee while he stared at the ceiling. If Vivian had been as insecure as everyone seemed to indicate, wouldn't she have been watching for signs that everything was not right with Covey?

Phone calls. Did Tina ever call Covey at home, and if so, was Vivian aware of it? Vivian's phone bill. For sure she was the one who paid the expenses. Would Covey have ever been dope enough to call Tina from his home? He would have to check that out.

Something else. Vivian's lawyer, the one who prepared the new will after the marriage. It would be worth ambling over to see him.

The phone rang. It was Deb. "I was listening to the news," she said. "There was a big story about an investigation into Vivian Carpenter's death. Did you expect that?"

"I just heard about it." Briefly Nat filled his wife in on his meeting with Jack Shea and what he was planning to do now. He had long ago learned that Deb was an excellent sounding board for him.

"The phone bills are a good idea," Deb said. "I'll bet anything that he wouldn't be dumb enough to call a girlfriend's apartment from home, but you say this Tina is a waitress at the Wayside Inn. Calls from his house to the Inn wouldn't be listed, but you could ask whether Tina got many personal calls there and if anyone knows who made them."

"Very smart," Nat said admiringly. "I've certainly educated you to think like a cop."

"Spare me. But another thing. Go to Vivian's beauty parlor. They're hotbeds of gossip. Or better yet, maybe I should start going there. I might hear something. You told me she went to Tresses, didn't you?"

"Yes."

"I'll make an appointment for this afternoon."

"Are you sure this is strictly business?" Nat asked.

"No, it isn't. I've been dying to get my hair frosted. They do a good job but they're expensive. Now I don't have to feel guilty. Bye, dear."

40

*A*fter Adam's question about Menley's not wanting Amy to know she'd been on the widow's walk, they had not talked any more but lay unhappily side by side, not touching, each aware that the other was awake. Just before dawn Menley had gotten up to check the baby. She found Hannah sleeping contentedly, the blankets cozy around her.

In the faint glow of the night-light, Menley stood over the crib, drinking in the exquisite little features, the tiny nose, the soft mouth, the lashes that cast shadows on the round cheeks, the wisps of golden hair that had begun to curl around the baby's face.

I can't swear that I *wasn't* on the widow's walk when Amy thought she saw me, but I do know that I would never neglect or forget or hurt Hannah, she thought. I have to understand Adam's concern, she warned herself, but he must realize that I will *not* have a baby-sitter reporting about me to his old buddy Elaine.

That resolve firmly made, it was easier to settle back

into bed, and when Adam's arm crept around her, she did not pull away.

At eight o'clock Adam went out for fresh bagels and the newspapers. As they ate and sipped coffee, Menley was aware that they were both trying to put aside the last vestiges of tension. She knew that when he left for New York this afternoon, neither one of them wanted to have the remnants of a quarrel still hanging between them.

He offered her her pick of the newspapers.

She smiled. "You know you want to start with *The New York Times.*"

"Well, maybe."

"That's fine." She opened the first section of the *Cape Cod Times* and a moment later said, "Oh boy, look at this." She slid the paper across the table.

Adam scanned the story she was pointing to, then jumped up. "Damn it! They're really gunning for Scott. Right now there must be a hell of a lot of pressure on the DA to call for a grand jury."

"Poor Scott. Do you think there's a chance they'd actually indict him?"

"I think the Carpenter family is howling for blood, and they've got plenty of pull. I've got to talk to him."

Hannah had had enough of the playpen. Menley picked her up, held her on her lap and gave her the end of a bagel to gnaw on. "Feels good, doesn't it?" she asked. "I think you've got a couple of teeth on the way."

Adam was holding the phone. "Covey's not home and he didn't leave his machine on. He should know enough to keep in touch with me. He has to have seen the paper."

"Unless he went fishing early," Menley suggested.

"Well, if he did, I hope there's nothing in his house that the police will find interesting. You can bet your boots that before the day is over some judge will be signing a search warrant." He slammed down the receiver. "Damn!"

Then he shook his head and walked over to her. "Listen, bad enough I have to go to New York. There's nothing I can do until Covey calls me, so let's not waste our time. You girls game for the beach?"

"Sure. We'll get dressed."

Menley was wearing a flowered cotton robe. Adam smiled down at her. "You look about eighteen," he commented. He smoothed her hair, then rested his hand on her cheek. "You're an awfully pretty lady, Menley McCarthy Nichols."

Menley's heart melted. One of the good moments, she thought—the kind I used to take for granted. I love him so much.

But then Adam asked, "What time did you say Amy is coming?"

She had planned to tell him this morning that this would be Amy's last day, but she didn't want to start a quarrel. Not now. "I asked her to be here around two," she said, trying to sound casual. "I'll work on the book this afternoon after I come back from the airport. Oh, I forgot to tell you. Jan Paley found some interesting facts about Captain Andrew Freeman. She's dropping in around four."

"That's great," he said, stroking her head. She knew Adam's enthusiastic reaction was an indication of his desire to have her surrounded by people.

Just don't suggest that I ask Jan to stay the night, she thought bitterly, clutching the baby as she pushed his hand away and got up.

41

*S*cott Covey did not realize how deeply the meeting with Adam the previous day had upset him until he took the boat out early Tuesday morning. The word was that the blues were running off Sandy Point. When the sun rose at 6:00 A.M. he was anchored in the location where they'd supposedly been spotted.

As he sat patiently holding the rod, Scott forced himself to think of the warnings Adam Nichols had given him. And Adam had said he was going to have his own investigator on him to find any "blemishes" he might have in his background.

It occurred to him that he had not spoken to his father and stepmother in five years. It's not my fault, he thought. They moved to San Mateo; her family is all around, and when I go out there's no room for me to stay overnight. But there might be questions about why his family had not come to either the wedding reception or the funeral service. He decided to call his father and ask for his support.

It was another beautiful August day in a string of sunny, low-humidity days. The horizon was dotted with boats ranging in size from dinghys to yachts.

Vivian had wanted a sailboat. "I just bought this one so I could get used to handling a boat on my own," she'd explained. "That's why I called it *Viv's Toy.*"

Now, riding in the boat with that name painted on the side, he felt weighted down. When he'd been walking down the dock this morning, Scott had seen several men standing next to the boat, looking at it and talking quietly. Speculating about the accident, no doubt.

As soon as this was settled, he'd change the name. No. Better than that. He'd sell the boat.

A strong tug on his line brought him sharply back to the present. He had a big one to land.

Twenty minutes later a thirty-two-pound striped bass was thrashing wildly on the deck.

Perspiration streaming from his forehead, Scott observed its dying struggle. Then revulsion seized him. He cut the line, managed to get a grip on the flailing fish and threw it back into the ocean. He had no stomach for fishing today, he decided, and headed for home.

On impulse Scott went to Clancy's in Dennisport for lunch. It was a cheerful, gregarious place, and he felt the need to be in the company of a lot of other people. He sat at the bar and ordered a beer and a hamburger. Several times he noticed the glances other people directed at him.

When the stools next to him were vacated, two attractive young women grabbed them. They quickly opened up a conversation by explaining that this was their first visit to the Cape and asked him if he could tell them the fun places to go.

Scott swallowed the last of his hamburger. "You're in one of the best," he said pleasantly and signaled for his bill. That's all I need, he thought. With my luck Sprague will come waltzing in and see me talking to these girls.

At least tonight he'd be able to relax. Elaine Atkins

and her boyfriend had invited him to dinner at the
Captain's Table in Hyannis. They were bringing
Menley Nichols too, and she'd been genuinely kind
to him.

On the way home he decided to stop for a paper. He
tossed it on the seat beside him and did not open it
until he was in the house. That was when he saw the
front page headline: CARPENTER FAMILY DEMANDS
ANSWERS.

"Oh, Christ," he murmured and rushed to the
phone. His call was to Adam Nichols, but there was
no answer.

An hour later the front doorbell pealed. He went to
the door and opened it. A half-dozen grim-faced men
were standing there. Scott only recognized one of
them, the detective from Chatham who'd questioned
him earlier.

In a daze he saw a piece of paper waved before him,
then heard the frightening words, "We have a search
warrant for these premises."

42

Menley got back from dropping Adam at the airport at quarter of two. The phone was ringing as she
opened the door, and still clutching Hannah in one
arm, she rushed to answer it.

It was her mother calling from Ireland. After the first joyous exchange, she found herself trying to reassure her mother that all was well. "What do you mean you have a feeling that something's wrong, Mom? That's crazy. The baby's great . . . We're having a wonderful time . . . The house we've rented is fascinating . . . We're even thinking of buying it . . . Weather's wonderful . . . Tell me about Ireland. How's the itinerary I made out for you?"

She had been to Ireland a half-dozen times on writing assignments and had helped plan her mother's trip. It was a relief to hear that the arrangements were highly satisfactory. "And how are Phyllis and Jack enjoying it?"

"They're having a great time," her mother said. Then she lowered her voice, adding, "Needless to say Phyl is hell-bent on looking up her family tree. We spent two days in Boyle while she was going through old county records. But score one for her. She did locate her great-grandfather's farm in Ballymote."

"I never doubted she would," Menley said, laughing, then tried to persuade Hannah to coo and gurgle for Grandma.

Before the conversation ended, Menley again assured her mother that she was feeling fine, that she'd hardly had a trace of PTSD.

"And wouldn't it be nice if that were true?" she asked Hannah ruefully when she hung up the phone.

Amy arrived a few minutes later. Menley greeted her coolly and knew Amy was perceptive enough to pick up the change in her attitude.

While Amy put Hannah in her carriage and took her outside, Menley settled down to the Sprague files. A note Phoebe Sprague had written about the meeting house built in 1700 intrigued her. After the building statistics—"20 ft by 32 and 13 feet in the walls," the names of the men who were appointed to "get the

144

timber and frame the house," "to bring boards and planks" and "to buy more finishing"—Mrs. Sprague had written, "Nickquenum (Remember House) was much larger than the meeting house, which probably caused a great deal of discontent in the town. People were undoubtedly ready to believe the worst of Mehitabel Freeman."

Then in what was clearly a later memo she had penciled in, "Tobias Knight," followed by a question mark.

The builder. What was the question about him? Menley wondered.

Shortly before three an agitated Scott Covey phoned, looking for Adam. The police had arrived with a search warrant. He wanted to know if there was anything he could do to stop them.

"Adam tried to reach you this morning," Menley said, and gave him Adam's New York office number. "I do know this," she told him, "once a judge issues a warrant, no lawyer can get it canceled, but it can be challenged later in court." Then she added softly, "I'm so sorry, Scott."

Jan Paley arrived promptly at four. Menley had the feeling of being on firm ground when she greeted the handsome older woman. "It's so kind of you to do research for me."

"Not at all. When Tom and I became interested in this house, we used to talk to Phoebe Sprague about it. She was fascinated by the story of poor Mehitabel. I'm glad Henry lent you Phoebe's papers." She glanced at the table. "I can see you are caught up in them," she said, smiling as she surveyed the stacks of files.

Menley checked on Amy and the baby, put on a kettle for tea, then placed cups and sugar and milk at the end of the table.

"Believe it or not, I have a computer and printer

and all the trimmings set up in the library, but there's something so inviting about this kitchen, or keeping room I guess I should call it, that I'm happiest working here."

Jan Paley nodded in understanding. She ran her hand over a protruding brick on the face of the massive fireplace. "I can see you're very into the spirit of the house. In the early days the keeping room was the only room they really lived in. The winters were so bitterly cold. The family slept in the bedrooms under piles of quilts and then rushed down here. And think about it. When you have a party at home, no matter how much room you have, the guests will usually manage to work their way into the kitchen. Same principle. Warmth and food and life."

She gestured toward the pantry door opposite the fireplace. "That used to be the borning room," she said. "It's where the woman gave birth or where the sick person was brought to be nursed back to health or to die. Obviously it made sense. The fire kept that room warm as well."

For a moment her eyes brightened, and she blinked back tears. "I hope you do decide to buy this place," she said. "It could make a wonderful home, and you have the feel for it."

"I believe I do," Menley agreed. It was on the tip of her tongue to tell this intelligent, sympathetic woman about the unexplainable business of the figure on the widow's walk, of Hannah being moved during the night to the cradle and the sound of the train rushing through the house, but she could not. She did not want anyone else to look at her as though speculating on her emotional stability.

Instead she busied herself at the stove, where the kettle was now whistling, poured boiling water into the teapot to warm it and reached for the tea cannister.

"You know how to make a cup of tea," Jan Paley observed.

"I hope so. My grandmother had a heart attack if anyone used teabags. She said that the Irish and the English always knew how to make a proper cup."

"A lot of the early sea captains carried tea as part of their cargo," Jan Paley commented. As they sipped the tea and nibbled on cookies, she reached for her oversized shoulder bag. "I told you I'd found some interesting material on Captain Freeman." She brought out a manila envelope and handed it to Menley. "Something that occurred to me: Captain Freeman's mother was a Nickerson. From the beginning the various branches of the family began to spell the name differently—Nickerson, Nicholson, Nichols. Was your husband a descendant of the first William Nickerson?"

"I have no idea. I do know his ancestor came over in the early sixteen hundreds," Menley said. "Adam never was terribly interested in tracing the line."

"Well, if you do decide to buy this house, he might become interested. Captain Freeman could turn out to be a thirty-fifth cousin, generations removed."

Jan watched as Menley began to read quickly through the material from the Brewster Library. "The coup I promised is on the last page."

"Great." Menley reached for a file on the table. "This is some of the data I've culled so far. I'd like you to take a look at it."

As she turned to the last page of the Brewster material, Menley heard Jan Paley's disappointed protest: "Oh, look, you already have the captain's picture, and I thought I was going to give you a treat by digging it up for you."

Menley felt her lips go dry.

Jan was looking at the sketch Menley had made

when she envisioned how she would portray the mature Captain Andrew Freeman in the new David book.

She was staring down at the copy Jan had made of the sketch of Captain Andrew Freeman at the wheel of his schooner.

The faces were identical.

43

Scott Covey carried a beer out onto the deck while the team of policemen and detectives searched his home. His face set in grim lines, he sat with his back to the Sprague house. The last thing he needed was to see Henry Sprague watching what he had helped set in motion. *If Tina's name hadn't come into this, the cops wouldn't be here now,* was the thought that he could not shake off.

Then he tried to reassure himself. He had nothing to worry about. What did they expect to find? No matter how much they searched, there was nothing in the house to incriminate him.

Adam Nichols had told him to stay put until everything about Viv's death and will was settled, but Scott knew he was beginning to hate this house and to hate the Cape as well. He knew that for him it would always be like living in a goldfish bowl.

He'd worked last winter in the office of a struggling

playhouse in Boca Raton, Florida. He had liked it there, so that was where he would buy a home when this was all over. Maybe he would even buy into that playhouse, too, instead of starting a new one here, the way he and Viv had planned.

Think ahead, he urged himself. They have nothing on me and nothing to go on except suspicion and jealousy and dirty minds. There is nothing that will stand up in a court of law.

"This place is clean," an investigator from the district attorney's office told Nat Coogan.

"It's too clean," Nat snapped as he continued to go through the desk. What little personal mail they had found was addressed to Vivian, letters from friends congratulating her on her marriage; postcards from cousins traveling in Europe.

There was a small, neat pile of bills, all marked paid. No mortgage; no credit card installments; no car loan: sure keeps things simple, Nat mused. Also helps one to stay mobile, with nothing to tie him down.

The phone bill was not very high. He knew Tina's phone number but there had not been a single call to it in the three months of the marriage.

He also had Vivian's lawyer's phone number. There were no calls to him in the last three months.

The bank records were somewhat interesting. Vivian kept a single checking account in the local bank, and it was in her name only. If Covey had his own money, he didn't keep it locally. If he had been dependent on her for cash, she had been doling it out to him. Of course, a good lawyer could argue that the lack of records in the house validated Covey's story that his wife had not admitted to him the extent of her holdings.

The Carpenters had told Nat about the house being stripped of pictures of Vivian. Nat found them in the guest room. Covey had also prepared a box to return to the family. He had not included any pictures in which he appeared with Vivian. Nat grudgingly acknowledged that that did show sensitivity.

On the other hand, the pictures of Covey and Vivian together were piled on the floor of a storage closet. Not exactly the place you keep sentimental objects, he thought.

Vivian's clothes were packed neatly in her expensive luggage. Who was going to be the recipient? he wondered. Not Tina. She was too heavy for them. Nat's bet was that the clothes and suitcases were headed for a secondhand shop.

He hadn't really expected that they would come across the emerald ring. Even if Covey had it, he wouldn't be stupid enough to keep it where it could be found. Vivian apparently wasn't really into jewelry. They had found her engagement ring, some chains and bracelets and earrings, all in a small jewelry box in the master bedroom. Nothing, including the engagement ring, had any significant value.

Nat decided to make his own inspection of the garage. Attached to the house, it was a good-sized structure, capable of holding two cars. Shelves in the back were neatly stacked with diving and fishing gear, an ice chest, some tools—the usual paraphernalia. The diving gear Vivian had been wearing when her body washed in was still being evaluated.

Covey and Vivian had only one car, a late-model BMW. Nat knew that it had belonged to Vivian. The more he'd seen this afternoon, the more he'd thought of his mother's disgust when her older sister married years ago. "Jane's worked all these years for everything she has," his mother had fumed. "What did she see in that miserable leech? He went into the marriage with one set of underwear."

It looked to Nat as though Covey had brought about

the same amount of worldly goods to his union with Vivian.

Then his eyes brightened. The BMW was on the left side of the garage. The floor on the right side was stained with oil.

Nat got down on his knees. There was no sign of oil drippings from the BMW, and he knew there were no oil stains in the driveway.

Who had parked here, not once but a number of times, he wondered, and why would a visitor's car be driven into the garage? One reason, of course, would be to ensure that no one would know it was there.

Nat knew that his next stop would be to see if Tina's car leaked oil.

44

*D*eb Coogan was having a marvelous time. Usually she washed her own short, curly hair, toweled it dry and went every six weeks or so to the small hairdresser's at the other end of town to have it shaped. This was her first visit to Tresses, the premier beauty salon in Chatham.

She was relaxed, thoroughly enjoying the luxurious pink-and-green interior of the chic salon, the prolonged shampoo that included a neck massage, the frosting that brought gold highlights to her medium-brown hair, the hot-oil manicure and the first-time pedicure. Deciding that it was her civic duty to try to get into conversation with as many operators as possible, she'd elected to have all these services.

Any fear she had that the salon's employees might be reluctant to talk disappeared quickly. Everyone in the place was buzzing with the news that Scott Covey might be a suspect in his wife's death.

Deb found it easy to get Beth, who shampooed her hair, to talk about the late Vivian Carpenter Covey, but all she learned was that Beth nearly fainted when she read that Vivian was worth so much money. "Never a tip to me and just a chintzy one to the hairdresser. And take my word for it. One drop of water got near her ear and she'd howl about her sensitive eardrums. I ask you, how sensitive could they be? She was always bragging about learning to scuba dive."

The hairdresser was a bit more charitable. "Oh, we all had a turn having Vivian as a client. She was always worried that she didn't look just right. And it was always the operator's fault, of course, if she thought she didn't. It's really a shame. She was a pretty woman but shifted between being on her Carpenter family high horse and getting upset about everything. She'd drive a saint crazy."

The manicurist was also gossipy but, unfortunately, not especially helpful: "She was crazy about that husband of hers. Isn't *he* gorgeous? One day he was crossing the street to pick her up, and one of our new girls saw him through the window. She said, 'Excuse me, I'm going to run out and throw myself in front of that hunk.' She was joking, of course, but wouldn't you know she was just finishing Vivian's nails? Talk about going through the roof. Vivian yelled at her. 'Why does every tramp in the world want to make a play for my husband?' "

Want to make a play, Deb thought. That suggests

he did not take them up on it. "When did that happen?" she asked.

"Oh, about two or three weeks before she drowned."

It was when she was having her pedicure that Debbie knew her afternoon had not been an extravagant waste. The pedicures were given in a separate, screened-off area with two raised chairs side by side over footbaths.

"Try to keep your toes still, Mrs. Coogan," said Marie, the pedicurist. "I don't want to cut you."

"I can't help it," Debbie confessed. "I have very ticklish toes."

Marie laughed. "So does one of my other clients. She almost never has pedicures, but when she was getting married we all told her she absolutely had to have pretty feet."

Recognizing an opening, Debbie brought up Vivian's name. "When you think that Vivian Carpenter only lived three months after she was married . . ." She sighed and let her voice trail off.

"I know. It was awful, wasn't it. Sandra, the client I was telling you about, the one who never wants to have pedicures?"

"Yes."

"Well, the day she had one for her wedding, she was sitting right in this chair and Vivian was next to her. They started talking. Sandra's the kind who tells you all her business."

"What was she talking about that day?"

"She was telling Vivian that she was on her way to her lawyer's office to meet her fiancé to sign a very tight prenuptial agreement."

Debbie sat up straighter. "What did Vivian say?"

"Well, she said something like, 'I think if you can't go into a marriage loving and trusting each other, you shouldn't go into it.' "

Marie applied lotion to Debbie's feet and began to massage them. "Sandra wasn't the kind to take that lying down. She told Vivian that she'd been married once before, and they broke up after three years. Sandra has a couple of boutiques. Her ex claimed he helped her a lot because—get this—at night she talked about her expansion plans to him. He got a big settlement. Sandra said when she married him he didn't know what the word 'boutique' meant and he still didn't know what it meant when they separated. She told Vivian that when one spouse has money and the other doesn't, if the marriage breaks up, the one with money pays through the nose."

"What did Vivian say?" Debbie asked.

"Vivian looked kind of upset. She said that that was very interesting and a good point. She said, 'Maybe I'd better call my lawyer.' "

"Was she joking?"

"I don't know. With her you never could tell." Marie pointed to the trays of polish. "Same color as your fingers, strawberry sorbet?"

"Please."

Marie shook the bottle, unscrewed the cap and with careful strokes began to paint Debbie's toenails. "Such a shame," she sighed. "Underneath, Vivian was really a nice person, just so insecure. That day she was talking to Sandra was the last time I ever saw her. She died three days later."

45

The captain's table restaurant, housed in the Hyannis Yacht Club, overlooked the harbor.

As a longtime member of the club and frequent customer of the restaurant, John had secured a desirable table in the dining room's glassed-in addition. He insisted that Menley sit facing the window so that she could enjoy the view of Nantucket Sound, the graceful sailboats, the sleek yachts and the ponderous island steamships that brought tourists back and forth from Martha's Vineyard and Nantucket.

When Menley had left Remember House at quarter of seven, Hannah was already tucked in for the night. Now as she sipped champagne, a thought haunted her. Was there a likeness of Captain Andrew Freeman in the Sprague files, one that she had glimpsed and that had made a subconscious impression on her as she was going through that vast mound of papers? That was what she let Jan Paley believe. And then she wondered, how often in the last few days had she used the words "unconscious" and "subconscious"? She reminded herself that even the infrequent tranquilizers she was taking could make her feel fuzzy.

She shook her head to push away the distracting thoughts. Now that she was at the restaurant, she was glad she had come. Maybe that was why Adam was anxious for her to have people around. She used to be a truly outgoing person, but after Bobby's death, it had become a real effort to try to seem cheerful and interested in anyone or anything.

During her pregnancy with Hannah, she'd been writing the last David book and was glad to be totally involved with finishing it. She had found that when she wasn't busy, she would start to worry that something might go wrong, that maybe she would miscarry or the baby would be stillborn.

And since Hannah's birth, she'd been battling the harrowing episodes of PTSD—flashbacks, anxiety attacks, depression.

A pretty dreary litany of problems for a man like Adam who has a superstressful job to live with, she thought. Earlier she had been so resentful of Adam's transparent efforts to make her go out, to have Amy stay overnight. Now she desperately wished he were beside her at this table.

Menley knew she was at last looking like her old self. Her waistline was completely back to normal, and tonight she had chosen to wear a pale gray silk suit with a bolero jacket and wide-cut slacks. Charcoal gray cuffs accentuated the charcoal gray camisole. Her hair, bleaching from the sun, was tied back in a simple knot at the nape of her neck. The silver-and-diamond choker and matching earrings Adam had given her when they were engaged complemented the outfit. She realized that it felt good to dress up again.

It had been a not-unpleasant surprise to find that Scott Covey was John and Elaine's other guest. Menley was aware of the appreciation in his eyes when the maître d' brought her to the table. A part of his charm, she acknowledged to herself, was that Scott seemed to be oblivious to his astonishing good looks. His manner

vas, if anything, a trifle shy, and he had the gift of
paying close attention to whoever was speaking.

He referred briefly to the search warrant. "Your
advice was right, Menley. When I reached Adam, he
told me he couldn't do anything about it, but he did
tell me to stay in closer touch and leave the answering
machine on all the time."

"Adam's a very decisive guy," Elaine smiled.

"I'm damn glad he's in my corner," Covey said,
but then added, "let's not spoil the evening by talking
about it. One consolation about having nothing to
hide: It's a terrible invasion when the police are ran-
sacking your home to try to prove you're a criminal,
but there's a big difference between being outraged
and being worried."

Heatedly, Elaine snapped, "Don't get me started.
The Carpenters should have shown half the concern
for Vivian when she was alive as they think they're
showing now that she's dead. I tell you, when that
poor kid bought her house three years ago, she seemed
so alone. I brought over a bottle of champagne later,
and it was pathetic how grateful she was. She was just
sitting there by herself."

"Elaine," John warned.

When she saw the tears welling in Scott's eyes,
Elaine bit her lip. "Oh God, Scott, I'm so sorry.
You're right. Let's change the subject."

"I will," John beamed. "We're having our wedding
reception here, and you two are the first to be officially
notified that the exact time is four o'clock on Saturday, November twenty-sixth. We even decided on the
menu: turkey stew." His laugh was a *heh-heh-heh*
sound. "Don't forget, that's two days after Thanksgiving." He squeezed Elaine's hand.

Elaine looked like a bride, Menley thought. Her
white cowl-neck dress was set off by a pearl-and-gold
necklace. Her soft-brushed blond hair flattered her

thin, somewhat angular face. The large pear-shape
diamond on her left hand was a clear and present sig
of John's generosity.

And the downside, Menley decided over dessert, i
that John *does* love to talk about insurance and shoul
not tell jokes. She was used to Adam's quick, shar
wit, and it was excruciating to hear John begin, ye
again, "That reminds me of a story about . . ."

At one point, during a tedious recital, Scott Cove
raised an eyebrow to her, and she felt her lips twitch
Coconspirator, she thought.

But John was a solid, good man, and a lot of wome
probably envied Elaine.

Still when they rose from the table, Menley wa
more than ready, even anxious, to get home. Joh
suggested that he and Elaine follow her to the door t
make sure she arrived safely.

"Oh, no, please, I'm fine." She tried not to soun
irritated. I'm developing too much of a knee-jerk reac
tion to any hint of protection, she thought.

Hannah was peacefully asleep when Menley arrive
home. "She's been great," Amy said. "Do you wan
me to come by tomorrow around the same time, Mrs
Nichols?"

"No, that won't be necessary," Menley sai
evenly. "I'll be in touch." She regretted the hurt sh
saw in Amy's crestfallen face but realized that sh
was looking forward to being alone with Hannah unt
Adam got back from New York tomorrow.

It was harder to go to sleep tonight. It wasn't tha
she was nervous. It was just that in her mind she kep
going through the pile of pictures and sketches i
Phoebe Sprague's files. She'd thought she'd barel
glanced at them. They were mostly sketches of earl
settlers, some of them unnamed, and landmark build

ings; property maps; sailing ships—an unsorted mish-mash, really.

Was it possible that she'd come across one that didn't have a name attached to it and subconsciously copied it when she was trying to envision Captain Andrew Freeman? His looks weren't that unusual. A lot of the early-eighteenth-century seamen had short, dark beards.

And then by coincidence, I'd actually drawn his face? she mocked herself. *Subconsciously, unconsciously*—those words again, she thought. Dear God what is happening to me?

Three times before 2:00 A.M. she got up to check on Hannah and found her in a sound sleep. In just a little over a week up here, she looks bigger, Menley mused as she lightly touched the small outstretched hand.

Finally she felt her own eyes growing heavy and knew she soon would be drifting off. She settled back in bed and touched Adam's pillow, missing him acutely. Had he phoned tonight? Probably not. Amy would have told her. But why hadn't he tried around ten-thirty? He knew she'd be home by then.

Or I could have called him, Menley thought. I should have let him know I'd enjoyed the evening. He might have been afraid to call me for fear I'd be complaining about going out.

Oh, God, I just want to be myself, I just want to be normal.

At four o'clock the sound of a train roaring toward her thundered through the house.

She was at the railroad crossing, trying to get through it in time. The train was coming.

She bolted up, shoved her fingers in her ears, trying to drown out the sound, and stumbled wildly to the nursery. She had to save Bobby.

Hannah was screaming, her arms flailing, her legs kicking the blankets away.

The train was going to kill her too, Menley thought, her mind racing to grasp some sense of reality in all the confusion.

But then it was over. The train was going away, the clickedy-click of the wheels vanishing into the night.

Hannah was screaming.

"Stop it," Menley shouted at the baby. "Stop it. Stop it!"

Hannah screeched louder.

Menley sank down on the bed opposite the crib, trembling, hugging herself, afraid to trust herself to pick up Hannah.

And then from downstairs, she heard him calling her, his voice excited and joyous, summoning her to him, "Mommy, Mommy."

Arms outstretched, sobbing his name, she rushed to find Bobby.

August 10th

46

The district attorney called a meeting for Wednesday afternoon at his office in the Barnstable courthouse. Scheduled to be present were the three officers from his staff who had participated in the search of the Covey house, the medical examiner who had conducted the autopsy, two expert witnesses from the Coast Guard group in Woods Hole—one to testify about the currents the day Vivian Carpenter drowned, the second to discuss the condition of the diving gear she was wearing—and Nat Coogan.

"That means I get an early start today," Nat told Debbie on Wednesday morning. "I want to take a look at Tina's car and see if it drips oil, and I want to talk to Vivian's lawyer to see if she contacted him."

Deb was placing a new batch of waffles on her husband's plate. Their two sons had already finished breakfast and taken off for their summer jobs.

"I shouldn't feed these to you," she sighed. "You're supposed to lose twenty pounds."

"I need the energy today, doll."

"Sure you do." Debbie shook her head.

From the breakfast table Nat looked admiringly at the glints of light in her hair. "You do look great," he said. "I'll take you out to dinner tonight to show you off. By the way, you never did tell me how much it cost to get all that done."

"Eat your waffles," Debbie said as she passed him the syrup. "You don't want to know."

Nat's first stop was the Wayside Inn. He poked his head in the dining room. As he had hoped, Tina was working. Then he went to the office, where he found only the secretary.

"Just a question," he said, "about Tina."

The secretary shrugged. "I guess it's all right. They let you look at her file the other day."

"Who would know if she received many personal calls here?" Nat asked.

"She wouldn't have received them. Unless it's a real emergency, we take a message and the waitress calls back on her break."

I guess it's a blind alley, he thought. "Would you happen to know what kind of car Tina drives?"

She pointed out the window to the parking lot in the back of the building. "That green Toyota is Tina's."

The car was at least ten years old. Rust spots on the fenders were deteriorating into breaks in the steel. Grunting as he squatted down, Nat peered at the undercarriage. Glistening drops of oil were clearly visible. There were stains on the macadam.

Just as I thought, he exulted. He labored to his feet and looked inside through the driver's window. Tina's car was sloppy. Tape cassettes were scattered on the front passenger seat. Empty soda cans were clumped on the floor. He looked through the back window. Newspapers and magazines were strewn on the seat. And then, half covered by paper bags, he saw two empty pint-sized oil cans on the floor.

He hurried into the office again. "One last question —by any chance does Tina take a turn at the reservations desk?"

"Well, yes, she does," the secretary replied. "She's assigned there from eleven to eleven-thirty, during Karen's break."

"So she could have received personal calls there?"

"I suppose so."

"Thank you very much." Nat's step was buoyant as he headed for his next stop, a chat with Vivian's lawyer.

Leonard Wells, Esquire, had a comfortable suite of offices a block from Main Street in Hyannis. A reserved-looking man in his fifties, with frameless glasses that magnified thoughtful brown eyes, he was crisply dressed in a beige lightweight suit. Nat had the immediate impression that Wells was the kind of man who never opened his collar and loosened his tie in public.

"You are aware, Detective Coogan, that I've already been visited by the district attorney's staff, the Carpenter family's attorney and the representative of the insurance company that carried the policy on the emerald ring. I fail to understand how much more I can contribute to the investigation."

"Perhaps you can't, sir," Nat said pleasantly. "But there's always the chance that something has been overlooked. I do, of course, know the terms of the will."

"Every cent Vivian had, as well as her home, boat, car and jewelry, were inherited by her new husband." Frosty disapproval dripped from Wells' voice.

"Who was the beneficiary of her prior will?"

"There was no prior will. Vivian came to me three years ago, at the time she inherited the principal of her trust, five million dollars."

"Why did she come to you? I mean, surely her family has lawyers."

"I'd done some work for one of her friends, who apparently was quite satisfied with me. And Vivian said at the time that she did not want to be represented by her family's legal advisors. She asked my advice about which bank I would suggest she go to in order to open a safety deposit box. She wanted the name of a conservative broker with whom she could review her considerable stock portfolio. She asked my advice about her potential heirs."

"She wanted to make out a will?"

"No, she specifically did *not* want to make one out. She wanted to know who would inherit in case of her death. I told her it would be her family."

"She was satisfied with that?" Nat asked.

"She told me she didn't want to leave it as a gift to them because they didn't deserve it, but since there was no one in the world she gave a damn about, they might just as well have it de facto. Of course, all that changed when she met Covey."

"Did you urge her to have a prenuptial agreement?"

"It was too late. She was already married. I did urge her to sign a more complex will. I pointed out that the way the will stood, her husband would inherit everything, and that she should write in provisions for unborn children. She said she'd face that issue when she became pregnant. I also urged her to consider the fact that if the marriage did fail, there were steps she should be aware of that would protect her assets."

Nat looked around the room. Paneled walls with a fine patina; law books stacked neatly on floor-to-ceiling shelves behind the mahogany desk. Handsomely framed English hunting scenes; an Oriental area rug. The overall effect was harmonious good taste, an appropriate background for Leonard Wells. Nat decided he liked this man.

"Mr. Wells, did Vivian consult with you often?"

"No. I do understand that she took my advice to keep only a relatively modest checking account in the local bank. She was satisfied with the securities expert I recommended and had quarterly meetings with him in Boston. She left the key to her safety deposit box in my office. When she occasionally came in to get it, we'd exchange pleasantries."

"Why did she leave her safety deposit box key here?" Nat asked.

"Vivian tended to be careless. Last year she lost the key twice and had to pay a heavy replacement fee. Since the bank is right next door, she decided to make us custodians. While she was alive she was the only one with access. Since her death, of course, the contents have been taken out and listed, as I'm sure you know."

"Did Vivian call you three days before she died?"

"Yes. The call came while I was on vacation."

"Do you know why she was contacting you?"

"No, I don't. She wasn't looking for her key and would not speak to my associate. She left word for me to phone as soon as I returned. Unfortunately, by then she'd been missing two days."

"What was her manner when she spoke to your secretary? Did she seem upset?"

"Vivian was always upset if people she wanted to see weren't readily available to her."

Not much help there, Nat thought. Then he asked, "Did you ever meet Scott Covey, Mr. Wells?"

"Only once. At the reading of the will."

"What did you think of him?"

"My opinion, of course, is just that. Prior to meeting him, I'd already decided in my own mind that he was a gold digger who had charmed a vulnerable, highly emotional young woman. I still feel that it is a disgrace that an entire Carpenter fortune will be enjoyed by a stranger. There are plenty of distant Carpenter cousins who could use a windfall. I confess that afterward I felt differently. I was most favorably impressed by Scott Covey. He seemed genuinely heartsick about his wife's death. And unless he's a magnificent actor, he was stunned to realize the extent of her fortune."

47

*H*enry Sprague had a bad taste in his mouth. Tuesday afternoon he'd observed the police cars when they pulled up to Scott Covey's driveway. Feeling like a Peeping Tom, he had watched from the side window as what he assumed to be a search warrant was handed to Covey. Later, when he and Phoebe were sitting on the deck, he had been uncomfortably aware of Covey sitting on his deck, his posture reflecting dejection and despair.

If it weren't for seeing that Tina woman in the Cheshire Pub, I wouldn't have one single reason to suspect Scott Covey, Henry had reminded himself during the sleepless night.

He remembered back to the first time he had met Phoebe. She had been a doctoral candidate at Yale. He had an M.B.A. from Amos Tuck and was in the family import-export business. From the minute he laid eyes on her, the other girls he had dated became unimportant. One of them, her name was Kay, had really been hurt and had kept calling him.

Suppose I had agreed to see Kay after I was married, just to talk it out, and someone misinterpreted the meeting? Henry thought. Could that be the case here?

On Wednesday morning, he knew what he had to do. Betty, their longtime cleaning woman, was there, and he knew he could trust her to keep an eye on Phoebe.

Sensing that he might be told to stay home, he did not phone Scott. Instead at ten o'clock he walked across the lawn and rang the back doorbell. Through the screen he could see Scott, seated at the kitchen table, drinking coffee and reading the newspaper.

Henry reminded himself that Covey had no reason to look pleased when he realized who his visitor was.

He came to the door but did not open it. "What do you want, Mr. Sprague?"

Henry did not mince words. "I feel I owe you an apology."

Covey was wearing a sports shirt, khaki shorts and leather thongs. His dark blond hair was damp, as though he'd just showered. His frown disappeared. "Why don't you come in?"

Without asking, he got another mug from the cabinet and poured coffee. "Vivian told me that you're a coffee-holic."

It was good, even excellent, coffee, Henry was pleased to note. He took the seat opposite Covey at the small table and sipped quietly for a few moments. Then, choosing his words carefully, he tried to convey to Scott his regret that he had told the detective about meeting Tina that afternoon in the pub.

He liked the fact that Covey did not demur. "Look, Mr. Sprague, I understand that you did what you felt you had to do. I also understand where the police are coming from and the attitude of Viv's family and friends. I do have to point out, Viv didn't have many friends who really cared about her. I'm just glad if you can begin to realize it's tough as hell to be missing my wife so much and at the same time have people treat me like a murderer."

"Yes, I think I'm beginning to understand."

"You know what's really scary?" Scott asked. "It's the way the Carpenters are stirring everyone up; there's a damn good chance I'll be indicted for murder."

Henry stood up. "I've got to get back. If there's anything I can do to help you, count on me. I should not have allowed myself to be talked into gossiping. I can promise you this: If I'm asked to testify, I'll say loud and clear that from the day you and Vivian were married, I witnessed the transformation of a very unhappy young woman."

"That's all I ask of you, sir," Scott Covey said. "If everyone would tell the simple truth, I'd be all right."

"Henry."

Both men turned as Phoebe opened the screen door and walked in. She looked around, her eyes clouded. "Did I tell you about Tobias Knight?" she asked vaguely.

"Phoebe . . . Phoebe . . ." Jan Paley was a few steps behind her. "Oh, Henry, I'm so sorry. I dropped by for a minute and I told Betty to go ahead with her work, that I'd sit with Phoebe. I turned my back and . . ."

"I understand," Henry said. "Come along, dear." He shook Scott's hand reassuringly, then put his arm around his wife and patiently led her home.

48

Menley's frantic search of the downstairs rooms had not revealed where Bobby's voice was coming from. Finally Hannah's wails had penetrated her consciousness, and she had made her way back to the nursery. By then Hannah's sobs had become gulping hiccups.

"Oh, sweet baby," Menley had murmured, shocked into awareness that Hannah had been crying for a long time. She had picked up her daughter, wrapped the covers around her and dropped onto the bed opposite the crib.

Crawling under the quilt, she had slid her shoulder strap down and put the baby's lips to her breast. She had not been able to nurse, but her breast pulsated as the tiny lips sucked at her nipple. Finally the hiccups had subsided, and Hannah had slept contentedly in her arms.

She wanted to keep the baby with her, but exhaustion was a cloud that pushed Menley into a stuporlike state. As she had done a few days ago, she placed a pillow in the cradle, laid Hannah on it, tucked the blankets around her, and fell into a dead sleep herself, her hand on the cradle, one tiny finger encircling her thumb.

* * *

The ringing of the phone woke her at eight o'clock. Hannah was still asleep, she noted, as she rushed to the master bedroom to answer it.

It was Adam.

"Don't tell me you and Hannah are still in bed? How come she never sleeps late for me?"

He was joking. Menley knew it. The tone of his voice was amused and affectionate. Then why was she so quick to look for a double meaning in everything he said?

"You always bragged about the fresh ocean air," she said. "Looks as though Hannah has started to believe you." She thought about the dinner. "Adam, I had a lovely time last night."

"Oh, I'm glad. I was afraid to ask."

Just as I suspected, Menley thought.

"Anyone else there besides you and Elaine and John?"

"Scott Covey."

"That was nice. I told him in no uncertain terms that I needed to be able to reach him. Did he talk about the search?"

"Only that it was intrusive but not worrisome."

"Good. How are you doing, honey?"

I'm doing just fine, Menley thought. I imagined I heard a train roar through this house. I imagined I heard my dead child calling me. And I let Hannah scream for half an hour while I searched for him.

"Fine," she said.

"Why do I get the feeling that you're holding something back?"

"Because you're a good lawyer, trained to look for hidden meanings." She forced a laugh.

"No episodes?"

"I said I'm fine." She tried not to sound irritated or panicky. Adam could always see through her. She tried to change the subject. "Dinner really was pleasant, but Adam, whenever John utters the words, 'That reminds me of a story,' run for the hills. He does go on and on.''

Adam chuckled. '' 'Laine must be in love. Otherwise she wouldn't put up with it. The airport at five?''

"I'll be there."

After Hannah had been bathed and fed and was temporarily content in the keeping-room playpen, Menley called the psychiatrist in New York who was treating her for post-traumatic stress disorder. "I'm in a bit of trouble," she said, trying to sound matter-of-fact.

"Tell me about it."

Carefully choosing her words, she told Dr. Kaufman about waking up, imagining she was hearing the sound of the train, thinking she'd heard Bobby calling.

"And you decided not to pick up Hannah when she was crying?"

She's trying to find out if I was afraid I'd hurt the baby, Menley thought. "I was trembling so much I was afraid that if I picked her up, I'd drop her."

"Was she crying?"

"Screaming."

"Did that upset you very much, Menley?"

She hesitated, then whispered, "Yes, it did. I wanted her to stop."

"I see. I think we'd better increase your medication. I reduced it last week, and it may have been too soon. I'll have to Express Mail it to you. I can't prescribe out of state over the phone."

I could have her send it to Adam's office, Menley thought. He could bring it up. But I don't want Adam to know I spoke to the doctor. "I don't know if I gave you the address here," she said calmly.

When she hung up the phone, she went over to the table. Yesterday, after Jan Paley left, she'd glanced quickly through Phoebe Sprague's file of pictures, looking for one of Captain Andrew Freeman. Now she spent the next several hours going through all the files specifically looking for a picture. But she couldn't find one.

She compared her drawing with the one Jan had brought. Feature for feature, it was a perfect match. The only difference was that the sketch from the Brewster Library showed the captain at the wheel of his ship. How did I know what he looked like? she wondered again.

She reached for her sketchpad. A mental image of Mehitabel was filling her mind, demanding to be released. Wind-blown, shoulder-length brown hair; a delicate heart-shaped face; wide, dark eyes; small hands and feet; smiling lips; a blue linen gown with long sleeves, a high neck and a lace bib, the skirt billowing to the side.

She drew with swift, sure strokes, her trained fingers skillfully transferring the image to paper. When she was finished she held it against the sketch Jan had brought and realized what she had done.

In the Brewster Library sketch, a trace of Mehitabel's flowing skirt flared out behind the figure of the captain.

Menley grabbed her magnifying glass. The small marks on Andrew Freeman's sleeve as shown in the Brewster drawing were the tips of fingers—Mehitabel's fingers. Had she been standing behind her husband on his ship when the unknown artist sketched him nearly three hundred years ago? Did she look anything like the way I visualized her? Menley wondered.

Suddenly frightened, she buried the three sketches in the bottom of one of the files, picked up Hannah and walked outside into the sunlight.

Hannah cooed and pulled her mother's hair, and as Menley gently disentangled the small fingers, a hought came to her: last night when I woke up to the oaring of the train, Hannah was screaming.

"Did the train wake you up too?" she cried. "Was hat why you were so frightened? Oh, Hannah, what s happening to us? What kind of craziness are you icking up from me?"

49

District attorney Robert Shore conducted the meetng in the conference room of his offices in the Barntable County Courthouse. He sat at the head of the able, the medical examiner, detectives and expert vitnesses along the sides. He had placed Nat Coogan t the opposite end, a tribute to the extensive work the letective had done on the case.

"What have we got?" Shore asked and nodded to Nat to begin laying out his facts.

Step by step, Nat presented the facts he had assemled.

The medical examiner was next. "The body was nutilated by marine scavengers. You are particularly nterested in the condition of her hands. The fingertips f both hands were gone, which is to be expected. In drowning it's one of the first places crabs will attack. he rest of the fingers of the left hand are intact. A narrow gold band, her wedding ring, was on the ring finger."

He held up a picture taken at the autopsy. "The right hand tells a different story. Besides the missing fingertips, the ring finger had been eaten to the bone between the knuckle and hand. That suggests it had suffered a previous trauma that caused the blood to rise to the surface and attract the scavengers."

"The husband claimed that the morning of the day she died, Vivian had been twisting and turning her emerald to get it off," Nat said. "Would that have caused the trauma?"

"Yes, but she must have been yanking at it mighty hard."

District Attorney Shore took the picture from the medical examiner. "The husband admits she was wearing the emerald on the boat but claims she must have switched it to the ring finger of her left hand. If it were loose, could it have slipped off in the water?"

"Certainly. But it never would have slipped off past the knuckle of the right hand. But here's something else." The medical examiner held up another autopsy photo. "There isn't much of her right ankle left, but there are some marks consistent with rope burn. It's possible she was tied up at some point and even dragged for a considerable distance."

Shore leaned forward. "Deliberately?"

"Impossible to tell."

"Let's talk about the alcohol content in her body."

"Between the vitreous humor, or in layman's words, eye fluid, and the blood, we've ascertained she'd consumed the equivalent of three glasses of wine. She'd have been listed as 'under the influence' if she'd been driving."

"In other words," Shore said, "she had no business scuba diving in that condition, but there's no law against it."

The two expert witnesses from the Coast Guard group in Woods Hole were next. One was carrying maritime charts, which he set up on a stand. With the aid of a pointer, he presented his findings. "If she disappeared here"—he indicated a spot a mile from Monomoy Island—"her body should have been washed toward the Vineyard and located somewhere around here." Again he pointed. "The other alternative is that, given the violent currents caused by the squall, she might have been washed into the Monomoy shore. One place she would not have been is where she was found, in Stage Harbor. Unless," he concluded, "unless she got caught in a fishing net and dragged there, which is also possible."

The expert on diving equipment spread out the gear Vivian Carpenter had been wearing the day of her death. "This stuff was pretty worn," he commented. "Wasn't she supposed to be rich?"

"I think I can speak to that," Nat said. "Vivian gave her husband new diving gear as a wedding present. His story is that she wanted to use his old rig to see if she liked diving. If she did, she'd buy a top-of-the-line set like his."

"Reasonable, I guess."

Tina's possible connection to Scott was discussed, with the district attorney playing devil's advocate. "Tina's engaged now?" he asked.

"Yes, to her old boyfriend," Nat said, then told them of his impression of Fred Hendin. Next he talked about the oil on the garage floor at Scott Covey's house.

"Pretty nebulous as evidence, I'd say," he admitted. "A good defense attorney—and Adam Nichols is tops—could blow that away."

The records taken from the Covey home were laid out. "Covey sure did his homework," Shore grunted.

"There's nothing there. But what about Vivian? Where did she keep all.her personal records?"

"In her safety deposit box," Nat said.

"And the husband wasn't a signatory on it?"

"No."

At the conclusion of the meeting, there was reluctant agreement that, based on the present facts, it would be almost impossible to get a grand jury to hand up an indictment of Scott Covey.

"I'm going to call Judge Marron in Orleans and ask him to schedule an inquest," Shore decided. "That way all the facts will be publicly aired. If he thinks we've got enough, he'll make a finding of evidence of criminal negligence or foul play and then we convene the grand jury."

He stretched. "Gentlemen, an informal poll. Forget what's admissible or not admissible for a jury. If you were voting innocent or guilty, how say you?"

He went around the table. One by one they quietly answered. "Guilty . . . Guilty . . . Guilty . . . Guilty . . . Guilty . . . Guilty . . . Guilty."

"Guilty," Shore agreed decisively. "It's unanimous. We may not be able to prove it yet, but we all believe Scott Covey is a murderer."

50

*A*dam's client, Susan Potter, wept quietly as she sat opposite him in his office at the Park Avenue law firm of Nichols, Strand and Miller. Twenty-eight years old, slightly plump, with dark red hair and blue-green eyes, she would have been very attractive if her features were not distorted by fear and stress.

Convicted of manslaughter in the death of her husband, she had been granted a new trial through Adam's appeal. It would begin in September.

"I just don't feel as though I can go through it again," she said. "I'm so grateful to be out of prison, but the thought that I might have to go back . . ."

"You won't," Adam told her. "But Susan, get this straight—have no contact with Kurt's family. Slam the phone down if his parents call you. Their goal is to get you to say something provocative, something that they can even loosely interpret as a threat."

"I know." She stood up to go. "You're on vacation and this is the second time you've come down because of my case. I hope you know how much I appreciate it."

"When we get you off for good is when I'll accept your words of appreciation." Adam walked around his desk and escorted her to the door.

As he opened it, she looked up at him. "I thank God every day of my life that you're handling my defense."

Adam saw the hero worship in her eyes. "Keep your chin up, Susan," he said matter-of-factly.

His fifty-year-old secretary, Rhoda, was in the outer office. She followed him back into his private room. "Honest to God, Adam, you do turn the ladies on. All your female clients end up falling in love with you."

"Come on, Rhoda. A lawyer is like a psychiatrist. Most patients fall in love with their shrink for a while. It's the arm-to-lean-on syndrome."

His words echoed in his ears as he thought about Menley. She had suffered another anxiety attack; he was sure of it. He could pick up the stress in her voice as clearly as someone with perfect musical pitch could detect an off-key note. It was part of his training, part of the reason he was a successful lawyer. But why wouldn't she talk about it? How bad had the attack—or attacks—been? he wondered.

The widow's walk. The only access to that precarious perch was a narrow ladder. Suppose she tried to carry Hannah up there and became dizzy. *Suppose she dropped the baby.*

Adam felt his throat close. The memory of Menley's face as she looked down at Bobby in the casket haunted him. Menley's sanity would never survive losing Hannah.

He knew what he had to do. Reluctantly he phoned his wife's psychiatrist. His heart sank when Dr. Kaufman said, "Oh, Adam, I was debating whether to call you. I didn't realize you were in town. When are you going back to the Cape?"

"This afternoon."

"Then I'll send Menley's new prescription over to you to take up to her."

"When were you talking to Menley?" he asked.

"Today." Dr. Kaufman's tone changed. "You didn't know that? Adam, why are you calling me?"

He told her that he was afraid Menley was having episodes of PTSD that she was not admitting to him. The doctor did not comment.

Then Adam told her how the baby-sitter had seen Menley on the widow's walk, and that Menley denied being there.

"Did she have Hannah with her?"

"No. The baby was with the sitter."

There was a pause. Then, speaking carefully, the doctor said, "Adam, I don't think Menley should be alone with Hannah, and I *do* think you should bring her back to New York. I want to admit her to the hospital for a little while. It's better to be safe. We don't need any more tragedies in your family."

51

*A*my had spent the day at Nauset Beach with her friends. On the one hand it had been fun to be with them. On the other, however, she had been saving her baby-sitting money toward the purchase of a new car to use at college, and she was still short of having the amount she needed. Her father had promised that he would pay half, but she had to make up the difference.

"I know I could give it to you," her father often told her, "but remember what your mother used to say: 'You appreciate what you work for.' "

Amy did indeed remember. She remembered everything her mother said. Mom hadn't been at all like Elaine, Amy thought. She'd been what most people would call plain: no makeup, no high-fashion clothes, no airs. But she'd been real. Amy remembered how when Dad told those long-winded stories, she'd say, with affection, "John, dear, get to the point." She didn't laugh the way Elaine did, giggling uncontrollably, acting like he was Robin Williams or something.

Yesterday Amy had known that Mrs. Nichols was angry at her. She realized now she shouldn't have told her father about seeing Mrs. Nichols on the widow's walk, and about Mrs. Nichols denying she had been there. Of course, her father had told Elaine, who told Mr. Nichols; she had been in the room when Elaine phoned him.

But one thing had been bothering Amy. When she had been with her in the house yesterday, Mrs. Nichols had been wearing shorts and a white cotton shirt. But in that impression of her on the widow's walk, she'd been wearing some sort of long dress.

It had startled Amy and made her wonder suddenly if maybe Mrs. Nichols was a little crazy. She'd heard Elaine tell her father that Mrs. Nichols was probably in the midst of a nervous breakdown.

But what if Mrs. Nichols was right, that it was only an optical illusion because of the metal on the chimney? When she thought about it, Amy realized that only a few minutes after she thought she saw that figure, Mrs. Nichols came out of the house dressed in the shorts and tee shirt.

The whole thing was kind of scary and spooky, Amy thought. Or maybe I've just heard too many stories about Remember House, and just like Carrie Bell, I think I'm seeing things.

She wanted to try to explain to Mrs. Nichols. She looked at her watch. It was four o'clock. Yes, she'd phone.

Mrs. Nichols answered on the first ring. She sounded a little breathless. "Amy, I'm sorry, I can't talk right now. I'm on my way to the airport, and Hannah is in the car."

"It's just I'm so sorry if you thought I was talking about you," Amy stammered. "I didn't mean to do that. What I mean is, you see . . ." She tried to explain about the dress and that she was sure she'd been mistaken. "You came out of the house right afterward."

Then she waited. There was a pause before Mrs. Nichols said, "Amy, I'm glad you called. Thank you."

"I really miss working for you. I'm so sorry."

"It's all right, Amy. Are you free to baby-sit tomorrow? I really must study all the data I have from Mrs. Sprague, and I'll need you to watch Hannah."

52

*H*enry Sprague took his wife for a walk along their favorite strip of beach, the one that eventually ran in front of Remember House. It was quarter past six when they saw Adam and Menley with their baby at the water's edge. They stopped to visit.

"I just got back from New York," Adam explained, "and I had to get some sand in my shoes right away. Come up and have a glass of wine with us."

It had been a bad day for Phoebe. After she and Henry and Jan Paley came back from Scott Covey's, she had been terribly agitated. She'd gone into the office and searched for her files, accusing Henry and Jan of stealing them. Henry reasoned it might be a good idea if she saw them where they were now while he explained again why Menley had them. And he wanted to tell Adam about talking to Scott.

He accepted the invitation, and they followed the Nicholses up from the beach to the house. As they crossed the lawn, he explained to Menley what he wanted to do.

Menley listened, her heart sinking, praying that Phoebe would not insist on taking her data back.

But in the keeping room, Phoebe Sprague only seemed pleased to see the neat stacks of files and papers and books. Lovingly she ran her fingers over them, and as her husband and Menley and Adam watched, her face cleared. The vague expression in her eyes receded. "I wanted to tell her story," she murmured as she opened the file of sketches.

Menley saw that Phoebe intended to look at all the pictures. When Phoebe came to the ones Menley had sketched, she held them up and cried, "Oh, you copied them from the painting I have of Mehitabel and Andrew together on the ship. I haven't been able to find that one. I thought I'd lost it."

Thank God, Menley thought. There *is* a picture I might have copied. With this damn medication, I know my head isn't on straight.

Phoebe stood for a moment, studying Mehitabel's face. She could feel herself stepping backward, being drawn into dark confusion, becoming lost again. She willed her mind to keep going. Her husband loved her, she thought, but he didn't believe her. That's why she died. I've got to warn Adam's wife. That's the plan for *her*.

Plan! Plan! She tried to hold on to the thought, but it had become meaningless.

Mehitabel. Andrew. Who else? Before her mind became cloudy and gray and empty again, she managed to whisper to Menley, "Mehitabel innocent. Tobias Knight. Answer in Mooncussers file."

53

Graham and Anne Carpenter received the phone call from the district attorney late Wednesday afternoon. They'd started to play golf but had quit after the ninth hole because Anne wasn't feeling well.

Graham realized that it might have been a mistake to pressure the authorities to openly accuse Scott Covey of being responsible for Vivian's death. The media was delighted to have a juicy news story and had laid out every detail of Vivian's life they could find.

Now the tabloids were referring to her as "the poor little rich girl," "the outcast," "the pot-smoking rebel." Details of their private lives were being distorted and held up for public ridicule and entertainment.

Anne was crushed and humiliated and bitter. "Maybe we should have left it alone, Graham. We couldn't bring her back, and now they're destroying her memory."

At least the inquest would clear the air, Graham thought as he made their five o'clock martinis and carried the tray to the sunporch, where Anne was resting.

"A bit early isn't it?" she asked.

"A little," he agreed. "That was the district attorney on the phone. The judge in Orleans is calling an inquest for Monday afternoon."

In response to her alarmed expression, he said, "At least the circumstances will be aired. It's a public hearing, and after all the facts are presented, we want the judge to decide one of three ways: no evidence of foul play; no evidence of negligence; no evidence of criminal negligence."

"Suppose the judge decides there is no evidence of negligence or foul play?" Anne said. "We'll have gone through this disgusting publicity for nothing."

"Not for nothing, dear. You know that."

From inside they heard faint ringing. A moment later the housekeeper came to the door, carrying the cellular phone. "It's Mr. Stevens, sir. He said it's important."

"That's the investigator the insurance company put on Covey," Graham said. "I insisted on being informed immediately of anything he found."

Anne Carpenter watched as her husband listened intently and then asked rapid-fire questions. When he hung up, he looked exhilarated.

"Stevens is in Florida, at Boca Raton. That's where Scott spent last winter. Apparently he was visited a number of times by a flashy-looking brunette named Tina. Her last visit was a week before he came up here and married Vivian!''

54

As soon as she'd picked up Adam at the airport, Menley had a feeling that something had unsettled him. She understood what it was when they were preparing for bed and he gave her the package of medicine from Dr. Kaufman.

"Which one of you called the other?" she asked evenly.

"I called the doctor, who was trying to decide whether or not to call me."

"I think I'd rather talk about it in the morning."

"If that's what you want."

It was the way they had most often gone to bed in the year after Bobby's death and before she became pregnant with Hannah, Menley thought. An impersonal kiss; lying apart; disparate emotions separating them as effectively as a bundling board.

She turned on her side and pillowed her face in her hand. A bundling board. Odd that she'd made that comparison. She'd just come upon the definition of that fixture of colonial times. In the winter, when a young man and woman were courting, the house was frequently so cold that the couple would be allowed to lie together in the same bed, fully clothed, swathed in blankets and with a long wooden plank firmly in place between them.

How much did Dr. Kaufman tell Adam? Menley wondered. Did she feel it was her obligation to let him know about the flashback when I thought I heard the train and Bobby calling me?

Then Menley froze. Had the doctor told Adam that Hannah's crying had been profoundly disturbing, that I didn't trust myself to touch her? Did Adam tell the doctor about the widow's walk? I didn't bring that up to her.

Dr. Kaufman and Adam may be afraid I'll hurt Hannah, Menley thought. What did they decide to do? Would they insist on a full-time baby-sitter or nurse always being present when Adam wasn't there?

No, she thought, there was another, more terrible possibility. With a sinking heart, Menley was sure she had hit on the right answer. Adam will take me to New York, and Dr. Kaufman will sign me into a psychiatric hospital. I cannot let that happen. I cannot be away from Hannah. That would destroy me.

I am getting better, she told herself. I did manage to go over the railroad crossing when I drove Adam to the airport this week. Even the other night, when I thought I heard Bobby calling, I did come out of it by myself. I did go back to Hannah. I did not hurt her, and I did comfort her. And I want to stay here.

Being careful not to disturb Adam, Menley drew the blanket closer around her neck. In happier times if she woke up chilly she would simply slide into the warmth of Adam's arms. Not now. Not like this.

I simply can never allow Adam to see any sign of my anxiety, she told herself. I've got to beat him to the punch in the morning and say that I'd like to have Amy around all day to help with Hannah. In a day or two I'll have to tell him how much better I feel, that maybe the doctor was right, that the medication shouldn't have been reduced so quickly.

I don't like being dishonest with him, but he's not being honest with me, she thought. Elaine's call about dinner the other afternoon had been arranged ahead of time.

It will be so much easier to have a baby-sitter around all day in this house. I won't have the feeling of her being underfoot the way I do in the apartment. And Hannah is thriving here.

The new book is a fascinating project. Working always keeps me on an even keel. A David book with Andrew as the boy who grows up to become the captain of his own ship could be my best. I feel it.

I don't believe in ghosts, but Jan Paley's story about people who claim a presence in their old houses intrigues me and would intrigue readers. It would make a great historical article for *Travel Times*.

And I want to tell Mehitabel's story. Phoebe insists she is innocent and that the proof is in the Mooncusser file. That poor girl was condemned as an adulteress, publicly flogged, despised by her husband, and her baby was taken from her. Bad enough if she'd been guilty but unimaginable if she was innocent. I want to find the proof of her innocence, if it exists.

Do I feel a kinship with her because my husband may be conspiring with my psychiatrist to separate me from my baby and because I'm innocent of what they believe about me, that I'm not capable of caring for her?

This must be the way it is for Scott Covey, she told herself. People watching, whispering, trying to find a way to lock you up. A smile tugged at her lips when she thought of Scott's raised eyebrow and hint of a wink as they listened to John labor through one of his interminable stories at dinner the night before.

Finally Menley felt herself relaxing and drifting off. She awakened with a start, not sure of how long she'd slept. She'd make sure Hannah was covered. As she slid out of bed, Adam jumped up and asked sharply, "Menley, where are you going?"

She bit back an angry retort and tried to sound off-hand. "Oh, I woke up because I was chilly and thought I'd check the baby. Have you been awake, dear? Maybe you've looked in to see if she's covered."

"No, I've been asleep."

"I'll be right back."

There was a musty smell in the room. Hannah had turned over and was sleeping with her bottom raised, her legs tucked under her. Her blankets were scattered on the floor. The stuffed animals that had been on the dresser were arranged around her in the crib. The antique doll was propped in a sitting position in the cradle.

Frantically Menley tossed the toys back on the dresser, picked up the blankets, and shook them out.

"I didn't do that, Hannah," she whispered as she covered her daughter. "I didn't do that."

"What didn't you do, Menley?" Adam asked from the doorway.

55

*T*hursday morning was cloudy, and a sharply cool breeze sent the residents of Chatham scurrying to their closets for long-sleeved shirts and jackets. It was the kind of day that Marge, Elaine's assistant, claimed "gave her pep."

The Atkins Real Estate Agency had a number of new listings, and Elaine had personally gone around to make flattering shots of the properties. She had developed and enlarged the photos, and the day before she had brought them into the office.

Feeling the coolness in the air when she awoke, Marge decided to go to the office early and take advantage of an uninterrupted hour to rearrange the display windows. She arrived there at seven-thirty and began removing the existing photos.

At ten of nine she was finished and standing out on the sidewalk, critically surveying her handiwork. Very nice, she thought, as she admired the effect.

The pictures were unusually good and showed the properties to excellent advantage. There was a lovely old Cape on Cockle Cove Ridge, a charming saltbox on Deep Water Lane, a contemporary on Sandy Shoes Lane and a dozen other lesser, but attractive, properties.

The most important listing was a waterfront estate on Wychmere Harbor. Elaine had hired the aerial photographer she always used to take a panoramic shot of that property. Marge had put it in the center of the window, in place of the framed Remember House aerial photo.

From behind her, Marge heard the sound of applause. She turned quickly.

"I'll buy all of them," Elaine said as she got out of her car.

"Sold!" Marge waited as Elaine walked up and stood beside her. "Honestly, what do you think?"

Elaine studied the exhibit. "I think they look great. I suppose it was time to take out my favorite, the Remember House shot."

"I honestly think so, especially since you're so sure the Nicholses are going to buy it."

Elaine preceded her into the agency. "I'm afraid that remains to be seen," she said soberly. "I'm getting the impression that Menley Nichols isn't a bit well."

"I never met her," Marge said, "but Adam Nichols is a lovely man. I remember how sad he looked when he came up here last year and you took him around. He rented the Spark cottage, near your house, didn't he?"

"That's right." Elaine spotted the photo of Remember House, propped against a chair. "I've got an idea," she said. "Let's send this over to Scott Covey. If everything gets straightened out for him, I wouldn't be surprised if he elected to stay on the Cape, and he and Vivian were crazy about that place. At least that way he'll keep the house in mind. Just in case the Nicholses don't take it."

"But suppose he isn't interested? If the property goes back on the market, you'll be sorry you gave it to him, Elaine."

"I've got the negative. I can make other copies."

She went into her own office. Marge began to transfer the pictures she'd taken from the window to the oversized album on the reception area table. The tinkling front door bell announced their first visitor.

It was the delivery boy from the florist. He was carrying a vase of long-stemmed roses.

"For Miss Atkins," he said.

"I never dreamed they were for me," Marge commented. "Take them in to her. You know the way."

After he left, Marge went in to admire the flowers. "Absolutely beautiful. This is getting to be a frequent occurrence. But what the heck is that?"

There was a streamer in the bouquet, with the number 106 pasted on it. "I know you're not that old, Elaine."

"John's just being sweet. That's how many days until we're married."

"He's a romantic, and God knows there are few of them left. Elaine, do you think the two of you will want to have a child?"

"He already has one, and I like to think that Amy and I are getting closer."

"But Amy's seventeen. She's going off to college. It would be different if she were a baby."

Elaine laughed. "If she were a baby, I wouldn't be marrying John. I'm just not that domestic."

The phone rang. "I'll get it." Elaine picked it up. "Atkins Real Estate, Elaine Atkins speaking." She listened. "Adam! . . . Is that bad? I mean an inquest sounds so intimidating. Of course I'll go over my testimony. Lunch with you would be fine. One o'clock? See you then."

When she hung up she told Marge, "It sounds like good news. They're convening an inquest on Vivian Covey's death, which means the media can be present. So this will be a chance for all of us to go to bat for

Scott." She got up. "Where's the Remember House picture?"

"By my desk," Marge told her.

"Let's messenger it over to him with a note."

On her personal stationery, she quickly penned a few sentences in her clear, decisive handwriting.

Dear Scott,

I just heard about the inquest and welcome the chance to let the world know how happy you and Vivian were that beautiful afternoon when you were looking at Remember House. You enjoyed the view so much I wanted you to have this picture to remind you of it.

Yours,
Elaine.

56

*A*t ten o'clock on Thursday morning, as the breakfast service was winding down, Tina Aroldi used her fifteen-minute break to rush into the office of the Wayside Inn. The secretary was there alone.

"Jean, what was that detective doing looking under my car yesterday?" Tina demanded.

"I don't know what you mean," the secretary protested.

"You sure do know what I mean. Don't bother to lie. A couple of the busboys saw him through the window."

"There's nothing to lie about," Jean stammered. "The detective asked me to point out your car, then he came back and wanted to know if you ever answered the phone for reservations."

"I see."

Preoccupied, Tina went back to her station in the dining room. A few minutes after one, she was not pleased to see Scott's lawyer, Adam Nichols, come in with Elaine Atkins, the real estate broker, who often brought clients to the inn.

She saw Nichols gesturing toward her. Great. He wanted to be sure she was their waitress. The hostess seated them at one of her tables, and reluctantly, pad in hand, Tina went over to greet them.

She was surprised at the warm smile Nichols gave her. He sure is attractive, Tina thought, not drop-dead handsome, but there was something about him. You got a feeling he'd be a pretty exciting guy to be with. And you could tell he was smart.

Well, he might be smiling today, but the other morning when he came in with Scott, he sure hadn't been smiling, Tina reflected. He was probably one of those guys who was nice when he needed you.

She responded coolly to his greeting and asked, "Can I get you anything from the bar?"

They each ordered a glass of chardonnay. When she left them, Elaine said, "I wonder what's with Tina today?"

"I suspect she's nervous about being dragged in to testify at the inquest," Adam responded. "Well, she has to get over that. The district attorney is certainly going to subpoena her, and I want to make sure she creates a favorable impression."

They ordered hamburgers and shared a side order

193

of onion rings. "It's a good thing I don't have lunch with you often," Elaine said. "I'd put on twenty pounds. I usually have a salad."

"This is like the good old days," Adam told her. "Remember how after our summer jobs we'd all load up on junk food, pile into that wreck of an outboard motorboat I had and call it our sunset sail?"

"I haven't forgotten."

"The other night, at your house with the old gang, I felt as though fifteen or twenty years had disappeared," Adam said. "The Cape does that to me. You do too, 'Laine. It's nice to feel like a kid sometimes."

"Well, you've had a lot to worry about. How is Menley doing?"

He hesitated. "She's doing okay."

"You don't look or sound as though you mean it. Hey, this is your old buddy you're talking to, Adam. Remember?"

He nodded. "I always could talk to you. The doctor thinks it would be wise to bring Menley back to New York and hospitalize her."

"You don't mean a psychiatric hospital, I hope."

"I'm afraid so."

"Adam, don't jump the gun. She seemed great at the party and at dinner the other night. Besides that, when I spoke to John, he said that Amy was going to be over at your place all day from now on."

"That's the only reason I'm able to be here. Menley told me this morning that she wants to work on her book, and she knows I'll be busy getting ready for the inquest, so she wanted to hire Amy for the entire day for a while."

"Then don't you think you should leave it at that? You're home in the evening."

"I guess so. I mean, this morning, Menley was herself. Relaxed, funny, enthusiastic about her book. You'd never think she's been experiencing post-traumatic stress—hallucinations, actually. Yesterday she told the doctor that she thought she heard Bobby calling her. She left Hannah screaming while she searched the house."

"Oh, Adam."

"So for her own good and for Hannah's safety, she has to be hospitalized. But as long as Amy can be there and I have to prepare for the inquest, I'll wait. After that, however, I'll take Menley back to New York."

"Will you stay there yourself?"

"I simply don't know. From what I understand, Doctor Kaufman wouldn't want me to visit Menley for a week or so. New York is damn hot, and our regular baby-sitter is away. If Amy helps out, minding Hannah during the day, I can certainly take care of her myself at night, so I may come back up here for at least that week."

He finished the last of the hamburger. "You know, if we really had wanted to make this like old times, we should have been drinking out of beer cans instead of wine glasses. No matter, I think I'll settle for coffee now."

He changed the subject. "Since the inquest is a public hearing, I can give a list of the people I want called to testify. That doesn't mean the district attorney won't frame his questions to try to put Scott in a bad light. Let's go over the sort of thing you might be asked."

They finished the coffee and had a second cup before Adam nodded in satisfaction. "You're a good witness, Elaine. When you're on the stand, emphasize how lonely Vivian seemed when she bought the house, how happy she was at her wedding reception; and talk about when she and Covey were house hunting, and all their plans for a baby. It's okay to let them know that Vivian had more than her share of New England thrift. That would help to explain why she didn't buy new diving gear right away.''

When he was paying the check, he looked up at the waitress. "Tina, you finish work at two-thirty. I'd like to talk to you for about fifteen minutes after that.''

"I have an appointment.''

"Tina, you're going to receive a subpoena to appear in court next week. I suggest you discuss your testimony with me. I can assure you that if the judge rules unfavorably, it will be because he thinks you were the motive for Vivian's murder and maybe he'll even suspect you were involved. Being an accessory to murder is pretty serious.''

Tina paled. "I'll meet you at the soda place next to the Yellow Umbrella Bookshop.''

Adam nodded.

He walked down the block to the real estate agency with Elaine. "Hey," he said, looking in the display window, "where's the picture of my house?''

"Your house?''

"Well, maybe. Just keep in mind I have an option that I may decide to exercise.''

"Sorry. I sent the picture over to Scott. I have to hedge my bets. If you don't buy it, there's a good chance he might. And Jan Paley could use the sale. She and Tom sank a lot of money in that renovation. I'll have another copy made up for you. I'll even throw in a really nice frame.''

"I'll hold you to that.''

Tina was clearly on the defensive when she spoke with Adam. "Listen, Mr. Nichols, I've got a nice boyfriend. Fred isn't going to like my having to testify in this thing.''

"Fred has nothing to say about it. But he could help you.''

"What do you mean?''

"He could verify that you two had dated for a while last summer, then broken up over Scott; that you got back together and now you're getting married."

"We didn't get back together right away. I dated other guys last winter."

"That's all right. The point is, I'd like to talk to Fred and decide whether he'd be a good witness."

"I don't know . . ."

"Tina, please get this straight. The faster Scott's name is cleared, the better it will be for you."

They were sitting at one of the small tables outside the soda shop. Tina toyed with the straw in her soda. "That detective is making me very nervous," she burst out. "Yesterday he was looking under my car."

"That's the sort of thing I need to know," Adam said quickly. "What was he looking for?"

Tina shrugged. "I don't know. I'm getting rid of it soon. Damn thing leaks like a sieve."

When they separated, Adam took Fred's phone number but promised he would wait to call until this evening, after Tina had a chance to explain what was going on.

He got in the station wagon and sat for a few minutes, thinking. Then he reached for the car phone and dialed Scott Covey's number.

When Covey answered, Adam said abruptly, "I'm on my way over."

57

*P*hoebe had had a restless night. Several times a nightmare caused her to cry out in her sleep. One time she had screamed, "I don't want to go in there," another time she'd moaned, "Don't do that to me."

Finally, at dawn, Henry had managed to coax her into taking a strong sedative, and she had settled into drugged slumber.

Over his solitary breakfast, Henry tried to figure out what might have upset her. Yesterday, she had seemed relaxed when they walked on the beach. She appeared to enjoy the visit with Adam and Menley at Remember House. She'd been glad to see her files there, and had sounded absolutely lucid when she told Menley that the answer was in the Mooncusser file.

What answer? What did she mean? Clearly some aspect of her research had surfaced in her mind and she was trying to communicate it. But she'd also been clear when she talked about the sketch Menley had made of Captain Freeman and Mehitabel.

Henry brought his coffee into Phoebe's study. He'd received a letter from the director of the nursing home, suggesting that he select some mementos for Phoebe to have in her room when she went to live there. The director wrote that familiar objects, particularly those involving long-term memory, helped increase awareness in Alzheimer patients. I ought to start deciding what to pack for her, he thought. This is the place to look.

As always, sitting at Phoebe's desk brought back with knifelike sharpness the reality of how different things were for them now, as compared to a few years ago. After Phoebe retired from teaching, she'd spent every morning in here, happily absorbed in her research, working much as he imagined Menley Nichols worked.

Wait a minute, Henry thought. That picture of the captain and his wife Phoebe talked about yesterday was in the extra-large folder. That wasn't with the data I gave Menley. I didn't know another picture of them together existed. It seems to me that folder had a lot of other material on the Freemans and Remember House. Where would Phoebe have kept it? he wondered.

He looked around the room, taking in the floor-to-ceiling bookshelves, the end table by the sofa. Then he thought—of course, the corner cupboard.

He walked over to it. The open shelves of the fine antique held rare samples of early Sandwich glassware. He remembered how Phoebe had collected each of them lovingly, and he decided that a few of the pieces should be among the items she had with her in the nursing home.

The cabinet under the shelves was jampacked with books and papers and folders. I didn't realize she had all this stuff in here, Henry mused.

In the bewildering hodgepodge, he did manage to find the folder he was looking for, and in it the sketch of Captain Freeman and Mehitabel. The billowing of her skirt and the sails suggested a strong, cool wind. She was standing a little behind him rather than alongside, as though he were sheltering her. His face was strong and firm, hers soft and smiling; her hand was resting lightly on his arm. The unknown artist had caught the chemistry between them. You can tell they were lovers, Henry thought.

He glanced through the folder. Several times the word "mooncusser" caught his eye. This may be what Phoebe intended Menley to read, he decided.

"Oh, is that where I left the doll?"

Phoebe was in the doorway, her hair disheveled, her nightgown stained. Henry remembered that he had left the bottle of liquid sedative on the bedside table. "Phoebe, did you take more medicine?" he asked anxiously.

"Medicine?" She sounded surprised. "I don't think so."

She stumbled over to the cabinet and crouched beside him. "That's where I put the Remember House doll," she said, her tone excited and pleased.

She pulled papers from the deep bottom shelf, letting them scatter on the floor. Then she reached into the back of the cabinet, and pulled out an antique doll dressed in a long yellowing cotton gown. A lace-edged bonnet with satin streamers framed the delicately beautiful china face.

Phoebe stared at it, frowning. Then she handed it to Henry. "She belongs in Remember House," she said vaguely. "I meant to put her back, but I forgot."

58

*A*fter lunch, Amy sat in front of the baby swing, playing with Hannah. "Clap hands, clap hands till Daddy comes home. Daddy has money and Mommy has none," she singsonged as she patted Hannah's hands together.

Hannah gurgled in delight, and Menley smiled. "That's a pretty sexist nursery rhyme," she said.

"I know," Amy agreed. "But it sticks in my head. My mother used to sing it to me when I was little."

Her mother's on her mind a lot, poor kid, Menley thought. Amy had arrived promptly at nine that morning, almost pathetically glad to be back. Menley knew her attitude reflected more than a desire to earn the baby-sitting money. She seemed genuinely happy to be there.

"My mother claims she tried to avoid singing to us," Menley commented as she scrubbed the sink. "She's tone deaf and didn't want to pass it on to my brother and me. But she did." She swished water in the sink.

"Honestly, Hildy isn't very much use," she complained. "That cleaning woman who was just leaving when we arrived here left this place spotless. I wish she had come back."

"Elaine was mad at her."

Menley turned and looked at Amy. "Why was she mad at her?"

"Oh, I don't know," Amy said hurriedly.

"Amy, I think you *do* know," Menley said, sensing that this might be important.

"Well, it was just that Carrie Bell was scared that morning you arrived. She said she had heard footsteps upstairs, but there was no one there. Then, when she went into the nursery, the cradle was rocking by itself, or so she claimed. Elaine said that was ridiculous and she didn't want those kind of stories spread about the house, because it's for sale."

"I see." Menley tried not to sound excited. That's three of us she thought. Amy, Carrie Bell and me. "Do you know how I can reach Carrie?" she asked.

"Oh, sure. She's cleaned our house for years."

Menley reached for a piece of paper and jotted down the number Amy rattled off. "I'm going to see if she can come over again, and I'll ask Elaine to cancel Hildy."

Since it was still very cool, they agreed that Amy would bundle Hannah up and take her for a walk in the carriage. "Hannah likes to know what's going on," Amy said, smiling.

And don't we all, Menley thought as she settled down at the table and reached again for the Mooncusser file. For a moment she stared reflectively into space. This morning Adam had not bothered to mince words. "Menley," he had said, "I'm sure if you phone Dr. Kaufman you'll find she agrees with me. While you're having such shattering anxiety attacks and flashbacks I have to insist that Amy stay here with you and Hannah when I'm out."

Menley remembered the effort with which she had bitten back an angry reply. Instead she had simply pointed out that it was her idea to have Amy with them, so he didn't need to be so overbearing. Even so, Adam had watched until Amy's car came into the driveway, then he had rushed out to have a word with her. After that he had closeted himself in the library, preparing for the inquest. He left the house at twelve-thirty, saying he'd be back late in the afternoon.

He talked privately to Amy because he doesn't even trust me to keep my word, Menley thought. Then she forced those thoughts from her mind and determinedly settled down to work.

Before lunch she'd been trying to make sense of the Mooncusser file, preparing her own notes, which she'd culled from the data Phoebe Sprague had put together.

She reread those notes:

The fifteen miles of treacherous currents and blind channels and shifting shoals that were the Chatham coastline were the undoing of countless vessels. They foundered and broke apart in blizzards and storms or sailed into sandbars, wrecking their hulls and sinking in the violent waters.

"Mooncussers" was the name given to the wreckers, who would rush to loot the cargos and snare the spoils. They would sail their small boats to the dying ship, carrying pinch bars, saws and axes, and would strip it clean of cargo and lumber and fixtures. Barrels and trunks and household goods were hoisted over the sides onto the waiting craft.

Even men of the cloth were wreckers. Menley had come across Phoebe's notes about the minister who in the middle of his sermon looked out the window, saw a ship in distress and immediately informed his congregation of the fortuitous happening. "Start fair," he'd yelped and rushed out of the meeting room, followed closely by his fellow scavengers.

Another story Phoebe had noted was of the minister who, when handed a note about a sinking ship, ordered his parishioners to bow their heads in silent prayer, while he himself slipped out in search of plunder. Returning five hours later, his booty tucked away, he found his obedient, stiff-necked and weary congregation still in place.

Wonderful stories, Menley thought, but what have they got to do with Tobias Knight? She continued to read; an hour later she finally came to a reference to him. He was listed as denouncing "the plundering gangs who stripped clean the cargo of flour and rum from the beached schooner *Red Jacket,* depriving the Crown of its salvedge."

Tobias was put in charge of that investigation. There was no mention of the success or failure of his mission.

But what is the connection to Mehitabel? Menley wondered. Certainly Captain Freeman wouldn't have been a wrecker.

And then she came upon another reference to Tobias Knight. In 1707 there was an election to replace him as selectman and assessor and to appoint Samuel Tucker to complete the building of the sheep pound that Knight had begun. The reason: "Tobias Knight no longer apeering in our midst to the greate disadvantage of the congregation."

Phoebe Sprague had noted: "Probably the 'greate disadvantage' was that they'd already paid him to build the pound. But what happened to him? No record of his death. Did he leave to avoid being pressed into service? 'Queen Anne's War,' the French and Indian war, was being fought. Or was his disappearance tied to the Crown investigation that began two years earlier?"

The Crown investigation! Menley thought. That's a new twist. Tobias Knight must have been quite a character. He threw Mehitabel to the winds. He led the search to recover the spoils from the *Red Jacket*, which meant he was investigating his own townspeople, and then he disappeared, leaving the sheep pound unfinished.

She got up and glanced at the clock. It was half past two. Amy had been out alone with the baby for nearly two hours. Concerned, she jumped up, went to the kitchen door and was relieved to see the carriage just turning onto the dirt road that marked the beginning of the property.

Will I ever get to the point where I'm not overly worried about Hannah? she wondered.

Stop thinking like that, she cautioned herself. You haven't even glanced at the ocean since you got out of bed, she thought. Take a look at it. It always does something for you.

She walked from the keeping room to the main parlor and opened the front windows, relishing the blast of salt-filled air. Tossed by the sharp breeze, the water was a mass of whitecaps. Cool as she knew it must be on the beach, she found herself yearning to walk there and feel the water on her ankles. How had Mehitabel felt about this house? She could visualize the way she would write the story.

They returned from the China trip and found the house completed. They examined it, room by room, remarking with joy on the posts and beams and paneling, the fine arrangement on the fireplaces of the bricks Andrew had commissioned from West Barnstable, the pilasters and carving that surrounded the great front door, with its crosslike panels.

They'd delighted in the fanlight they had admired in London, the way it cast lovely patterns over the entrance hall. Then they descended the steep slope to see their house as it would be observed from the beach.

"Tobias Knight be a fine builder," Andrew said as they stood looking up. The water was lapping at Mehitabel's skirt. She gathered it up and stepped onto dry sand, commenting, "I would love to feel the water on my ankles."

Andrew laughed. "A chill water it is, and you with child. I think it not advisable."

"Mrs. Nichols, are you all right?"

Menley spun around. Amy was in the doorway, Hannah in her arms. "Oh, of course, I'm fine. Amy, you're going to have to forgive me. When I write or sketch, I'm in a different world."

Amy smiled. "That's the way Professor Sprague used to describe writing when she visited my mother."

"Your mother and Professor Sprague were friends? I didn't know that."

"My mother and father belonged to a camera club. They were good amateur photographers. My father still is, of course. They met Professor Sprague through the club, and she and my mother got really friendly." Amy's tone changed. "That's where my father met Elaine. She's a member too."

Menley's throat went dry. Hannah was patting Amy's face. But she envisioned Amy looking different. Slimmer. Not as tall. Her blond hair darker, her face small and heart shaped. Her smile tender and sad as she kissed the top of the baby's head and rocked her in her arms. That was the way she would portray Mehitabel in the weeks between her baby's birth and the day she lost her.

Then Amy shivered. "It's really freezing cold in here, isn't it? Is it all right if I make a cup of tea?"

59

When Adam arrived at Scott's house, he found him hosing down the garage. He frowned when he saw that Covey had been concentrating on an oil-stained area. "You're being very industrious," he observed.

"Not really. I've been meaning to do this for a while. Viv took a course on car maintenance a couple of years ago and fancied herself a mechanic for a while. She had an old Caddy, and she liked to pump her own gas and change the oil."

"Did the Caddy have an oil leak?" Adam asked quickly.

"I don't know whether it had a leak or if Viv was spilling half the oil. She always parked that car in this space. She bought the BMW after we were married."

"I see. Do you happen to know if the police took any pictures of the garage floor when they were here?"

Scott looked startled. "What's that supposed to mean?"

"Detective Coogan was looking under Tina's car yesterday. It has an oil leak."

Abruptly Scott turned off the hose and slammed it down. "Adam, can you understand what this is like for me? I'm going nuts. I have to tell you that as soon as the inquest is over, I'm getting out of here. Let them think what they want. They will anyhow."

Then he shook his head, as though clearing it. "Sorry. I shouldn't take it out on you. Come on inside. It's chilly out here. I thought August was supposed to be the best month of the year on the Cape."

"Other than being cool today, I haven't seen any weather to object to so far," Adam said mildly.

"Sorry again. Adam, I have to talk to you." He turned abruptly and led the way into the house.

Adam refused the offer of a beer, and while Scott went to get one for himself, used the time to study the living room carefully. It looked as though it needed a good straightening, but that could have been the result of the search. The police were not famous for restoring the premises they had searched to pristine order.

But there was something else Adam noted, an emptiness about the room. There was nothing personal anywhere, no photographs, no books, no magazines. The furniture wasn't shabby, but it was neither attractive nor coordinated. Adam remembered that Elaine had told him Vivian had bought the place furnished. It didn't look as though she had done anything to put her stamp on it, and if Scott Covey's personality was reflected in the room, Adam certainly couldn't spot it.

He thought of the keeping room of Remember House. In the two weeks they had been there, Menley had given it an inviting atmosphere, and she'd done it effortlessly. Geraniums lined the windowsills. The outsized wooden salad bowl was heaped with fruit. She had lugged a battered rocker from the small parlor and set it by the fireplace. A wicker basket that had probably been used for carrying logs was serving as a container for magazines and newspapers.

Menley was a natural homemaker. Adam thought uncomfortably of how he had dashed out this morning to warn Amy to stay with Menley until he got back. Menley wouldn't have sent Amy home, he told himself. She's just as concerned about those anxiety attacks as I am. She called Dr. Kaufman yesterday. She had even suggested having Amy in all day.

What was keeping Covey? How long did it take to pour a beer? And what in hell am I doing here? Adam asked himself. This is my vacation. My wife needs me and I let myself get talked into taking on this case.

He walked into the kitchen. "Any problem?"

Scott was sitting at the table, his arms folded, the beer untouched. "Adam," he said tonelessly. "I haven't been straight with you."

60

Nat Coogan decided it would be a good idea to pay a second visit to Fred Hendin. Armed with the information that the insurance investigator had shared with him, he arrived at Hendin's home at four-thirty.

Hendin's car was in the driveway. Nat was not delighted to see that Tina's green Toyota was parked behind it. On the other hand, it might be interesting to observe them together, he thought.

He sauntered up the walk and rang the bell. When Hendin came to the door, he was visibly displeased. "Did I forget we had an appointment?" he asked.

"We don't," Nat said pleasantly. "Is it okay if I come in?"

Hendin stood aside. "It's not okay if you keep upsetting my girlfriend."

Tina was sitting on the couch, dabbing at her eyes with a handkerchief. "Why do you keep bothering me?" she demanded.

"I have no intention of bothering you, Tina," Nat said evenly. "We're conducting an investigation into a possible homicide. When we ask questions, it's to get answers, not to harass people."

"You're talking to people about me. You're looking at my car." Fresh tears gushed from her eyes.

You're a lousy actress, Nat thought. This is show-and-tell for Fred's benefit. He glanced at Hendin and saw irritation and sympathy on his face. And it's working, he thought.

Hendin sat down beside Tina, and his work-roughened hand closed over hers. "What's this about the car?"

"Haven't you noticed that Tina has a fairly serious oil leak?"

"I noticed it. I'm giving Tina a new car for her birthday. That's in three weeks. No point wasting money fixing up the other one."

"The floor of Scott Covey's garage has a pretty big oil stain," Nat said. "It didn't come from the new BMW."

"And it didn't come from my car," Tina snapped, her eyes suddenly dry.

Hendin stood up. "Mr. Coogan, Tina told me there'd be an inquest. Covey's lawyer is coming to talk to me, and I'm going to tell him exactly what I'm telling you now, so listen good. Tina and I broke up last summer because she was seeing Covey. She dated a lot of guys over the winter, and that's not my business. We've been back together since last April, and

210

there hasn't been a night I haven't seen her, so don't try to make a big romance out of her bumping into Covey in that bar or stopping by his house to offer sympathy when his wife was missing."

He slung an arm around Tina's shoulders, and she smiled up at him. "It's a damn shame that you're spoiling all my surprises, but I have another one for this little lady. Besides the car, I bought her an engagement ring that I was going to give her on her birthday, but with the way things are, she's going to have it on her finger when we go into court next week. Now get out, Coogan. You and your questions make me sick."

61

So this is where the defense falls apart, Adam thought. In Vivian Carpenter's kitchen. "What do you mean you weren't being straight with me?" he snapped.

Scott Covey studied his untouched glass of beer. He did not look at Adam as he said, "I told you that I didn't see Tina from the time I married Vivian except that day in the pub and when she came here to offer condolences. That's true. What isn't true is the impression I gave you that she and I called it quits last summer."

"You saw her after you left the Cape last August?"

"She came down to Boca five or six times. I've been wanting to tell you; I'm sure your investigator will find out anyhow."

"The investigator I want is on vacation till next week. But you're right. He would have found out. And so will the district attorney's office, if they haven't already."

Scott pushed back his chair and got up. "Adam, I feel like a louse saying this, but it's true. I did break off with Tina last August. It wasn't just that I was seeing Viv. It was that Tina wanted to get serious and I didn't. Then when I got to Boca, I realized that I missed Viv a lot. Usually these summer romances fizzle. You know that. I phoned Viv and realized she felt the same way about me. She came down to Boca, we met in New York a few times and by spring we both were sure we wanted to get married."

"If you're telling the truth now, why didn't you tell it from the beginning?" Adam shot the question accusingly.

"Because Fred doesn't know that Tina was still seeing me over the winter. It didn't bother him that she dated other guys, but he really hates me because she dropped him for me last summer. That was the real reason she asked me to meet her. She wanted to see me face to face and hear me promise never to tell anyone that she'd been down to Florida."

"Did you see her after she walked out of the pub that day?"

Scott shrugged. "I called her and said that whatever she had to talk about, she'd have to say it on the phone. Then when I heard what it was, I laughed. I asked her who she thought I was going to tell about her coming to Boca. What kind of jerk did she think I was?"

"I think we're going to need a few witnesses at the inquest to testify that Tina was chasing you, and not

212

the other way around. Is there anyone you can suggest?''

Scott brightened. "A couple of the other waitresses at the Daniel Webster Inn. Tina used to be friendly with them, but then they got mad at her. She told me they were sore because some of the regular customers who are big tippers requested to be seated at one of her tables.''

"Tina seems to play all the angles," Adam said. "I hope her friend Fred doesn't mind having it publicly aired that she was lying to him." Why did I get myself into this? he wondered again. He still believed that Scott Covey's wife died in a tragic accident, but he also believed that Covey had been using Tina until Vivian decided to marry him. This guy may be innocent of murder, but it doesn't keep him from being a sleaze, he thought.

Suddenly this smallish kitchen seemed to close in on Adam. He wanted to get back to Menley and Hannah. They would have only a few days together before he had to take Menley to the hospital in New York. He would have to begin to prepare her for that. "Give me the names of those waitresses," he said abruptly.

"Liz Murphy and Alice Regan."

"Write them down. Let's hope they still work there." Adam turned and left the kitchen.

As he passed the dining room he glanced in. A large framed picture was on the table; it was the aerial view of Remember House Elaine had had in the window. He went over to examine it.

Beautiful photography, he thought. The house seemed majestically aloof. The colors were spectacular—the rich green-leaved branches of the trees surrounding the house, the purple-blue hydrangeas bordering the foundation, the blue-green ocean, tranquil with a lazy surf. You could even see strollers on the beach and a small boat anchored just below the horizon.

"I'd love to have this," he commented.

"It's a gift from Elaine," Scott said quickly. "Otherwise I'd give it to you. She seems to think that if you don't buy Remember House, I'd be interested."

"Would you be?"

"If Viv were alive, yes. As it stands, no." He hesitated. "What I mean is, in my present frame of mind, no. Maybe I'll feel differently if a judge clears me."

"Looking at this picture would certainly be an incentive to buy the place. It is for me," Adam said. Then he turned to leave. "I'm on my way. We'll talk later."

He was getting into his car when Henry Sprague waved him over. "I've found more material that I think Menley would be interested in," he explained. "Come in; let me give it to you."

The file was on the foyer table. "And Phoebe is very insistent that this doll belongs in Remember House. I don't know why she thinks that, but would you mind taking it with you?"

"Menley will probably be delighted to see it," Adam said. "It certainly is a genuine antique. Don't be surprised if it shows up sketched in her book. Thanks, Henry. How's Phoebe today?"

"Napping right now. She didn't have a good night. I don't know if I told you; I'm putting her in the nursing home as of the first of the month."

"You didn't tell me. I'm sorry."

As Adam tucked the file under his arm and picked up the doll, he was startled by a scream. "She's having another nightmare," Henry said, and rushed toward the bedroom, Adam behind him.

Phoebe was lying on the bed, her hands covering her face. Henry bent over and took her hands in his. "It's all right, dear," he said soothingly.

She opened her eyes, looked up at him, then turned her head and saw Adam holding the doll. "Oh, they did drown her," she sighed. "But I'm glad they decided to let the baby live."

62

Menley phoned Carrie Bell at four o'clock. Carrie's initial cautious response when Menley identified herself was replaced by genuine warmth when she realized the reason for the call.

"Oh, that's wonderful," she said. "I sure can use the money. I've lost a lot of work these two weeks."

"A lot of work?" Menley asked. "Why is that?"

"Oh, I shouldn't have said that. I'll be over tomorrow morning bright and early. Thank you, Mrs. Nichols."

Menley told Amy about the conversation. "Do you know what she could have meant about losing a lot of work?"

Amy looked uncomfortable. "It's just that Elaine recommends her to people who are selling or renting their houses. Carrie goes in for a couple of days and is really good at making a house look great. But Elaine says that, because she's a terrible gossip, she's not sending her out on new jobs. She even tried to get my father to fire her."

* * *

Over dinner, Menley told Adam about that conversation. "Don't you think that was mean?" she asked as she ladled a second helping of chili onto his plate. "From what Amy tells me, Carrie Bell is a hardworking single mother, supporting a three-year-old."

"This is your best chili ever," Adam commented. "To answer you, I know Carrie's good. She cleaned the cottage I took last year when I came up alone. But I also know that Elaine is a hard worker. It's no accident that she's as successful as she is, because she doesn't leave anything to chance. If she thinks Carrie Bell's gossip is hurting her chances of selling houses, Carrie's out of a job. Oh, did I mention that besides the food I like the ambience?"

Menley had turned off the overhead light and put the wall sconces on the dim setting. They were sitting opposite each other at the refectory table. All Phoebe Sprague's research data and books, as well as Menley's own notes and sketches, were now in the library.

"I decided that since we always eat in here, it's a shame to have it so cluttered," she explained.

That was only part of the truth, she acknowledged to herself. The rest was that when Adam had gotten home late in the afternoon and given her the heavy file he'd gotten from Henry Sprague, she had glanced through it and been shocked to see the sketch of Mehitabel and Andrew on the ship. It was exactly as she had visualized them. There has to be another picture of them in all this stuff, she thought, and I must have seen it. But it was one more example of forgetting something important.

That was when she decided to put the Remember House research aside for a few days and get the *Travel Times* article out of the way. She'd phoned Jan Paley, who agreed to line up some historical homes for her to visit.

"The stories you told me about the houses where

people sense a presence would be perfect," she had told Jan. "I know the editor would love it." *And I want to know what those people have to say,* she'd thought.

"Did you do much writing today, or are you still digging through Phoebe's files?" Adam asked.

"Neither actually; I was working on something else." She told him about her call to Jan and what she planned to do.

Did I rush that explanation? Menley wondered. *It sounded so rehearsed.*

"Ghost stories?" Adam smiled. "You don't believe in that nonsense."

"I believe in legends." She noticed the chili had disappeared from his plate. "You were hungry. What did you have for lunch?"

"A hamburger, but that was a long time ago. 'Laine was with me. We went over her testimony for the inquest."

There was always something affectionate, even intimate, about the way Adam spoke when he referred to Elaine. She had to ask. "Adam, were you ever involved with Elaine, I mean more than as a big buddy?"

He looked uncomfortable. "Oh, we dated on and off as kids, and sometimes when I spent time at the Cape during law school, we got together."

"And never since then?"

"Oh, hell, Men, you don't expect me to kiss and tell. Before I met you, I used to bring the girl I was dating up here for a long weekend when my mother still had the big place. Other times I came alone. If neither one of us was busy, 'Laine and I would go out. But that was years ago. No big deal."

"I see." *Get off it,* Menley told herself. *The last thing you need to start is a discussion on Elaine.*

Adam was stretching his hand across the table. "I'm

with the only girl I've ever really loved and wanted to be with," he said. He paused. "We've had more ups and downs in five years than most people experience in a lifetime. All I care about is getting through them and being on firm ground again."

Menley touched her fingertips to his. She pulled them back. "Adam, you're trying to tell me something, aren't you?"

With increasing horror, she listened as he told her his plan:

"Men, when I spoke to Dr. Kaufman, she said that she thought you would benefit from aggressive therapy. It's one thing to have a flashback to the accident. It's another to think you heard Bobby calling and run through the house looking for him. She wants you to be an inpatient for just a short time."

It was exactly what she had feared.

"I'm getting better, Adam."

"I know how hard you're trying. But after the inquest it would be better if we took her advice. You know you trust her."

In that moment she hated him and knew it showed in her face. She turned and saw that he had put the antique doll in Hannah's high chair. Now it stared at her with fixed china blue eyes, a parody of the miracle that was Hannah.

"We're not talking about trusting Dr. Kaufman, we're talking about trusting *me*."

63

*J*an Paley had been surprised and pleased to receive the phone call from Menley Nichols that afternoon. Menley had asked about historical houses with legends attached to them. "By historical, I mean good examples of early architecture, and by legends, I mean stories about an unexplainable presence, a ghost," Menley told her.

Jan had readily agreed to be her guide. She'd immediately sat down and made a list of the places she would take her.

The old Dillingham house in Brewster was one they would visit. It was the second oldest house on the Cape. Over the years some of the people who rented it claimed to have gotten the impression of a woman passing the door of one of the bedrooms.

The Dennis Inn was another place to take her. The proprietors even had a nickname for the playful spirit who constantly wrought havoc in the kitchen. They called her Lillian.

They could visit Sarah Nye, the friend she had mentioned to Menley when they spoke at Elaine's party. Sarah was sure she was sharing her house with the lady for whom it had been built in 1720.

And what about the saltbox in Harwich that now

was an interior designer's shop on the entry level? The owners claimed they entertained a resident ghost and were convinced she was a sixteen-year-old who had died there in the nineteenth century.

Jan made some calls, set up appointments and phoned Menley back. "We're all set. I'll pick you up tomorrow morning at about ten o'clock."

"That's fine, and Jan, do you know anything about an antique doll that Phoebe Sprague was keeping? Henry told Adam that she insists it belongs in Remember House."

"Oh, did she find it?" Jan exclaimed. "I'm so glad. Tom discovered it under the eaves in the attic. God only knows how long it had been there. Phoebe wanted to show it to an antiques expert. Some research she had done suggested it actually might have belonged to Mehitabel. I didn't realize at that time that Phoebe's memory was beginning to slip. She put the doll somewhere and then couldn't find it."

"Why did she think it belonged to Mehitabel?" Menley asked Jan.

"Phoebe told me that a memoir she read mentioned that after her husband took her baby from her, Mehitabel could be observed standing on the widow's walk, holding a doll."

August 12th

64

Scott Covey spent most of Friday on the boat. He packed a picnic lunch, brought along his fishing rods and passed the most peaceful day he had enjoyed in weeks. The golden warmth of August had returned in full measure, replacing the chill that had dominated yesterday. The ocean breeze was balmy again. His lobster pots were full.

After lunch he stretched out on the deck, clasped his hands under his head and rehearsed the testimony he would give at the inquest. He tried to remember all the negatives Adam Nichols had warned him about and how he could refute every single one.

His involvement with Tina last winter was going to be his biggest problem. Without seeming like a louse and a cad, how could he let the judge understand that she had been the one pursuing him?

And then something Vivian had told him came into his mind. In late June, when he had talked her through one of her periodic fits of tearful insecurity, she had sighed, "Scott, you're the kind of great-looking guy women naturally fall for. I try to understand that. I know other people instinctively understand it too. It's not your fault; you can't help it."

"Vivy," he said aloud, "I'm going to have you to thank for getting me through this inquest."

Looking up at the sky, he put his fingers to his lips and blew her a kiss.

65

*A*ll little ducks in a row, Nat Coogan thought as he went over the list of witnesses they had subpoenaed for the inquest. He was in the district attorney's office in Barnstable.

The DA, Robert Shore, was sitting behind his desk, going over his own notes. He had scheduled a conference at noon to coordinate final preparations for the inquest. "All right. We're going to get some bitching that we haven't given much notice to the people we've subpoenaed, but that's the way it goes. This is a high-profile case, and we can't let it drag on. Any problems?"

The meeting lasted an hour and a half. By then the two men were in agreement that they had a good case to present to the judge. But Nat felt he had to issue some words of warning: "Listen, I've seen this guy in action. He can cry on cue. He may not have made it as an actor on stage, but trust me—he might be able to earn his Tony in district court."

66

*O*n Friday morning, Adam left Remember House as soon as Amy arrived. "I have to interview the waitresses who might balance any testimony about Tina visiting Scott in Florida," he explained to Menley.

"Jan is picking me up at ten," she said mechanically. "I should be back around two or two-thirty. Carrie Bell will be cleaning today, so she and Amy will both be in the house with Hannah. Is that satisfactory?"

"Menley!" He went to put his arms around her, but she turned and walked away from him.

"Do you want to tell me what's wrong?" Jan asked Menley as they drove over the bridge from Morris Island to the road that led to the lighthouse and Route 28.

"What's wrong is that my husband and my psychiatrist seem to agree that I belong in a padded cell."

"That's ridiculous."

"Yes, it is. And I'm not going to let it happen. Let's leave it at that. But, Jan, I have the feeling that Phoebe is trying to communicate something to me. The other day when she was at the house and saw her files, she looked at them, and I think she really understood what they were.''

"It's possible," Jan agreed. "There are times when Phoebe does seem to have breakthroughs of memory.''

"Her tone of voice was so urgent. She said that Mehitabel was innocent. Then she said something like, 'Tobias Knight. Answer in Mooncusser file.' Does that mean anything to you?''

"Not really. We know Tobias built Remember House, and that's about it. But when I was thinking of places to take you today I learned that he also built one of the oldest houses in Eastham. If you have time, we could swing by and take a look at it. It's run by the Eastham Historical Society, and they may have collected some information on him.''

67

"*T*ina met Scott Covey in here," Liz Murphy told Adam. "He came in for dinner with some of the people from the playhouse, and she played up to him like crazy. And nobody knows how to play up to a guy better than Tina.''

Adam was interviewing the young waitress in the office of the Daniel Webster Inn in Sandwich. "That was in July of last year?''

"Early July. Tina was going around with Fred at the time. What a nice guy he is. But boy, she put the skids on him when Scott came into the picture."

"Did you think Scott was serious about Tina?"

"Heck no. We all agreed that Scott had big plans for himself. He wasn't going to ever settle down with someone who worked for a living. We told her she was crazy to dump Fred for him."

"As far as you know, did Tina see Scott over the winter?"

"She knew he was in Boca Raton, and she wanted to get a job there. But I guess he told her that if things worked out, he'd be back up on the Cape."

"And she knew he was going around with Vivian Carpenter?"

"She knew it and she didn't care."

Exactly what Scott told me, Adam thought. "Did Vivian know about Tina?"

"Unless Scott told her, I don't know how she would know."

"Do you know why Tina quit her job here?"

"She told me that Scott had gotten married and she was starting to see Fred again and wanted to be free evenings to be with him. She said that Fred gets up so early for work that he's in bed at ten o'clock at night. She wanted a job where she worked breakfast and lunch, but that wasn't available here."

"Liz, you're going to be subpoenaed as a witness at the inquest. Don't worry about it. The district attorney will ask you pretty much the same questions I've just asked."

The other waitress, Alice Regan, came on at eleven, so Adam waited to see her. Her story verified what Liz Murphy had told him. He knew the district attorney would hit Tina hard on choosing to work in Chatham, at a restaurant frequented by an ex-lover, but that would make Tina look bad, not Scott.

Adam drove down Route 6A and stopped at the Courthouse. In the district attorney's office, he submitted the names of Liz Murphy and Alice Regan to be added to the list of witnesses he wanted subpoenaed. "I may have one or two more," he told an assistant DA.

His next stop was in Orleans, to interview a fisherman whose boat had been swamped in the same squall that took Vivian Carpenter's life.

68

Carrie Bell bustled around the keeping room, dusting the inside of the cabinets as she chatted with Amy. "That is one adorable baby," she said. "And so good."

Amy was feeding Hannah her lunch.

As though she understood the compliment, Hannah turned a dazzling smile on Carrie and put her fist in the jar of peaches.

"Hannah!" Amy protested, laughing.

"And she's going to look a lot like her brother," Carrie announced.

"I think so too," Amy agreed. "That picture on Mrs. Nichols' dresser shows a real resemblance."

"It shows up even more in the video of Bobby that Mr. Nichols had up here last year." Carrie lowered her voice. "You know, I used to clean that little cottage he rented near Elaine's house. Well, one time I went in, and Mr. Nichols was watching a video of Bobby running to his mother. I swear, the look on his face almost broke my heart."

She picked up the antique doll. "You don't want to be taking this in and out of the high chair, Amy. Why don't I just put it in that old cradle in the baby's room? It kind of looks as though it belongs there."

69

*B*y one o'clock, a dozen pages of Menley's notebook were filled, and she had two hours of interviews on her tape recorder.

As Jan drove down Route 6 toward Eastham, Menley mused on the similarities in the experiences she had heard. "Everyone we talked to seems to feel that if there is something unexplainable in their house, it's a benevolent presence," she said. "But your friend in Brewster, Sarah, has never had any manifestation except that first one."

Jan looked at her. "Meaning?"

"Sarah told us that early one morning when she and her husband were asleep in bed, the sound of someone coming up the stairs awakened her. Then the door opened and she saw the imprint of footsteps on the carpet.''

"That's right."

Menley flipped through her notebook. "Sarah said she felt a sense of comfort. Here's how she put it, 'It was like when you're a small child, and your mother comes into the room and covers you.' "

"Yes, that was the way she expressed it."

"And then she said she felt a pat on her shoulder, and it was as though someone were speaking, but she was hearing with her mind, not her ears. She knew it was Abigail Harding, the lady for whom the house had been built, and Abigail was telling her how happy she was that her home had been restored to its original beauty."

"That's always been the way Sarah described that experience."

"My point," Menley continued, "is that there was a reason for Abigail to contact Sarah. She had something to tell her. Sarah says she's never experienced anything specific again, and that when she has that feeling of a benevolent presence now, she may be simply sensing a tranquil atmosphere in the house. I think what I'm trying to say is that maybe some kind of unfinished business keeps a presence anchored to earth."

"It's possible," Jan agreed.

They stopped for a quick lunch at a small waterfront restaurant in Eastham, then went to see the house Tobias Knight had built in that town. It was on Route 6, surrounded by restaurants and shops.

"The location can't compare with Remember House," Menley remarked.

"Most of the captains' houses were set back from the water. The early settlers respected those nor'easters. But the house is similar to Remember House, if not quite as fancy. This one dates back to 1699. As you can see, there's no fanlight.''

"The captain and Mehitabel brought the fanlight from England," Menley said.

"I didn't know that. You must have found that bit of information in Phoebe's material.''

Menley did not answer. They went inside, stopped at the reception desk, picked up the literature on the house and then walked through the rooms. The beautifully restored mansion was similar in layout to Remember House. "The rooms are larger here," Jan observed, "but Remember House has finer detail.''

Menley was silent on the drive back to Chatham. Something was bothering her, but she wasn't sure what it was. Now she was anxious to get home and have a chance to talk to Carrie Bell before she left.

70

*F*red Hendin worked on a carpentry crew with a small builder in Dennis who specialized in renovations. Fred liked the work, especially enjoying the feel of wood in his hands. Wood had a mind of its own as well as an inherent dignity. He viewed himself in much the same way.

Now that waterfront property was worth a fortune, it paid to renovate the budget homes that were situated on prime lots. The waterfront house they were working on was one of those. It was about forty years old, and they were practically rebuilding it. Part of the project was to gut the kitchen, replacing those pressboard cabinets that builders used in cheap housing with custom cherrywood units.

Fred actually had his eye on a house opposite the one where he was working, a real handyman's special, with beach rights and a terrific view. He'd been watching the local real estate agents bring prospective buyers to see it, but none of them stayed long. They didn't look past the fact that the place was a mess. Fred knew that if he bought it and put in six months of hard work, he'd end up with one of the nicest homes anyone could want, plus he would have a good investment.

Only two weeks more till the end of August, he thought. Then the price would drop. Real estate activity pretty much died on the Cape during the winter.

Fred sat with the other guys in the crew, having lunch. They worked well together, and at breaks they shared a few laughs.

They began talking about the inquest into Vivian Carpenter Covey's death. Matt, the electrician, had done some work for Vivian in May, shortly after she was married. "Not an easy lady," he reported. "The day I was there her husband went to the store and stayed out a while. She sailed into him when he got back, said he wasn't going to make a fool of her. Told him to go pack his bags. Then she started crying and falling all over him when he reminded her she'd asked him to stop at the cleaners and that's what held him up. Believe me, that woman was a problem."

Sam, a recent addition to the crew asked, "Isn't there talk that Covey has a girlfriend, a waitress from around here who's a real hot number?"

"Forget it." Matt scowled as he glanced sideways at Fred.

Fred stuffed the napkin into his coffee container. "That's right. Forget it," he snapped, his previous good humor instantly gone. He pushed his chair back and left the table.

When he went back to work, it took him time to settle down. A lot of things were sticking in his craw. Last night after the detective left, Tina admitted that she'd been seeing Covey all last winter, making several trips down to Florida.

Does it matter? Fred asked himself as he hung the cabinets. As Tina had pointed out, she and Fred had not been dating then. But why did she have to lie about it? he asked himself. Then he wondered if she was also lying about seeing Covey after he was married. And what about in the past month since his wife died?

At the end of the day, when he arrived home to wait for Adam Nichols to keep their appointment, he was still wrestling with the question of whether or not he would ever be able to trust Tina again.

He wouldn't say anything to Covey's lawyer. For the present he would stick up for Tina and give her the engagement ring to wear at the inquest. From the way that detective talked, the police wouldn't mind involving Tina in a murder plot. She didn't seem to understand how serious all this had become.

No, he would stand by her for now, but if this bad feeling kept growing, he knew that as crazy as he was about Tina, he couldn't marry her. A man had to have his dignity.

Brooding, he thought about all the nice gifts he had given her this summer, like his mother's gold watch and pearls and pin. She kept them in that hollowed-out book that was really a jewelry box, on a shelf in her living room.

When the inquest was over, if he decided to call it quits with Tina, he would collect the engagement ring and them too.

71

*I*t was a busy afternoon at the agency. Elaine received two new listings from walk-ins and went out to inspect the properties. One of them she photographed immediately, a handsome replica of a square-rigger on Ryders Pond. "This should go fast," she assured the owner.

The other place had always been a rental and needed sprucing up. Tactfully she suggested that if the lawn were mowed and the shrubs trimmed, the overall effect could be enhanced. The house also needed a good cleaning. Reluctantly she offered to send Carrie Bell over—she had her drawbacks, but no one did a better job.

She called Marge on the car phone. "I'll go directly home. John and Amy are coming for dinner, and I want to develop the new pictures before I have to start cooking."

"You're getting very domestic," Marge kidded her.

"I might as well."

When she got home, Elaine made one more call, this time to Scott Covey. "Why not join us for dinner?"

"If you let me bring it. I just came in from the boat with a bucket of lobsters."

"I knew there was a reason I was calling you. Did you get the picture?"

"Yes, I did."

"You didn't even thank me," she teased. "But you know why I sent it."

"As a reminder, I know."

"See you later, Scott."

72

Carrie Bell was upstairs vacuuming when Jan dropped Menley off. Menley went up to her. "Amy has the baby out in the carriage, Mrs. Nichols," she explained. "Good as gold that baby is, let me tell you."

"She wasn't always that good." Menley smiled. She looked around. "Everything shines. Thanks, Carrie."

"Well, I like to leave things just right. I'm just about finished now. Do you want me to come next week?"

"I certainly do." Menley opened her pocketbook, took out her wallet and with a silent prayer began to steer the conversation where she wanted it to go. "Carrie, strictly between us, what frightened you the last time you were here?"

Carrie looked alarmed. "Mrs. Nichols, I know it's just my imagination, and like Miss Atkins says, I'm so heavy footed I probably stepped on a loose floorboard and that got the cradle rocking."

"Maybe. But you also thought you heard someone moving around upstairs. At least that's what Amy said."

Carrie leaned forward, and her voice lowered. "Mrs. Nichols, you promise you won't tell Miss Atkins a word about this?"

"I promise."

"Mrs. Nichols, I did hear something that day, and today I tried pounding my feet when I went into the nursery, and that cradle didn't budge."

"You didn't notice anything unusual today, then?"

"No. Nothing strange. But I'm a bit worried about Amy."

"Why? What happened?"

"Oh, nothing happened. I mean, just before Hannah woke up from her nap a little while ago, Amy was reading in the little parlor with the door closed. I thought I heard her crying. I didn't want to seem nosy so I didn't go in to her. I know she's worried about her father marrying Miss Atkins. Then later I asked her if anything was troubling her, and she denied it. You know how kids are. Sometimes they'll bare their souls. Other times they want you to MYOB."

"MYOB?"

"Mind your own business."

"Of course." Menley handed Carrie the folded bills. "Thanks very much."

"Thank you. You're a nice lady. And I tell you, I have a three-year-old, and I can understand how awful it must have been for you to lose that beautiful little boy. I got tears in my eyes when I saw that video of him last year."

"You saw a video of Bobby?"

"Mr. Nichols had it up here when he rented the cottage. Like I was telling Amy, he had the saddest expression watching it. It showed him in the pool with Bobby, and he lifted him out, and you called him, and he ran to you."

Menley swallowed over the lump in her throat. "That tape was made just two weeks before the accident," she said, trying to keep her voice steady. "I never could bear to watch it. It was such a happy day."

I want to see it now, she thought. I'm ready to see it.

Carrie put the money in her purse. "Miss Atkins was with Mr. Nichols that day, and he was telling her all about Bobby and how guilty he felt because he should have been with the two of you the day of the accident but played golf instead."

73

*I*t had been a good day's work, Adam thought as he drove onto the private road that led to Remember House. Unfortunately it wasn't over. It was nearly three o'clock now and at five he'd leave to meet Fred Hendin.

But at least he'd be home for a couple of hours, and

it was a perfect beach day. That is, if Menley was willing to go to the beach with him.

Amy's car was in the driveway. He had mixed feelings of relief and irritation. She was a nice, responsible kid, but it would be great to be alone with his family and not have someone always underfoot.

If I react this way, how does Menley feel, having someone around all the time? he wondered. Sick at heart, he realized that they were rapidly going back to the way it had been before the pregnancy with Hannah. Remote from each other. Both of them on edge.

There was no one in the house. Was Menley back yet, and if so, were they on the beach? He walked to the edge of the bluff and looked down.

Menley was sitting cross-legged on the blanket, Hannah propped against her. The perfect picture, Adam thought. Menley's hair was swirling behind her. Her slender body was tanned and lovely. She and Amy seemed to be deep in conversation.

Amy was lying on the sand facing Menley, leaning on her elbows, chin resting in her palms. It's got to be tough for her, he thought. Going away to college is always scary, and according to Elaine, she's still having a problem about her father remarrying. But Elaine had also said, "She doesn't know how lucky she is that John can afford to send her to Chapel Hill."

Elaine hadn't gone to college. At the end of the summer twenty-one years ago, when the rest of the crowd was heading for elite schools, her mother had just lost another job, so Elaine had gotten work as a typist in a real estate agency. Obviously she had done very well for herself, Adam reflected. Now she owned the agency.

At that moment Menley looked up. Adam scrambled down the steep path. When he reached them he had the feeling that he was an intruder. "Hi," he said, lamely.

Menley did not answer.

Amy sprang up. "Hi, Mr. Nichols. Are you home for good?"

"Yes, Adam, are you home for good?" Menley asked. "If you are, I know Amy would like to have a few hours to herself."

He decided to ignore her impersonal tone. "Go ahead, Amy. Thanks." He squatted down on the blanket and waited while Amy said good-bye to Hannah and Menley.

When she was out of earshot, he said, "I'll give her a chance to change, then I'll go up and get my bathing suit on."

"We'll come up with you. We've had enough of the beach."

"Damn it, Menley, knock it off."

"Knock what off?"

"Men, don't let this happen to us," he pleaded.

Hannah looked up at him uncertainly.

"It's all right, sweetheart," he said, "I'm just trying to make your mommy stop being mad at me."

"Adam, we can't reduce this to a tiff. I spoke to Dr. Kaufman. She's going to call us back at four-thirty. I am going to absolutely refuse to be hospitalized. I also have a call in to my mother in Ireland. I'm going to ask her to cut short her trip. If there is some way that you and Dr. Kaufman can sign me into a hospital against my will, then my mother, who is a registered nurse, will mind my baby, not your girlfriend 'Laine."

"What in the hell is that supposed to mean?"

"Adam, when you came up here last year, how much did you see of Elaine?"

"She's an old friend. Of course I saw her. And it meant nothing."

"As you said last night, you're not the kind to kiss and tell. But what was she doing watching vidoes of my little boy with you?"

"My God, Men, she happened to stop in when I was playing the tape. I wasn't just looking at Bobby in that video. I was looking at you."

"With your girlfriend."

"No, with an old buddy."

"Who has told her future stepdaughter that after you deposit me in a psychiatric hospital in New York, you'll be here with Hannah."

Adam stood up. "I'm going to change and go for a swim."

"Surely you're not planning to leave Hannah alone with me?"

He did not answer but turned and walked away.

Menley watched Adam climb the path. He was leaning forward, his hands in his pockets. She thought of what Carrie Bell had overheard him tell Elaine, that he felt guilty he hadn't been with her the day of the accident.

Adam had told her that right after Bobby died, and she had raged at him. "Don't try to make me feel better. You had a long-standing golf date. I didn't want you to change your plans for a last-minute invitation."

He'd never mentioned it to her again.

When Adam returned ten minutes later, she said, "Adam, I know myself. I am going to tell Dr. Kaufman that I am coming to grips with these anxiety attacks. I am also going to tell her that if you cannot and will not accept that fact, then our marriage is not going to last. The background of this house is of a husband who did not trust his wife. Don't perpetuate that mistake."

74

On the drive home, Amy puzzled over whether or not to warn her father that Carrie Bell might tell him that she had been crying. Mrs. Nichols had asked her about it. "I wasn't crying," she'd protested. "Honestly. Carrie's hearing things."

She thought that Mrs. Nichols believed her, but her father would probably believe Carrie. Her father was always worried about her these days. If only he'd stop telling her how wonderful it was going to be to have a new mother.

I'll be eighteen next month, Amy thought. I wish Dad would stop trying to sell Elaine to me. I'm glad he is getting married again, but I wish it weren't to her.

Tonight she had wanted to go out with the crowd to Hyannis. But Elaine had decided she was going to fix a home-cooked meal, so her father had half ordered, half begged Amy to go with him.

"Don't hurt Elaine's feelings," he had urged.

I can't wait to get to college, Amy thought as she drove through the Main Street traffic into the rotary. Then she sighed. Oh, Mom, why did you have to go and die on us?

Maybe that was the reason she felt so close to Mrs.

Nichols. Just the way she missed Mom, she knew Mrs. Nichols missed her little boy. But now Mrs. Nichols has Hannah.

And I have Elaine, she thought bitterly as she turned into her driveway.

But later she was glad her father had made her accompany him to Elaine's house. Scott Covey was there, and she helped him steam the lobsters he had brought. He was so nice, and even though he was having so many problems, he sure didn't take them out on anyone. He talked about Chapel Hill.

"One of the plays I toured in ran at the college for a couple of weeks," he told her. "Great town. You'll have a lot of fun."

During dinner, Amy noticed that they avoided any talk about the inquest. Elaine did ask if Carrie Bell had heard any more footsteps when she was cleaning today.

Amy seized the chance to get in something about the crying. "No, but in case she tells you she heard me crying, she was wrong."

"She heard crying?" Elaine asked. "Was it Menley?"

"Mrs. Nichols was out for a long time with Mrs. Paley, and when she came in she was fine." Amy did not want to talk about Mrs. Nichols with Elaine. She knew that Elaine thought Mrs. Nichols was on the verge of another breakdown. If I'd only brought my own car instead of going with Dad, she thought. I don't want to sit around here all night.

When Scott Covey started to talk about leaving, she saw her chance to get away. "Scott, would you mind dropping me off?" she asked, then tried to sound tired when she turned to her father. "Dad, I really have had a long day and I'd like to get home. Unless you want me to help with the dishes, Elaine."

"No, go right ahead. Taking care of a baby all day is work."

Now that she'd claimed to be tired, Amy realized there was nothing to do for the rest of the evening. She couldn't announce she was meeting her friends. There was nothing good on television, and she didn't want to ask Scott to drive her to rent a video. But wait a minute, she thought. Elaine has a terrific collection of old films. She lends them to Dad all the time.

"Elaine," she asked, "could I borrow one of your videos?"

"Any at all," Elaine said. "Take a couple of them. Just be sure to bring them back."

I know enough to return them, Amy thought resentfully. Her father was just starting to tell one of his long, pointless stories when she went into the family room.

The longest wall was covered with bookshelves. Fully half of them held videotapes, the titles facing out, in alphabetical order. Amy skimmed them and selected *The Country Girl* with Grace Kelly and *Horse Feathers*, the Marx brothers comedy.

She was about to leave when she remembered another oldie she'd always wanted to watch: *Birth of a Nation*. Was it here?

She read the *B* titles slowly and found it. As she took it from the shelf, several cassettes around it fell. Putting them back in place, she realized why they'd been sticking out. There was a cassette behind them, standing upright against the wall.

It was labeled BOBBY—EAST HAMPTON—LAST TAPE. Could this be the one of the Nicholses' little boy that Carrie Bell saw last year?

I'd love to see it, Amy thought. Elaine may not even realize it's here. It does belong to the Nicholses' and she might not want to lend it. I'll return it with the others and not say anything.

She dropped the cassettes in her shoulder bag and went back to the dining room.

Her father was just finishing his story.

Scott Covey was smiling politely. Elaine seemed convulsed with laughter. Amy wanted to strangle Elaine every time she heard that phony laugh. She thought, Mom would have said, "John, will you absolutely promise not to inflict that long-winded monologue on anyone again for at least a week?"

And then she would have laughed *with* Dad, not *at* him.

75

"No, I have not increased the medication," Menley told Dr. Kaufman. "I haven't found it necessary."

She was on the phone in the library, Hannah in her lap. Adam was on the extension in the keeping room.

"Menley, I have a feeling you regard Adam and me as the enemy," Dr. Kaufman said.

"No, that isn't true. I did not tell you about the baby-sitter seeing me on the widow's walk for the simple reason that I thought she was mistaken. And now she has come to that conclusion too."

"Then whom did Amy see?"

"My guess is that she saw no one. There's a metal

strip on that chimney. When the sun hits it, it gives an impression of someone moving."

"What about the flashback to hearing the train and Bobby calling you? You told me you were afraid to pick up Hannah."

"I didn't want her to cry anymore, but I was afraid to pick her up because I was trembling so much. I'm sorry I failed her at that moment. But even without a mother who's having an anxiety attack, babies are left to cry it out sometimes."

Hannah tugged her hair as she spoke. Menley bent her head. "Ouch."

"Menley!" Adam sounded startled.

"The baby is pulling my hair and I said 'ouch,' and Dr. Kaufman, please listen to what I'm trying to convey to you. Adam is ready to drop the phone and rush in here at the least hint of anything. I have to say I think you're treating the wrong patient."

She paused and bit her lip. "I'm going to get off now and let you two talk. Doctor, if you and Adam are able to sign me into a psychiatric facility against my will, you are going to wait until my mother is home from Ireland and can mind my baby. In the meantime, I will stay here in this lovely house and write my book. When I started having these anxiety attacks, you talked to both of us about the need for his support. Well, I don't feel that Adam has offered that to me, and I need it. The time will come, however, when I do not need it, and at that time I will neither need nor want him either."

She replaced the receiver quietly. "Well, Hannah," she said, "that's telling them."

It was exactly four-forty. At 4:43, Adam came to the door. "I always said I never wanted you to get mad at me." He hesitated. "I've got to see Fred Hendin now. I don't want to go. I'm sorry I got involved in this Covey case. But since we're being so stripped-down honest, I'd like to remind you that you were the one who urged me to help this guy out.''

''Granted,'' Menley said.

''But when I get back, I'd like to take you out for dinner. You feed her nibs while I'm gone, and we'll bring her along. We used to do that with Bobby.''

''Yes, we did.''

''One more thing. You have a call in to your mother. When she phones, don't ask her to interrupt her vacation. Dr. Kaufman believes you're doing fine and I agree. Have a baby-sitter or not. That's up to you.''

He was gone. Menley waited until she heard the sound of the keeping room door closing behind him before she said, ''Hannah, sometimes you just have to stand up to people. We're going to be fine.''

At six-thirty, just as she came out of the shower, her mother phoned from Wexford.

''Menley, they said it was urgent that I call you. What's wrong?''

Menley made a determined effort to sound cheery. ''Nothing's wrong, Mom. I just wanted to see how you were. Hannah's telling herself jokes. She's lying on my bed, giggling . . . No, I didn't have a special reason for calling . . . Jack and Phyllis okay?''

She was still on the phone when Adam came into the bedroom. She waved him over. ''Mom, let me brief Adam. He'll love it.'' Quickly she explained, ''Phyl is now tracing my father's family. She's back five generations to 1860. She discovered Adrian McCarthy, a scholar from Trinity College. The McCarthys have gone up in her estimation. The hunt continues.''

She handed him the phone. ''Say a quick hello to your mother-in-law.''

She studied Adam as he chatted with her mother,

realizing how tired he looked. This has not been much of a vacation for him, she thought.

When he hung up, she said, "We don't have to eat out. The fish market isn't closed yet. Why don't you run down and get something."

"Actually, I would like that. Thanks, Men."

He returned with bay scallops, freshly picked ears of small-kernel corn, beef tomatoes and French bread.

Hannah watched the sunset with them. After they settled her in her crib, they prepared dinner together. By unspoken agreement, they did not discuss the conversation with Dr. Kaufman.

Instead, Adam told her about the meetings he had had that day. "Those waitresses will be good witnesses," he said, "and so will Tina's boyfriend. But Men, I have to tell you, Scott Covey is coming through more and more as an opportunist."

"But surely not a murderer."

"No, not that."

After dinner they both read for a while. They were still sensitive from the things that had been said earlier, so they talked very little.

They went to bed at ten-thirty, both sensing that they still needed space from each other. Menley felt uncommonly tired and fell asleep almost immediately.

"Mommy, Mommy." It was the afternoon at East Hampton two weeks before Bobby died. They were spending the weekend with Louis Miller, one of Adam's law partners. Lou was taking videos. Adam had Bobby in the pool. He'd put him on the deck. "Go to Mommy," he'd instructed.

Bobby ran to her, his arms outstretched, his smile joyous. "Mommy, Mommy."

She swung him up and turned to the camera. "Tell us your name," she instructed.

"Wobert Adam Nikko," he'd said proudly.

"And what do people call you?"
"Bobby."
"And do you go to school?"
"Nertry schoow."
"Nertry schoow," she'd repeated and the sound of laughter closed the tape.

"Bobby. Bobby."
She was crying. Adam was leaning over her. "It's all right, Men."
She opened her eyes. "It was just a dream this time."
As Adam put his arms around her, they heard Hannah begin to fuss. Menley pulled herself up.
"I'll go in to her," Adam said, quickly getting out of bed.
He brought her back to their room. "Here she is, Mama."
Menley closed her arms around the baby. A sense of peace and healing came over her as Hannah snuggled close.
"Go to sleep, honey," Adam said quietly. "I'll put her nibs back in a couple of minutes."
She drifted off, remembering Bobby's happy, sunny voice. "Mommy, Mommy." By next summer Hannah would be able to call to her too.
After a while she felt Hannah being taken from her arms. A few minutes later Adam drew her to him and whispered, "Sweetheart, the one thing you mustn't do is deny you're having flashbacks."

August 13th

76

*L*ate Saturday morning, Nat Coogan dutifully accompanied his wife into town. Their anniversary was coming up, and Debbie had seen a painting at one of the galleries that she thought would be perfect over their fireplace.

"It's a panoramic view of the ocean and shore," she told him. "I think if I were looking at it every day, I'd feel I was living on the water."

"If you like it, buy it, Babe."

"No, you have to see it first."

Nat was no judge of art, but when he saw the watercolor, he thought it was a pretty amateurish job, certainly not worth the two hundred dollar price tag.

"You don't like it. I can tell," Debbie said.

"It's okay."

The dealer intervened. "The artist is only twenty-one years old and has a lot of promise. This painting may be worth money someday."

I wouldn't hold my breath, Nat thought.

"We'll think about it," Debbie said. When they were outside, she sighed. "It didn't look that good today. Oh, well."

The art shop was on a path off Main Street. "Buy

you lunch?" Nat asked when they reached the side-walk.

"You probably want to get out on the boat."

"No, that's all right. We'll go to the Wayside. Tina's working today and I like her to see me hanging around. One of our few good chances to nail Covey is to get her rattled when she's testifying."

They passed the Atkins Real Estate Agency. Debbie stopped and looked in the window. "I always check to see what waterfront estate they're showing this week," she told Nat. "After all, we might win the lottery someday. I was so sorry when they took out that aerial photograph of Remember House. That was my favorite. I think it inspired me to get interested in the watercolor."

"Looks as though Marge is about to put the one of Remember House back," Nat observed.

Inside the office, Marge was opening the showcase window, and as they watched, she put the handsomely framed photograph in an empty space in the display area. Noticing them, Marge waved and came outside to speak to them. "Hello Detective Coogan," she said. "Anything I can help you with? We've got some very attractive listings."

"Unofficial business," Nat told her. "My wife is enamored of that picture." He pointed to the aerial photo of Remember House. "Unfortunately, that listing is a little out of our price range."

"That picture has brought in more traffic," Marge commented. "Actually this is a copy of the one you saw. Elaine made it for Adam Nichols and I'm just putting it in the window until he comes for it. She gave the original to Scott Covey."

"Scott Covey!" Nat exclaimed. "What would he want with it?"

"Elaine says he's expressed interest in Remember House."

"I'd have thought he couldn't wait to get away from the Cape," Nat said. "Provided he's free to go."

Marge was suddenly uncomfortably aware that she might be wandering into dangerous territory. She had heard that Nat Coogan was investigating Scott Covey. On the other hand, that was his job, and he and his wife were nice people and in the future could become clients. His wife was still admiring the picture of Remember House. Marge remembered that Elaine had said she had the negative and could always make copies.

"Would you want to have a print of this photograph?" she asked.

Debbie said, "I certainly would. I have just the spot for it."

"I know Elaine would make one up for you," Marge volunteered.

"Then that's settled," Nat decreed.

At the Wayside Inn, they found that Tina had phoned in sick. "I am getting her rattled," Nat said. "That's good."

It was when they were finishing their lobster rolls that Debbie suddenly observed, "That isn't the same picture, Nat."

"What do you mean?"

"There was something different about the picture of Remember House we saw this morning, and I just figured it out. The one that had been in the window earlier had a boat in it. The one Marge just showed us didn't. Isn't that odd?"

77

*O*n Saturday morning, Adam reminded Menley to tell Amy they wouldn't be needing her that day. He had a meeting with a marine expert the harbormaster at Chatham had recommended. "I want someone to balance the people from Woods Hole who are going to raise a question about where the body washed in, but it shouldn't take long. I'll be home by twelve or one."

Half a loaf, Menley thought. He may not have believed that I didn't have a flashback when I dreamed of Bobby, but at least he's willing to leave me alone with the baby.

"I want to work this morning," she said. "I'll have Amy baby-sit till lunchtime."

"Your decision, dear."

Amy arrived just as he was leaving. She was dismayed to hear Menley ask, "Adam, where is that tape of Bobby at East Hampton? I'm ready to see it now."

"It's in the apartment."

"The next time you go down will you bring it up?"

"Of course. We'll watch it together."

Should I tell them I have it? Amy wondered. They might not like the idea that I was looking at it. No, it would be better to return it to Elaine's house as fast as she could. Mr. Nichols might remember that he'd left it at the Cape and ask Elaine for it.

When Menley went into the library and closed the door, she realized instantly that something was different about the atmosphere. It was so chilly. That must be it. This room didn't get the morning sun. Even so, she decided not to move the data back into the keeping room. She was wasting too much time going through the stacks of files. She would spread them out on the floor, the way she worked in her office at home, and fasten on each one a sheet of paper on which she'd written the contents in large, bold print. That way she could find what she was looking for easily, and when she was finished, she could just close the door on the mess instead of straightening it out.

She spent the first hour spreading the data around to her satisfaction, then opened the new file from Phoebe Sprague and began to analyze the contents.

The sketches were on top. Again she studied the one of the Captain and Mehitabel on the ship, then taped it to the wall by her desk. Alongside it she hung her own sketches of them and the drawing Jan had brought from the Brewster Library. Almost interchangeable, she thought. I must have come across something like this in the files.

She had already planned the way she would work. She began by combing through the new material for any and every reference to Tobias Knight.

The first time she saw his name was in connection with the carrying out of Mehitabel's punishment. "At ye town meeting in Monomoit on the third Wednesday of August in ye year of our Lord one thousand seven hundred and five, Mehitabel, the wife of Captain Andrew Freeman was presented and the judgment of ye court carried out in the presence of her husband, her accusers, her penitent partner in adultery and ye town people who ventured forth from their homes and duties to witness and be warned of the punishment of unchastity."

The third Wednesday in August, Menley thought. That would be around this time. And Andrew watched her tortured. How could he?

There was a note that Phoebe had made: "Captain Freeman sailed that night, bringing with him the six-week-old infant and an Indian slave as nursemaid."

He left her in that condition and took her baby from her. Menley looked up at her sketch of Andrew Freeman. You didn't look strong and sure that day, I hope, she thought. She ripped the sketch from the wall, reached for a charcoal pencil, and with quick, sure strokes altered the confident expression.

She had intended to depict cruelty, but try as she would, when she was finished, the face of Andrew Freeman was that of a man ravaged by grief.

Maybe you had the grace to regret what you did to her, she thought.

Amy had brought Hannah in for a bottle of juice. Holding the baby, she stood uncertainly in the keeping room. From the front of the house she thought she could hear the sound of soft sobbing. That's what Carrie heard yesterday, she thought. Maybe Mrs. Nichols came back earlier than we realized.

Mrs. Nichols kept up such a good front when people were around, but she really was depressed, Amy thought, wondering briefly if it was her responsibility to talk to Mr. Nichols about it.

Then she listened again. No, that wasn't Mrs. Nichols crying. The breeze had started up the way it did yesterday and was making the sobbing sound that echoed in the chimney. Wrong again, Carrie, Amy thought.

August 14th

78

On Sunday morning Adam insisted on going out for brunch after church. "We both ended up working last night, which wasn't the plan, and I have to spend at least an hour with Scott Covey this afternoon."

Menley could not refuse even though she wanted to stay at her desk. From town records in Phoebe Sprague's last file, she'd learned the circumstances of Mehitabel's death.

Captain Andrew Freeman had been gone for two years after he sailed, taking his infant daughter with him. Mehitabel had kept watch for him from the widow's walk of Nickquenum, as the house was known at that time.

When she spotted his sails, she had gone to the harbor to wait for him. "A piteous sight," according to a letter written by selectman Jonathan Weekes.

Clearly souferin, she homble knelt before him and begged for her babe. He told her his daughter-babe would never set eyes on an unchaste mother. He ordered Mehitabel begone from his home. But her sickliness and fatague was observed by all and she was caried there to be gathered that night to her heavenly account. It is said that Captain Freeman witnessed her death and that her last words were "Andrew, here I await my child and here cruelly wronged, I die sinless."

Menley discussed what she had learned with Adam as they had eggs Benedict at the Red Pheasant in Dennis.

"My father used to love this place," Adam said, looking around. "It's too bad he's not still here. He'd be a great help to you. He knew Cape history backward and forward."

"And God knows Phoebe Sprague knew it," Menley said. "Adam, do you think it would be all right to call the Spragues and see if Hannah and I could visit them while you're with Scott?"

Adam hesitated. "Phoebe says crazy things sometimes."

"Not always."

He made the call and came back to the table, smiling. "Phoebe's having a pretty good day. Henry said to come right over."

Eighteen days more, Henry thought as he watched Phoebe playing patty-cake with Hannah, who was sitting on Menley's lap. He dreaded the morning he would awaken without Phoebe beside him.

Today she was walking better. There was less of the uncertain shuffling that was her usual gait. He knew it wouldn't last. There were fewer and fewer moments of lucidity, but at least, thank heaven, there were no more nightmares. She'd slept fairly well the last couple of nights.

"My granddaughter loves patty-cake too," Phoebe told Hannah. "She's just about your age."

Laura was fifteen now. It was as the doctor said. Long-term memory was the last to go. Henry was grateful for the look of understanding Adam's wife exchanged with him. What a pretty girl Menley is, he thought. In these couple of weeks her hair had become sunstreaked and her skin lightly tanned. The coloration brought out the deep blue of her eyes. She had a lovely smile, but today he noticed a difference in her, an indefinable air of sadness that hadn't been there before.

Then, when he heard her talking to Phoebe, he wondered if she was letting the research on Remember House get to her. It certainly was a tragic story.

"I came across the account of Mehitabel's death," she was telling Phoebe. "I guess when she knew Andrew wouldn't bring her the baby, she just gave up."

There was something Phoebe wanted to say. It had to do with Mehitabel and what was going to happen to Adam's wife. She would be dragged into that murky place where Andrew Freeman had left Tobias Knight to rot and then she would be drowned. If only Phoebe could explain that. If only the faces and voices of the people who were going to kill Adam's wife weren't hazy shadows. How could she warn her?

"Go away!" she cried, as she pushed at Menley and the baby. "Go away!"

"Vivian's mother and father are going to make strong, emotional witnesses," Adam warned Scott. "They're going to paint you as a fortune hunter who had a flashy girlfriend visiting him the week before the marriage, and who, after murdering their daughter, ripped a ring from her finger as a final act of greed."

Scott Covey was showing the strain of the impending inquest. They were sitting opposite each other at the dining room table, Adam's notes spread between them.

"I can only tell the truth," he said quietly.

"The *way* you tell it is what matters. You've got to convince that judge that you're as much a victim of that squall as Vivian was. I do have a good corroborating witness, a guy who almost lost his grandson when their boat was swamped. He would have lost him if he hadn't grabbed the kid by the foot as he was going over the rail.''

"Would they have accused him of murdering the child if he hadn't been able to grab him?" Covey asked bitterly.

"That's exactly the thought we want to plant in the judge's mind.''

When he left an hour later, Adam said, "No one can predict the outcome of these hearings. But we've got a good shot. Just remember, don't lose your temper, and don't criticize Vivian's parents. Get across that, yes, they're grieving parents and you are a grieving husband. Keep 'husband' in mind when they try to paint you as a murdering opportunist.''

Adam was surprised to find Menley and Hannah waiting for him in the car. "I'm afraid I upset Phoebe,'' Menley told him. "I should never have mentioned Mehitabel to her. For some reason she got terribly agitated.''

"There's no explaining what brings on those spells,'' Adam said.

"I don't know about that. Mine are triggered by stimulus, aren't they?''

"It's not the same.'' Adam put the key in the ignition.

Mommy, Mommy. Such a joyous sound. The night she thought she'd heard Bobby calling her. Had she been dreaming of the way he'd sounded that day in East Hampton? Had she attached a happy memory to a flashback? "When do you have to go to New York again?'' she asked.

"We should hear the judge's decision either late tomorrow or Tuesday. I'll go down overnight Tuesday and stay until Thursday morning. But I swear that will be it on working this month, Men.''

"I want you to bring up the tape of Bobby at East Hampton.''

"I told you I would, honey.'' As Adam steered the car away from the curb, he wondered, what is that all about?

79

*F*red Hendin took Tina out for dinner on Sunday evening. She had said she had a headache when he called her in the morning, but agreed that fish and chips and a couple of drinks at Clancey's that evening would pick up her spirits.

They had a gin and tonic at the bar and Fred was surprised at how vivacious and animated Tina was. She knew the bartender and some of the patrons and kidded with them.

Fred thought she looked terrific in her red miniskirt and red-and-white top, and he could see that a number of other guys at the bar were giving her the eye. There was no doubt about it. Tina attracted men. She was the kind of woman a man could lose his head over.

Last year when they had been dating, she kept telling him that he was a real gentleman. Sometimes he wondered if that was a compliment. Then she dropped him like a hot potato when Covey came into the picture. Last winter when he tried to get back with her, she hadn't given him the time of day. Then suddenly in April she had called him. "Fred, why don't you drop around?" she had said as though nothing had happened.

Was she ready to settle for me only when she couldn't get Covey? he wondered, as Tina burst out laughing at a joke the bartender told.

He hadn't heard her laugh like that for a while. She seemed really happy tonight.

That's what it was, he realized suddenly. Even though she was nervous about testifying at the inquest, she seemed happy.

Over dinner, she asked him about the ring. "Fred, I would like to wear the engagement ring when I testify. Did you bring it?"

"Now you're trying to spoil what's left of the surprise. I'll give it to you when we get to your place."

Tina lived in a furnished apartment over a garage in Yarmouth. She wasn't much of a housekeeper and hadn't done much to personalize the place, but the minute they walked in, Fred noticed there was something different about the small sitting room. Some things were missing. She had a pretty good collection of rock music, but almost all the cassettes and CDs were gone. And so was the picture of her skiing with her brother's family in Colorado.

Was she planning a trip and not telling him about it? Fred wondered. And if so, was she going alone?

August 15th

80

Menley awakened at dawn to the faint sound of sobbing. She pulled herself up on one elbow and strained to listen. No, it must be a seagull, she thought. The curtains were moving restlessly, and the good scent of the ocean was in the room.

She settled back on the pillow. Adam was in a deep sleep, snoring lightly. Menley remembered something her mother had said years ago. She'd been reading an advice column, probably Ann Landers or Dear Abby, and a woman had written in to complain that her husband's snoring kept her awake. The response was that to some women a husband's snoring would be the most welcome sound in the world. Ask any widow.

Her mother had commented, "Isn't that the truth?"

Mom raised us alone, Menley thought. I never experienced firsthand the interaction between happily married people. I never knew what it was like to see married people face problems and get through them.

Why think about that now? she wondered. Is it because I'm beginning to see a vulnerability in Adam that I didn't know existed? In a way I've always handled him with kid gloves. He's the attractive, successful, sought-after man who could have had anyone, but it was me he asked to marry him.

She realized there was no use trying to go back to sleep. She slipped out of bed, picked up her robe and slippers and tiptoed out of the room.

Hannah showed no signs of awakening, so Menley went down the stairs noiselessly and entered the library. With luck she might have two quiet hours before Adam and Hannah got up. She opened the new file.

Halfway through it, she found a group of papers clipped together that dealt with shipwrecks. Some of them she had already read about, such as the 1717 wreck of the pirate ship *Whidaw*. The mooncussers had picked its cargo clean.

And then she saw a reference to Tobias Knight: "The biggest house-to-house search for booty before the *Whidaw* was when the *Thankful* was lost in 1704 off Monomoy." Phoebe noted, "Tobias Knight was brought to Boston for questioning. He was developing an unsavory reputation and was suspected of being a mooncusser."

The next page was an account of the wreck of Captain Andrew Freeman's *Godspeed*. It was the copy of a letter to Governor Shute written by Jonathan Weekes, a selectman. The letter informed His Excellency that " 'on the thirty-first of August, in ye year of our Lord one thousand seven hundred and seven,' Captain Andrew Freeman set sail against all advice, 'there being a northeast breeze which was certain indication of an approaching storm.' The one survivor, Ezekiel Snow, a cabin boy, 'tells us the captain was distraught and much deranged, shouting he must return his daughter-babe to her mother's arms. All knew the baby's mother was dead and became much alarmed. The *Godspeed*, driven to the shoals, there broke up with a grievous loss of life.'

"Captain Freeman's body washed into Monomoit and he was buried alongside his wife, Mehitabel, since, in the testimony of the cabin boy, he went to his Maker crying out his love for her.''

Something happened to make him change his mind, Menley thought. What was it? He was trying to bring the baby back to a mother already dead. He went to his Maker crying out his love for her.

81

*E*ven though it was obviously going to be a hot day, Scott Covey chose to wear a navy summer-weight suit, long-sleeved white shirt and subdued navy-and-gray tie to the inquest. He had debated about wearing his green jacket, khakis and a sports shirt but realized they would not convey the impression he wanted to make on the judge.

He was uncertain about wearing his wedding ring. Would it look as though he were grandstanding? Probably not. He slipped it on.

When he was ready to go, he studied himself in the mirror. Vivian had told him that she was jealous of his ability to tan. "I burn and peel, burn and peel," she had sighed. "You just get this gorgeous tan, and your eyes look greener and your hair blonder and that many more girls turn their heads to look at you."

"And I'm looking at you," he had teased.

He surveyed his reflection from head to toe and

frowned. He was wearing a new pair of Gucci loafers. Somehow they looked too picture perfect. He went to the closet and got out his old well-polished pair. Better, he thought, as he checked the mirror again.

His mouth suddenly dry, he said aloud, "This is it."

Jan Paley arrived to stay with Phoebe while Henry went to the inquest. "She was upset yesterday afternoon," Henry warned. "Something Menley said about Remember House disturbed her. I get the feeling she's trying to convey something to us and can't find the words."

"Maybe if I just talk about the house to her, it will come out," Jan suggested.

Amy arrived at Remember House at eight o'clock. It was the first time she had seen Mr. Nichols in a business suit, and she looked at him admiringly. He has a kind of elegance about him, she thought. He makes you feel that anything he does will be done well.

He seemed preoccupied, checking the papers in his briefcase, but he glanced up at her and smiled. "Hi, Amy. Menley's getting dressed and the baby is with her. Why don't you go upstairs and take over Hannah? We're starting to run late."

He was such a nice man, Amy thought. She hated to think that he was going to be wasting his time looking for the tape of little Bobby in New York when it was a few minutes away in Elaine's house. In a burst of confidence she said, "Mr. Nichols, can I tell you something, but don't let on you heard it from me?"

She thought he looked worried, but then he said, "Of course."

She explained about the tape, how she had noticed it, taken it home and put it back. "I didn't tell Elaine

262

I had borrowed it, so she might get mad if she found out. It was just that I wanted to see what your little boy was like," she said almost apologetically.

"Amy, you've saved me a lot of trouble. We don't have any other copies, and my wife would have been really upset if that one disappeared. I left the Cape last year in a hurry, and Elaine had to ship a couple of things down to me. It will be easy to ask her to look for it without involving you."

He looked at his watch. "I've got to get moving. Oh, here they come."

Amy could hear footsteps on the staircase, then Mrs. Nichols came hurrying in, Hannah in her arms. "I'm all ready, Adam, or at least I think I am. This kid kept wiggling to the edge of the bed. She's all yours, Amy."

Amy reached for Hannah as Mrs. Nichols smilingly added, "Temporarily, of course."

82

At 9:00 A.M. the courtroom in Orleans was filled to capacity. The media was out in full force. The extensive publicity around Vivian Carpenter Covey's death had attracted the sensation seekers who vied with friends and townspeople for the limited seating.

"It's like a tennis match," Nat heard one reporter whisper to another just before lunch.

It has to do with murder, not games, Nat thought, but we don't have enough to prove it today. The district attorney had presented the evidence well. Point by point he had built up his case: Covey's involvement with Tina until a week before he married Vivian; the bruised finger and missing ring; the failure to turn on the radio for the weather report; the fact that Vivian's body should not have washed in where it had been found.

The judge frequently had his own questions for the witnesses. With meticulous attention, he studied the charts and autopsy reports.

Tina made a discouragingly good witness for Covey. She readily admitted that he had warned her he was seeing Vivian, that she had gone to visit him in Boca Raton, hoping that he'd become interested in her again. "I was crazy about him," she said, "but I knew it was over when he married Vivian. He really was in love with her. I'm engaged to someone else now." From the witness chair, she smiled brilliantly at Fred.

During recess Nat saw the eyes of the spectators shift from Scott Covey, with his movie-star looks and poise, to Fred Hendin, squat and stolid with thinning hair and an air of profound embarrassment. You could read their minds. She had settled for Fred Hendin when she couldn't snare Covey from Vivian.

The testimony of Conner Marcus, the sixty-five-year-old resident of Eastham who had almost lost his grandson in the squall, might have clinched it even without Covey's testimony. "No one who wasn't out there can possibly understand how suddenly it came up," he said, his voice shaking with emotion. "One minute Terry, my little grandson, and I were fishing. Then the current got rough. Less than ten minutes

264

later the waves were washing over the boat, and Terry was almost pulled into the water. I get down on my knees every night and thank God that I'm not in the boots of that young fellow." Tears in his eyes, he pointed at Covey.

With quiet authority, Elaine Atkins described the change in Vivian Carpenter when she met Scott Covey, and the marital happiness she witnessed. "The day they looked at Remember House, they talked about buying it. They wanted a large family. But Vivian said she would have to sell the other house first."

Nat had never heard that before. And it gave credence to Covey's story that he had been kept in the dark about the extent of Vivian's inheritance.

They recessed for lunch. In the afternoon, Vivian's lawyer from Hyannis was called and proved to be a dryly credible witness for Covey. Henry Sprague came through solidly as a next-door neighbor who testified to the mutual devotion of the newlyweds. The insurance investigator could only confirm what Tina had already admitted: She had visited Covey in Boca Raton.

Both Carpenters testified. They admitted that their daughter had always had emotional problems and had great difficulty in keeping friends. They pointed out that at an imagined slight she would sever a relationship, and they introduced the possibility that something had happened to make Vivian turn on Scott and threaten to disinherit him.

Anne Carpenter talked about the emerald ring. "It never was too tight," she said emphatically. "Besides, Vivy was superstitious about it. She'd sworn to her grandmother that she'd never take it off. She used to hold it to the light and admire it." Asked to describe the ring, she said, "It was a beautiful, five-and-a-half carat Colombian stone with a large diamond on each side, and it was mounted in platinum.''

And then Covey got on the stand. He began his testimony in a composed voice. He smiled when he talked about the early days of dating Vivian. '' 'Getting to Know You,' was our favorite song,'' he said.

He talked about the emerald ring: ''It was bothering her. She kept tugging at it that last morning. But I'm absolutely sure she was wearing it on the boat. She must have switched it to her left hand.''

And finally the description of losing her in the squall. Tears came to his eyes, welled there, his voice broke, and when he shook his head and said, ''I can't stand thinking about how scared she must have been,'' there were many moist eyes in the courtroom.

''I have nightmares where I'm searching through the water for her and I can't find her,'' he said. ''I wake up calling out to her.'' Then he began to sob.

The judge's finding was that there was no evidence of negligence and no evidence of foul play was almost anticlimatic.

The media asked Adam to make a statement.

''This has been a terrible ordeal for Scott Covey,'' he said. ''Not only has he lost his young wife but he has been subjected to scandalous rumors and accusations. I hope this public airing has not only served to present the true circumstances surrounding this tragedy but will also allow this young man the peace and privacy he desperately needs.''

Scott was asked his plans. ''My father isn't well which is why he and my stepmother can't be here. I'm going to drive across the country to California to visit them. I'll stop in some of the cities where I've toured with shows and have friends, but mostly I just want time alone to decide what to do with the rest of my life.''

"Will you stay on the Cape?" a reporter asked.

"I don't know," he said simply. "It holds a lot of heartache for me."

Menley was standing to the side, listening. You've done it again, Adam, she thought with pride. You're wonderful.

She felt a light touch on her arm. A woman in her late sixties said, "I wanted to introduce myself. I'm Norma Chambers. My grandchildren love your books and were so disappointed when you withdrew from renting my house for August."

"Renting your house? Oh, of course, you mean the first house Elaine arranged for us to take. But when there was a problem with the pipes, she switched us to Remember House," Menley said.

Chambers looked astonished. "'There was no problem. I had the house rented the day after you gave it up. Wherever did you get that idea?"

83

*A*fter he testified, Henry Sprague phoned his house to see how Phoebe was doing. Jan urged him to stay until the end of the proceedings. "We're doing fine," she insisted.

It had not, however, been an easy day. Phoebe lost her balance going down the two steps to the backyard, and Jan barely managed to keep her from falling. At lunchtime, Phoebe picked up a knife and tried to eat the soup with it.

As Jan placed the spoon in her hand, she thought sadly of the many times she and Tom had dined here with the Spragues. In those days, Phoebe had been a gracious, witty hostess, presiding over a table bright with placemats and matching napkins and candles and a centerpiece she had created from flowers from her garden.

It was heartbreaking to realize that this woman who flashed her a look of pathetic gratitude for understanding that she hadn't known which utensil to use was the same person.

Phoebe napped after lunch, and when she awoke in mid-afternoon, she seemed more alert. Jan decided to try to find out what she might have been trying to convey about Remember House.

"The other day, Adam's wife and I went to talk to other people who have old houses," she began. "Adam's wife is writing an article about houses with legends attached to them. I think Remember House is the most interesting of all. Then we drove to Eastham and saw another house Tobias Knight had built. It's very much like Remember House but not as fancy, and the rooms are larger."

The rooms. Remember House. A musty smell came into Phoebe's nostrils. It smelled like a tomb. It was a tomb. She was at the top of a narrow ladder. There were piles of junk everywhere. She started to go through them, and her hands touched the skull. And the voices came from below, talking about Adam's wife.

"Inside the house," she managed to say.

"Is something inside Remember House, dear?"

"Tobias Knight," she mumbled.

84

Scott Covey urged Elaine and Adam and Menley and Henry to come back to his house for a glass of wine. "I won't keep you, but I do want to have a chance to thank you."

Adam glanced at Menley and she nodded. "A brief stop," he agreed.

Henry declined to stop at Covey's even for a few minutes. "Jan has been with Phoebe all day," he explained.

Menley was anxious to get back to Hannah but wanted a chance to ask Elaine about the reason she had switched them from renting Mrs. Chambers' house. Dropping by Scott Covey's place would give her the opportunity.

On the way there she and Adam discussed the inquest. "I wouldn't want to be Fred Hendin, with everyone listening to my fiancée talk about throwing herself at another man," she observed, "but he certainly stood up for her when he testified."

"If he's smart, he'll dump her," Adam said, "but I hope he doesn't. Scott's lucky that she backed up his story, but this inquest wouldn't preclude a grand jury being called if further evidence came out. Scott's got to be careful."

Scott opened a bottle of vintage bordeaux. "I hoped I'd be using it for this reason," he said. When it was poured he held up his glass. "This is not a celebration," he began. "It would only be that if Vivian were with us now. But I do want to toast you, my friends, for all that you've done to help me. Adam, you're the best. Menley, I know you urged Adam to help me. Elaine, what can I say except thank you."

He sipped and then said, "And now I want to share my future plans with you and only with you. I'm leaving here first thing in the morning, and I'm not coming back. I'm sure you can understand. I'll never walk down a street in this town without being pointed at and whispered about. I think that the Carpenters will be better able to get on with their lives if they don't run the risk of bumping into me. So Elaine, I'd like you to put this house on the market immediately."

"If that's what you want," Elaine murmured.

"I can't disagree with your thinking," Adam commented.

"Adam, I'll be on the road for a while. I'll phone your office next week, and if you have my bill ready I'll send you a check." He smiled. "Whatever it is, you were worth every penny."

A few moments later, Adam said, "Scott, if you're leaving early you'll want to pack."

Menley and Adam said their good-byes, but Elaine stayed behind to discuss details of leasing the house.

As they went down the walk to their car, Adam wondered why he didn't feel more triumphant. Why was his gut telling him he'd been had?

85

*A*fter the inquest, Nat Coogan did not have a celebratory glass of wine. Instead he sat in the family room, sipping a glass of cold beer, replaying the day in his mind. "This is what happens," he told Debbie. "Murderers get away with murder. I could spend the next two days citing cases where everybody knows the husband or the neighbor or the business partner committed the crime, but there just isn't enough proof to get a conviction."

"Will you keep working on the case?" Debbie asked.

Nat shrugged. "The trouble is, there's no smoking gun."

"In that case, let's plan our anniversary. Shall we have a party?"

Nat looked alarmed. "I thought I'd take you out for a fancy dinner alone and maybe we can check into a motel." He winked at her.

"The No-Tell Motel?" It was a long-standing joke between them.

Nat finished his beer. "Damn it, Deb," he said. "There *is* a smoking gun. And it's right under my nose. I know it is. But I can't find it!"

271

86

*A*s he drove Tina home from the inquest, Fred Hendin had the sickening feeling that he might never be able to hold up his head again. He hadn't missed the fact that the spectators were comparing him with that gigolo, Scott Covey. Fred knew Covey was a smooth-talking phony, but that didn't make it easier that Tina freely admitted she had thrown herself at him all winter.

When Fred was on the stand he had done the best he could to back her up, and the judge's decision showed that he didn't feel that the affair between Tina and Covey had any connection with Vivian Carpenter's death.

Fred knew Tina better than she knew herself. A couple of times in the corridor during recess, she had glanced at Covey. There had been a look in her eye that said it all. A blind man could see she was still crazy about him.

"You're very quiet, Freddie," Tina said, slipping her arm around his.

"I guess I am."

"I'm so glad this is over."

"So am I."

"I'm going to see if I can take some time off and

visit my brother. I'm sick of people whispering about me."

"I don't blame you, but Colorado is a long way to go just to get away."

"Not that far. About five hours from Logan Airport."

She leaned her head on his shoulder. "Freddie, I just want to go home now and collapse. Do you mind?"

"No."

"But tomorrow night, we'll have a nice dinner. I'll even cook."

Fred was painfully aware of how much he wanted to smooth the shiny dark hair that was tumbled on his sleeve. I'm nuts about you, Tina, he thought. That won't change. "Don't worry about cooking," he said, "but you can have a drink waiting for me. I'll be there by six."

87

"What made you question 'Laine about the house in Eastham?" Adam asked as they drove home from the visit to Scott Covey.

"Because she lied about the reason for switching us to Remember House. There was nothing wrong with the pipes in the other place."

"From what she said, the Chambers woman who owns it would never admit the constant trouble she has with the pipes."

"In that case, why did Elaine rent it to someone else?"

Adam chuckled. "I think I see the picture. 'Laine probably realized that we might be good candidates to buy Remember House. I bet that's why she switched us. She always knew there were more ways than one to skin a cat."

"Including lying? Adam, you're a terrific lawyer, but sometimes I wonder about your blind spots."

"You're getting mean in your old age, Men."

"No, I'm getting honest."

They were driving onto Morris Island and down Quitnesset Lane. The late afternoon was turning cooler. The leaves on the locust trees were rustling, and a few had begun to fall. "It must be pretty here in other seasons," Menley observed.

"Well, in two weeks we have to decide whether we want to find that out for ourselves."

Amy had just finished feeding Hannah. The baby lifted her arms joyously when Menley bent over her.

"She's sticky," Amy warned as Menley lifted her from the high chair.

"That's fine with me. I've missed you," she told Hannah.

"I've missed her too," Adam said, "but your blouse is washable and this suit isn't. Hi, Toots." He blew a kiss at Hannah but kept out of her reach.

Menley said, "I'll take her upstairs. Thanks, Amy. Tomorrow afternoon about two all right with you? After I drop off the breadwinner at the airport, I do want to get in about four hours' work."

Amy nodded, and when Menley was out of earshot

asked, "Did you speak to Elaine about the tape, Mr. Nichols?"

"Yes. She was sure she had returned it to me. You're positive you saw the right one?"

"You were all in it. You lifted Bobby out of the pool and told him to run to his mother. He called 'Mommy, Mommy' and then Mrs. Nichols asked him questions about his name and where he went to school."

"Nertry schoow," Adam said.

Amy saw the glint of tears in his eyes. "I'm so glad you have Hannah," she said quietly. "But that is the tape you're looking for, isn't it?"

"Yes, it is. Amy, Elaine doesn't like to admit to mistakes. Maybe you should just pick it up for me the next time you're at her house. It sounds like petty larceny, but it is ours, and I can't insist that she has it without perhaps causing trouble for you."

"I'd rather do it that way. Thanks, Mr. Nichols."

August 16th

88

*A*t six o'clock on Tuesday morning, Scott Covey loaded the last of his bags into the BMW and made one more inspection of the house. Elaine was going to send someone in to give it a thorough cleaning, so that was not his concern. He looked again through the drawers in the bedroom and the closets for anything he might have missed.

Wait a minute, he thought. He had forgotten the eight or ten good bottles of wine that were still in cartons in the basement. No sense leaving them for the cleaning woman.

One thing nagged him, however—the pictures of Vivy. He wanted to put everything that had happened this summer behind him, but it might look callous to leave them here. He carried them to the car too.

He had put out the garbage and recycling bags. He wondered if he should rip the picture of Remember House out of the frame and completely tear it up. Then he shrugged. Forget it. Garbage pickup was in an hour.

Yesterday at the inquest, he had asked Vivian's lawyer, Leonard Wells, to handle her estate and probate her will. Now that the judge had cleared him, the family couldn't delay the transfer of assets. Wells told him he would have to sell a chunk of securities for taxes. The government certainly wanted plenty of other people's money.

I guess no matter how much you inherit, you feel that way, Scott thought.

He drove the car out of the garage and around the house. He paused for an instant; then he stepped on the accelerator.

"Good-bye, Vivy," he said aloud.

89

*T*hey spent Tuesday morning on the beach, just the three of them. They had brought the playpen down for Hannah and kept it under the shade of the umbrella. Adam lay in the sun and read the papers. Menley had magazines in her beach bag, but she had also brought a sheaf of papers from Phoebe's file.

The papers had a rubber band around them and didn't seem to be arranged in any particular order. Menley was getting the impression that, as the Alzheimer's disease started to make inroads, Phoebe's research became progressively more disorganized. It seemed as though she must have been gathering material and simply dumping it into the file. There were even recipes, clipped a few years ago from the *Cape Cod Times*, attached to stories of the early settlers.

"Tough sledding," she murmured.

Adam looked up. "What is?"

"Phoebe's most recent notes. They date back about four years, I think. It's obvious she was having real problems then. The pity is she must have realized she was losing her faculties. Many of the memos to herself are so terribly vague."

"Let's see." Adam glanced through the papers. "Now that's interesting."

"What is?"

"There's a reference to this place. 'Laine told me it got to be called Remember House because during a storm the house acts like a bellows. The way the wind whooshes against it sounds like someone calling 'Re-mmmmbaaaa.' "

"That's what Jan Paley told me."

"Then according to this, they're both wrong. Here's a copy of a town record from 1705. It records the birth of a child to Captain Andrew Freeman and his wife, Mehitabel, a daughter named Remember."

"The baby's name was Remember?"

"And look at this. It's a town record from 1712. 'Said property known as Nickquenum, a dwelling house and chattels and homestead bounded easterly by ye bank or clift to the salt water, southerly by the land of Ensign William Sears, southwesterly by ye land of Jonathan Crowell and northerly by ye land of Amos Nickerson by the will of Captain Andrew Freeman was passed to his wife and if she be deceased to his descendants. Mehitabel his wife having predeceased him, the sole heir is a daughter Remember listed on ye record of birth in the year of our Lord one thousand seven hundred and five. The whereabouts of said child being unknown, ye dwelling that has come to be known as Remember House is to be sold for taxes.' "

Menley shivered.

"Men, what is it?" Adam asked sharply.

"It's only that there's a story about one of the settlers in the late sixteen hundreds, a woman who knew she was going to die when her baby was born and directed that it be called Remember so it would always remember her. I wonder if Mehitabel knew of that. She may have suspected she was going to lose her child."

"Then if we do buy the house, maybe we'd better

change its name back to the original. Have you any idea what Nickquenum means?''

"It's an Indian word that in essence means 'I am going home.' In the days of the early settlers, if a traveler was passing through hostile territory he only had to say that word and no one impeded him on his journey.''

"You must have learned that from your research.''

Did I? Menley wondered.

"I'm going for a quick swim," she said. "And I promise I won't go out too far.''

"If you do, I'll rescue you.''

"I hope so.''

At one-thirty she dropped Adam at the Barnstable airport. "Here we go again," he said. "When I get back Thursday, we are starting a real vacation. No more work for me. And if I mind her nibs during the morning, will you be ready to be a beach bum or do some exploring in the afternoon?''

"You bet.''

"We'll save Amy for a couple of dinners out.''

"Alone, I hope.''

On her way back from the airport, Menley decided to take a quick run to Eastham to see the Tobias Knight house again. "Now, Hannah," she instructed, "you must promise to behave. I need to get another look at this place. There's something that I don't understand.''

There was a different volunteer, an older woman, Letitia Raleigh, at the old house's reception desk today. It had been a quiet afternoon, she told Menley, and she had time to chat.

Menley offered Hannah a cookie. "It's as hard as a dog biscuit," she said, "but it feels good to her because she's teething. I'll make sure she doesn't drop crumbs."

Content, Hannah settled down and Menley opened the subject of Tobias Knight. "I can't find very much about him," she explained.

"He was a bit of a mystery man," Raleigh confirmed. "Certainly a wonderful builder and ahead of his time. This house is nice, but I understand the one he built in Chatham was a showplace for that period."

"I rent it," Menley said. "It is beautiful, but the rooms are smaller than those in this house."

"I don't understand that. The dimensions are supposed to be the same." Raleigh rummaged through the desk. "There's a bio here we don't usually pass out. It's not too flattering of him. Here's his picture. Presentable if pompous, don't you think? And something of a dandy for those days."

The drawing was of an even-featured man of about thirty with a whisp of beard and longish hair. He was wearing breeches, a doublet, a cape and a high-collared ruffled shirt, and his shoes had silver buckles.

She lowered her voice. "According to this bio, Tobias left Eastham under a cloud. He got in trouble when he became involved with a couple of the goodwives, and a lot of people were sure he had a wrecker business going . . . that's a mooncusser, you know."

She skimmed the brochure and handed it to Menley. "Apparently in 1704, a few years after Tobias settled in Chatham, he was questioned by the Crown when all the cargo from the *Thankful* was missing. Everyone was sure he was guilty, but he must have found a way to hide his loot. He disappeared two years later. The theory is that it got too hot for him around Chatham and he took off to start fresh somewhere else."

"What was the cargo?" Menley asked.

"Clothing, blankets, household goods, coffee, rum

—the reason it caused so much trouble is that it was all headed for the governor's mansion in Boston.''

"Where did they usually hide all the cargo?"

"In sheds, buried on the shore, and some of them even had hidden rooms within their houses. These rooms were usually behind the fireplace.''

90

On Tuesday morning, Nat Coogan left for work earlier than usual. As a matter of curiosity, he drove past Scott Covey's house to see if there was any sign of his getting ready to clear out. Nat had no doubt that now that the inquest was over and the decision favorable, Covey would shake the dust of the Cape from his shoes.

But early as he was, he could see that Covey was already gone. The shades were drawn and there were a couple of garbage bags on the side of the house for pickup. You don't need a search warrant to go through stuff that has been left for disposal, Nat thought as he parked his car.

One bag contained cans and bottles for recycling as well as sharp fragments of broken glass. The other had garbage and trash, including a frame with the rest of the broken glass stuck in it and a picture with long crisscross scratches. Oh my, my, Nat thought. There was the original aerial photo of Remember House, the one that had been in the real estate office window. Even in its mutilated condition it was clearer than the duplicate Marge had shown him in the office. But the section with the boat had been torn out. Why? Nat wondered. Why did he try to destroy it? Why not just leave it if he didn't want to be bothered carrying it? And why did he tear the boat out of the picture? And why was it missing from the copy print as well?

He put the mangled photo in the trunk of the car and drove to Main Street. Elaine Atkins was just opening up. She greeted him pleasantly. "I have that picture you want. I can get it framed if you like."

"No, don't bother," Nat said quickly. "I'll take it now. Deb wants to take care of the framing herself." He reached for the print. He studied it. "Terrific! That's great photography!"

"I agree. A panoramic aerial photo can be a real selling tool, but just on its own, this one is wonderful."

"At the department we sometimes need aerial work done. Do you use someone around here?"

"Yes, Walter Orr from Orleans."

Nat continued to study the print. It was the same version that Marge had put in the window three days ago. Nat said, "Am I wrong, or when the picture was in the window did it have a boat in it?"

"The negative got damaged," Elaine said quickly. "I had to do some patching."

He noticed her heightened color. And why are you so nervous? he wondered.

"What do I owe you?" he asked.

"Nothing. I do my own developing."

"That's very nice of you, Miss Atkins."

91

*T*uesday was not an easy day for Fred Hendin. Knowing that he was about to give up Tina for good was an assault on his senses. He was thirty-eight now and had dated a number of girls over the years. At least half of them would probably have married him.

Fred knew that by some standards he was a good catch. He was a hard worker who made a comfortable living. He had been a devoted son and he would be a devoted husband and father. People would have been surprised to know exactly how robust his bank account was, although he had always had the feeling Tina could sense it.

Right now if he called up Jean or Lillian or Marcia, he knew he would have a dinner date tonight.

The trouble was that he had genuinely fallen in love with Tina. He had always known she could be moody and demanding, but when he went out with her on his arm, he felt like a king. And she could be lots of fun.

He had to get her out of his mind. All day he was distracted, thinking about her and about having to give her up. The boss had even called him on it a couple of times. "Hey, Fred, stop daydreaming. We've got a job to finish."

He looked again at the house across the road; somehow it didn't have the same appeal today. Oh, sure, he probably would buy it, but it wouldn't be the same. He had imagined Tina in it with him.

But a man had his dignity, his pride. He had to end it with Tina. The papers today were filled with the details of the inquest. Nothing had been left out: the condition of Vivian's right hand; the missing emerald ring; Tina's visits to Covey in Florida. Fred had winced to find his own name mentioned as Tina's on-again-off-again boyfriend, and now fiancé. The account made him look like a fool.

Yes, he had to end it. Tomorrow, when he drove her to the airport, he would tell her. But one thing concerned him. It would be just like Tina to refuse to give his mother's jewelry back to him.

At six o'clock when he got to Tina's and found that as usual she wasn't ready, he had turned on the television and then opened the jewelry box.

His mother's pearls and watch and pin were there, as well as the engagement ring he had just given Tina. It had served her purpose, and she probably couldn't wait to get it off her finger, he thought. He put the pieces in his pocket.

And then he stared. Buried underneath Tina's inexpensive chains and bracelets, he glimpsed a ring. It was a large green stone with a diamond on each side, mounted in platinum.

He picked it up and studied it. Even a fool would have recognized the clarity and depth of that emerald. Fred knew he was holding the family ring that had been ripped from Vivian Carpenter's finger.

When Menley arrived home from visiting the Tobias Knight house, Amy was sitting on the steps. "You must have thought I'd forgotten about you," Menley said apologetically.

"I knew you didn't." Amy unbuckled Hannah from the car seat.

"Amy, yesterday I overheard you talking to my husband about the tape of Bobby. Tell me about that."

Reluctantly Amy recounted how she happened to have it.

"Where is it now?"

"Home. I took it from Elaine's house last night when I borrowed more movie tapes. I was going to give it to Mr. Nichols when he gets back Thursday."

"Give it to me in the morning."

"Of course."

92

On the day after the inquest, Graham and Anne Carpenter decided to go on a cruise. "We need to get away," Graham decreed.

Anne, deeply depressed by recent events, agreed listlessly. Their other two daughters had come out for the hearing, and Emily, the older one, said bluntly, "Mother, you must stop blaming yourself. In her own way poor Vivy loved you and Dad very much, and I don't think she'd want to see you like this. Go on a trip. Get away from all this. Have a great time with Daddy, and you two take care of each other."

Tuesday evening, after Emily and Barbara and their

husbands left, Anne and Graham sat out on the front porch, making plans for the trip. Anne's voice was brighter, and she laughed as they recalled some of the other cruises they had taken.

Graham had to put in words the way he felt: "It hasn't been pleasant for either of us to be depicted as horrible parents in the tabloids, and I'm sure they'll have a field day describing the inquest. But we did what we had to do, and I think that somewhere Vivian knows we tried to secure justice for her."

"And I pray she also knows we can do no more."

"Oh, look, there's Pres Crenshaw with Brutus."

They watched as their elderly neighbor walked slowly down the road past their gate, his German shepherd on a leash.

"Set your watch," Graham said. "Ten o'clock on the dot."

A moment later, a car drove past the gate. "Pres should be careful, that road is dark," Anne said.

They turned and went into the house.

93

Menley invited Amy to stay for dinner. She sensed something forlorn about the young girl. "I'm just making a salad and linguine with clam sauce," she explained, "but you're welcome to share it."

"I'd love to."

She really is a nice kid, Menley thought, and actually she's not that much of a kid. She's almost eighteen and has a quiet poise that really is attractive. Plus she is more responsible than most adults. But she sure doesn't like the idea of her father marrying Elaine.

That was a subject Menley had no intention of bringing up, however. What she did introduce was Amy's preparations for college.

Discussing her plans, Amy became animated. "I've talked on the phone to my roommate. She sounds nice. We've decided on spreads and curtains. Her mother will help her buy them, and I'll pay my share."

"What have you done about clothes?"

"Elaine said she'll drive to Boston someday and we'll have a—wait, how does she put it—a 'fun girl day together.' Isn't that awful?"

"Amy, don't fight her," Menley said. "She's going to marry your father."

"Why? She certainly doesn't love him."

"Of course she does."

"Menley, I mean Mrs. Nichols, my father is a very boring man."

"Amy!" Menley protested.

"No, I mean it. He's nice and kind and good and successful but that's not what we're talking about. Elaine doesn't love him. He gives her corny gifts, at least he gives them in a corny way, and she puts on the big act. She's going to make him miserable and she knows that I know it and that's why she can't stand me."

"Amy, I hope Hannah doesn't talk about her father like that someday," Menley said, shaking her head even as she acknowledged that Amy was right on target.

"Are you kidding? Mr. Nichols is the kind of guy

women want. And if you want to know something, the list starts with Elaine.''

When Amy left, Menley walked through the house, locking up. She turned on the local weather channel and learned that a storm was brewing that would hit the Cape tomorrow in the late afternoon or early evening. I had better make sure we have a flashlight and candles just in case, she thought.

The phone rang as she was settling at her desk in the library. It was Jan Paley.

"I missed you yesterday when you were at Scott Covey's house," Jan said. "I wanted you to know that Phoebe was talking about Tobias Knight again. Menley, I think you're right. She is trying to tell us something about him."

"I stopped by his Eastham house today after I dropped Adam off," Menley said. "The receptionist showed me his picture. Jan, Tobias looked like a sneak and a dandy. I can't imagine why Mehitabel ever would have bothered with him. Another interesting point is that, according to the dates we have, she was already at least three months pregnant with Andrew Freeman's child when she was denounced."

She paused. "I guess I'm really thinking aloud. I've had two pregnancies, and the last thing in the world that would have intrigued me during the first three months of either one of them is to become involved in a love affair."

"Then what are you thinking?" Jan asked.

"Tobias Knight was a mooncusser. He was being questioned by the Crown about the cargo of the *Thankful* around the time he was seen visiting Mehitabel at unseemly hours. Suppose he wasn't visiting her? Suppose she never knew he was around? If he hadn't confessed to carrying on with Mehitabel, they'd have looked for another reason for him to be here. Suppose he hid some of the *Thankful* cargo on these grounds, or even in this house?"

"Oh, I don't think in the house," Jan protested.

"The dimensions of the first-floor rooms here are smaller than in the Eastham place. But from the outside the house is the same size. I'm going to poke around a bit."

"I don't think it will do you much good. If there ever was a storage area, it's probably been boarded up for the last two hundred years. But it is possible that one did exist at some time."

"Did anyone ever suggest that this house might have had a hidden room?"

"Not to me. And the last contractor did an awful lot of work. He's Nick Bean, from Orleans."

"Do you mind if I talk to him tomorrow?"

"Of course not. And feel free to poke around. Good night, Menley."

When she replaced the receiver, Menley leaned back in the chair and studied the drawings of Mehitabel and Andrew. On the ship they had looked so happy together.

Mehitabel had died swearing her innocence, and a week later Andrew had set sail into an oncoming storm, frantic to bring his baby back and crying out his love for his wife. Was it possible that he had been convinced of Mehitabel's innocence and been driven out of his mind with regret?

Every instinct told Menley that she was on the right track.

She settled back at the desk but now was not interested in going through the files. Something Amy had said at dinner had to be faced. Elaine might be engaged to another man, but she was in love with Adam. I sensed it that night at dinner, Menley thought. Elaine didn't forget she had that tape. She deliberately withheld it, knowing that it was irreplaceable to us. What use was it to her except to be able to look at Adam?

Or did she find another use for it?

At ten o'clock she went upstairs, changed into a nightgown and robe, and phoned Adam at the apartment in New York.

"I was just about to call you to say good night," he said. "How are my girls?"

"We're fine." Menley hesitated but knew she had to ask the question that was on her mind. "Amy stayed for dinner, and she made an interesting observation. She thinks Elaine is in love with you, and I have to say I agree with her."

"That's ridiculous."

"Is it? Adam, please understand that after Bobby died, I wasn't much of a wife to you for a year. Last summer I asked you for a separation, and we'd probably be divorced right now if I hadn't learned I was pregnant with Hannah. You got pretty close to Elaine in that time we were apart, didn't you?"

"It depends on what you call close. We've always been there for each other since we were kids."

"Adam, forget the buddy routine. Haven't you pulled that on her before? You said she was a rock when your father died. And over the years when you didn't have another serious girlfriend, you'd call her up. Wasn't that the pattern?"

"Menley, you can't think that I was involved with Elaine last year."

"Are you involved with her now?"

"My God, Menley, no!"

"I had to ask. Good night, Adam."

Adam heard the click in his ear. When he got to the apartment he had realized what had been bugging him. One day last winter when Menley was out, he had watched the tape of Bobby. It was where he had left

290

it, in his desk drawer. He *had* brought it home last summer. Why did Elaine make a copy of it and not tell him about it?

94

On Wednesday morning, Nat brought his second cup of coffee into the family room and studied the two pictures of Remember House. He had painstakingly removed the mangled one from the frame, and now it was propped up on the mantel next to the copy Elaine had given him.

The destruction of the print he had taken from Scott Covey's garbage was even more apparent now that the picture was out of the frame. It looked as though the crisscross tears might have been made by a sharp knife or even a wedge of broken glass. There was a gaping hole where the boat had been.

The other print showed a faint smudge where the boat had been, as though Elaine had attempted to retouch the negative, but hadn't completed the job.

"Bye, Dad."

Nat's two sons, Kevin and Danny, sixteen and eighteen years old, stood in the doorway, grinning at him. "If you're trying to decide which one to buy, Dad, I'd vote for the one on the right," Kevin said.

"Someone sure didn't like the other one," Danny commented.

"I agree," Nat said. "The question is *why* didn't he like it? See you tonight, guys."

Debbie came in a few minutes later. "Still haven't figured it out?" she asked.

"Nothing makes sense. First of all, I can't believe that Elaine Atkins honestly thought that Scott Covey was in the market for that property. Then when he was clearing out, why didn't he just leave it in the house? Why go to all the trouble of smashing it and cutting out the boat? And why did Elaine blank out the boat in the copy? There has to be a reason."

Debbie picked up the torn photograph and turned it over. "Maybe you should talk to whoever took the picture. Look, his name is stamped on the back. Walter Orr. His phone number and address are here too."

"I know his name," Nat said. "Elaine gave it to me."

Debbie turned the pictures over again and smoothed the curling edges. "Look. The date and time this was taken is here on the bottom." She looked at the other picture. "It's not on the copy Elaine gave you."

Nat looked at the date. "July 15th at 3:30 P.M.!" he exclaimed.

"Is there anything significant about that date?"

"You bet there is," Nat said. "July 15th was the day Vivian Carpenter was drowned. Covey phoned the coastguard at 4:30 that afternoon." In two strides he was over to the phone.

A look of disappointment came over Nat's face as he listened to a recorded message. Then he gave his name and the phone number of the police station and finished by saying, "Mr. Orr, it is imperative I speak to you immediately."

When he hung up, he said, "Orr is on a job and will be back at four o'clock. So this will have to hold until then. But Deb, I just realized, when Marge offered us this copy, she said Elaine had the negative. And she's obviously already altered that. So if there is something to this, we may never find out what it is. Damn!''

95

*T*here was a restless feeling in the air when Menley awakened at seven o'clock on Wednesday morning. The breeze was damp, and the room still shadowed. The light that penetrated around the shades was subdued, and no rays of sun danced on the windowsills.

She had slept well. Even though Hannah's room was close by and she had left both doors open, she had kept the baby monitor on the night table next to her. At two she had heard the baby stirring and checked her, but Hannah didn't wake up.

And no dreams, no flashbacks, thank God, Menley thought as she reached for a robe. She walked to the windows that overlooked the water and pulled up the shades. The ocean was gray, the waves still mild as they lapped at the shore. Thin sunlight peered around the heavy clouds that drifted over the water.

Ocean and sky and sand and space, she thought. This wonderful house, this special view. She was enjoying getting used to all this space. After her father died, her mother had given her brother the smaller bedroom to himself and moved Menley's twin bed into her room. When Jack went to college it was Menley's turn to get a room of her own, and thereafter when Jack was home, he slept on the pullout couch in the living room.

I remember how when I was little, I used to draw pictures of pretty houses with pretty rooms, Menley thought as she looked out over the ocean. But I never visualized a home like this, a location like this. Maybe that's why the house Adam and I had in Rye never got to me the way this one does.

Remember House would be a home of the heart, she thought. I can see coming up here for Thanksgiving and Christmas and the kind of summers Adam experienced growing up, and for long weekends in other seasons. That's a perfect balance to all the plusses of living in Manhattan, with Adam's office minutes away.

What had been Mehitabel's plans for her life? she wondered. Many wives of sea captains sailed with their husbands all over the world and brought their young children with them. Mehitabel had sailed with Andrew after they were married. Before everything went wrong, had she been looking forward to other trips?

It would make sense if Tobias Knight did build some sort of storage area on the grounds or in the house and that was why he had been seen around here. I'm going to write the story that way, she decided.

Why do I feel so strongly about her this morning? she wondered. And then she understood the reason. On the third Wednesday in August all those years ago, Mehitabel was condemned as an adulteress, flogged and returned here to find her husband had taken her baby away. Today was the third Wednesday in August.

A moment later Menley did not need the baby monitor to inform her that Hannah was awake and hungry. "I'm coming, Crabby," she called as she hurried into the nursery.

Amy arrived at nine o'clock. It was obvious that she was upset. It didn't take long to find out what was wrong. "Elaine was at our house when I got home last night," she said. "Mr. Nichols had asked her about the tape of Bobby, and I guess she must have figured out that I borrowed it. She asked me for it.

"I wouldn't give it to her. I said it belonged to you and I had promised to give it back to you. She said it was a backup copy she'd made because Mr. Nichols was so distraught last year she was afraid he'd lose it, and she knew you hadn't seen it." Tears glistened in Amy's eyes. "My dad sided with Elaine. He's mad at me too."

"Amy, I'm sorry you've had a problem about this. But I don't believe that Elaine made a copy of that tape with me in mind. And I'm glad you didn't give it to her. Where is it now?"

Amy reached in her bag. "Here it is."

Menley held the cassette in her hand for a moment, then laid it on the refectory table. "I'll watch it later. I think it would be a good idea if you put Hannah in the carriage and went for a walk. When that storm breaks, it's supposed to last until sometime tomorrow afternoon."

Adam phoned an hour later. "How's it going, love?"

"Fine," she told him, "but the weather's changing. There's a storm predicted."

"Did Amy bring the tape of Bobby?"

"Yes."

"Have you watched it yet?"

"No. Adam, trust me. I'm going to watch it this afternoon while Amy is with Hannah, but I know I can handle it."

When she hung up, she looked at the computer screen. The last sentence she had written before the phone had begun to ring was, "It would seem that Mehitabel implored her husband to trust her."

At eleven o'clock she reached the contractor Nick Bean, who had renovated the house. An affable man, Bean was both open and informative about Remember House. "Priceless workmanship," he said. "Not a nail anywhere in the original construction. All mortise-and-tenon joints."

She asked him what he knew about hidden rooms in the homes of early settlers.

"I've come across them in some of these old places," he explained. "People glamorize them. Originally they were called 'Indian rooms,' the idea being that they were where the family hid from the Indians when they were attacked."

Menley could hear the amusement in his voice as he continued: "Only one problem. The Indians on the Cape weren't hostile. Those rooms were where bootleg cargo was kept or where people who were going on a trip would hide their valuables. Their version of a safety deposit box, I guess you could call it."

"Do you think it's possible Remember House has a hidden storage area?" Menley asked.

"It's possible," Bean confirmed. "Seems to me my last workman on the job mentioned something about that. There's a fair amount of space between the rooms and the center of the house, where the chimneys were built. But that doesn't mean we'd ever find one if it exists. It may have been boarded over to the point where it would take a genius to locate it. One place to start looking is the minister's cabinet in the parlor. Sometimes a removable panel behind it led into a storage area."

A removable panel. As soon as Menley hung up, she hurried to check the minister's cabinet in the main parlor. It was to the left of the fireplace. She opened it, and a musty smell assailed her nostrils. I should leave the door open and let it air out, she thought. But the back of the built-in cabinet had no seams to indicate an entrance to a storage area.

Maybe when we own the house we can explore this further, she thought. You just can't go around smashing walls. She went back to the desk but realized she was becoming more and more distracted. She wanted to see the tape of Bobby.

She waited until after lunch, when Amy brought Hannah up for her afternoon nap. Then she picked up the cassette and brought it into the library. A lump was already forming in her throat when she put the tape in the VCR and pressed the start button.

They had visited one of Adam's partners in East Hampton that weekend. Lou Miller had a video camera and had brought it out on Sunday afternoon after brunch. Adam had Bobby in the pool. She had been sitting at the umbrella table talking with Lou's wife, Sherry.

Lou took shots of Adam teaching Bobby how to swim. Bobby looked so much like Adam, Menley thought. They were having such a good time together. Then Adam lifted Bobby onto the deck. She remembered Lou turning off the camera and saying, "Okay, enough of the aquacade. Let's get some shots of Bobby with Menley. Adam, put him on the deck. Menley, you call him."

She heard her own voice next. "Bobby, come on over here. I want you."

I want you, Bobby.

Menley dabbed at her eyes as she watched her two-year-old, arms outstretched, running toward her, heard him calling her, *"Mommy, Mommy."*

She gasped. It was the same joyous voice she had heard when she thought Bobby was calling her last week. He had sounded so vibrant, so alive. It was the way he had just started to say "Mommy" that struck her now. She and Adam had joked about it. Adam had said, "Sounds more like Mom-me, with the emphasis on *me*."

That was exactly the way he had called to her the night that she'd searched the house for him. Had that been simply a vivid waking dream rather than a flashback? Dr. Kaufman had told her that happy memories would begin to replace the traumatic one. But the train whistle had certainly been a flashback.

The tape was rolling. Bobby flinging himself into her arms; turning him to the camera. "Tell us your name."

She began to sob as he said proudly, "Wobert Adam Nikko."

Tears choked her, and when the tape was finished, she sat for a few minutes, her face buried in her hands. And then a reassuring thought assuaged the pain: in another two years Hannah would be answering the same question. How would she pronounce Menley Hannah Nichols?

She heard Amy coming down the stairs and called to her. Amy came in, her expression concerned. "Are you okay, Mrs. Nichols?"

Menley realized that her eyes were still welling with tears. "I really am," she said, "but I'd like you to watch this with me."

Amy stood beside her as she rewound the videotape and played it again. When it was finished, Menley asked, "Amy, when Bobby was calling me, did you notice anything special about the way he sounded?"

Amy smiled. "You mean 'Mom-me'? It sounded as though he was saying, 'Hey, Mom, you come to me!' "

"That's what I thought. I just wanted to make sure I wasn't imagining that."

"Mrs. Nichols, do you ever get over losing someone you love?" Amy asked.

Menley knew Amy was thinking about her own mother. "No," she said, "but you learn to be grateful that you had the person at all, even though it wasn't long enough. And to quote my own mother, she always told my brother and me that she'd rather have had twelve years with my father than seventy years with anyone else."

She put an arm around Amy. "You'll always miss your mother the way I'll always miss Bobby, but we've both got to keep that thought in mind. I know I'm going to try."

Even as she was rewarded by Amy's grateful smile, Menley was struck by the thought that both times she had awakened to the sound of the train whistle, Hannah had heard it too.

The calling, the train. What if she hadn't imagined it?

96

Graham and Anne Carpenter spent most of Wednesday packing. At two o'clock, Graham saw the mail van go by and walked down to the mailbox.

When he took out the mail he glanced into the box and was surprised to see a small package in the far-back corner. It was wrapped in brown paper and tied with twine, so he knew it wasn't one of those soap samples that regularly made an appearance in the box.

The package was addressed to Anne, but there was no postage and no return address on it. Graham carried it up to the house and brought it to the kitchen, where Anne was talking to the housekeeper. When he told them about finding it, he saw a look of concern cross his wife's face.

"Do you want me to open it for you?" he asked.

Anne nodded.

He saw her expectant expression as he cut the twine. He wondered if she was thinking the same thing he was. There was something distinctly odd about the neatly lettered, tightly sealed package.

When he opened it, his eyes widened in shock. The fine deep green of the heirloom emerald ring gleamed through a plastic sandwich bag.

The housekeeper gasped, "Isn't that . . . ?"

Anne grabbed the bag and pulled out the ring, folding it in her hand. Her voice was shrill, on the verge of hysteria as she cried, "Graham, where did this come from? Who brought it here? Remember, I told you that emeralds always find their way home?"

97

Nat Coogan was in his car on the way to Orleans when he received a call at 3:15 from the district attorney's office. An assistant DA informed him that the emerald ring had been returned to the Carpenters' house last night and that at exactly 10:00 P.M. an elderly neighbor, Preston Crenshaw, had noticed a strange car slow up at the Carpenters' mailbox.

"We can't be sure that whoever was in the car left the ring, but it gives us something to go on," the assistant DA told him. "Mr. Crenshaw's description of the vehicle he saw is pretty good. A dark green or black Plymouth, Massachusetts plates with a 7 and a 3 or 8 in the numbers. We're running a check."

Plymouth, Nat thought. Dark green or black. Where had he seen one recently? Then he remembered. It had been in Fred Hendin's driveway, and then he had seen Fred and Tina in it after the inquest. "Tina Arcoli's boyfriend, Fred Hendin, drives a dark green Plymouth," he said. "Run a check on his plates."

He waited. The assistant DA came back on the phone, sounding triumphant. "Hendin's license plate number has both a 7 and a 3 in it. The boss says he wants you to go along when we pick him up for questioning."

"Then let's meet at Hendin's house at five o'clock. I'm on my way to something that may turn out to be another lead."

The aerial photographer, Walter Orr, had picked up his messages and returned Nat's call. Nat was to meet him in his office at four o'clock.

It's unraveling, Nat thought exultantly, snapping the phone back on the dashboard.

Ten minutes later he was turning off Route 6 onto the Orleans exit. Five minutes after that he was in Orr's office in the center of town.

Orr was about thirty, a brawny man who looked more like a dockworker than a photographer. He was in the process of making coffee. "Long day," he told Nat. "I was doing a shoot in New London. Believe me, I was glad to get back here. That storm is going to hit us in a couple of hours, and I wouldn't want to be flying in it.''

He held out a mug. ''Coffee?''

Nat shook his head. ''No thanks.'' He took out the mangled aerial photo. ''You took this?''

Orr studied it briefly. ''Yes, I did. Who slashed it?''

''That's part of what we're investigating. I understand Elaine Atkins hired you to take it and that she has the negative.''

''That's right. She specifically wanted the negative and paid extra to get it.''

''All right, take a look at this print.'' Nat unrolled the copy that Elaine had given him. ''You see the difference?''

''Sure. The boat's been taken out. Who did that? Elaine?''

''That's what I'm told.''

''Well, it's hers to mess around with, I guess.''

''On the phone you told me that when you take aerial photos, the exact time and date is being registered on the film.''

''That's right.''

Nat pointed to the lower right-hand corner of the original photo. ''This is marked Friday, 15 July, 3:30 P.M.''

''And the year is above it.''

''I see that. The point is that this is the absolutely accurate time the photo was made. Is that right?''

''Absolutely.''

''I need to get a blowup of that missing boat. How many photos did you shoot, and is there another one that's similar?''

Orr hesitated. ''Listen, is this important to you? You think the boat is carrying drugs or something?''

''It might be important to a lot of people,'' Nat said.

Orr pressed his lips together. ''I know you're not here because you want to admire my photography.

Just between us, I did sell Elaine the whole roll of film, but I made a duplicate negative of this shot for myself. I wouldn't have sold it to anyone else, but it's damn good photography. I wanted it as a sample of my work."

"That's very good news," Nat said. "Can you make another print, fast?"

"Sure. Exactly like this one?"

"Yes, exactly like the original, but it's really the boat I'm interested in."

"What do you want to know about it?"

"Everything that your skills can reveal to me." He scribbled the number of his cellular phone on the back of his card and handed it to Orr. "As soon as possible. I'll be waiting for your call."

98

*F*red Hendin was picked up shortly after five o'clock and brought to the district attorney's office in the courthouse. Quietly and courteously, he answered the questions that were flung at him. No, he had never met Vivian Carpenter. No, he had never met Scott Covey either, although he had seen him hanging around the Daniel Webster Inn last year. Yes, he was engaged to Tina Arcoli.

The ring? He had no idea what they were talking

about. He hadn't been in Osterville last night. He had been out with Tina and then gone directly home to bed.

Yes, at the inquest he had heard a lot of talk about a missing ring. The *Cape Cod Times* yesterday gave a description of it. Nearly a quarter of a million dollars was a lot of ring. Whoever gave it back was certainly honest.

"I've got to get out of here," Fred told his interrogators. "I'm driving my fiancée to Logan Airport. She's got a flight to Denver at nine o'clock."

"I think Tina's going to miss her flight, Fred," Nat said. "We're going to bring her in now."

He watched as the telltale flush appeared on Fred's neck and worked its way up to his face. They were getting to him.

"Tina wants to visit her brother and his family," Fred said angrily. "All this business has upset her."

"It's upset a lot of people," Nat said mildly. "If you have sympathy for anyone, I suggest you start with the Carpenters. Don't waste it on Tina."

Nat drove with Bill Walsh, an investigator from the district attorney's office, to Tina's home. At first she refused to let them in, then finally opened the door.

They found her surrounded by luggage. The living room obviously had been stripped of personal belongings. She had no intention of coming back, Nat thought.

"I have no time for you," Tina snapped. "I have to make a plane. I'm waiting for Fred."

"Fred's at the district attorney's office, Tina," Nat told her. "We have to talk to him, and it's very important that we talk to you as well. If everything gets straightened out quickly, you can still make your plane."

Tina looked startled. "I have no idea why you want to talk to Fred or me. Let's get this over with fast."

99

Menley walked Amy to the door. "Dad and I are going to Elaine's for dinner tonight," she said. "We're supposed to talk out my relationship with her."

"You mean to try to get it on a more even keel?" Menley asked.

"Last night she said something about not walking into such a hostile situation." Amy shrugged. "I'm going to tell her that I'll be in college in a couple of weeks and if there's a problem about my being around on school breaks, then I'll stay away. My grandmother still lives in Pennsylvania; she'll be glad to have me. At least then I won't have to watch Elaine make a jerk out of Dad."

"Sometimes it gets worse before it gets better," Menley said, opening the door. A gust of wind swept through the room. "I'm glad Adam isn't flying today," she commented.

After Amy left, Menley fed Hannah, bathed her, then watched the six o'clock news from Boston with the baby in her lap. At quarter past six a bulletin ran across the bottom of the screen. The storm would break at about seven, and a particular warning was issued to residents of the Cape and area islands.

"We'd better get the candles and flashlights out," Menley told Hannah. The sky was completely overcast. The water, dark gray and angry, was now crashing on the shore. The first drops of rain began to beat against the window. She went from room to room, turning on lights.

Hannah began to fuss, and Menley settled her in her crib, then came back downstairs. Outside the wind was increasing in velocity, and she heard the faint call that it made as it whooshed around the house: *Remmmmbaaaa . . .*

Adam phoned at quarter of seven.

"Men, the dinner I was staying for got canceled at the last minute. I grabbed a cab to the airport to make the direct flight. We were on the runway when they got word Barnstable Airport is closed. I'll take the shuttle to Boston and rent a car there. With luck I'll be home between nine-thirty and ten."

Adam was coming home tonight! "That's terrific," Menley said. "We'll weather the storm together."

"Always."

"You haven't had a chance to eat, have you?" she asked.

"No."

"I'll have dinner waiting. It probably will be by candlelight, and not just for effect."

"Men . . ." He hesitated.

"Don't be afraid to ask if I'm all right. Yes, I am."

"Did you watch the tape of Bobby?"

"Twice. Amy watched it with me the second time. Adam, remember how Bobby had just started to say 'Mom-me'?"

"Yes I do. Why, Men?"

"I'm not sure."

"Men, they're boarding. I'll have to go. See you in a little while."

Adam hung up and ran for the departure gate. He had watched the tape that he found in the library of the apartment. "Mom-*me*." It almost sounded as though Bobby were calling Menley to him. Oh Christ, Adam thought, why didn't I get back to the Cape before the airport closed.

100

Nat and Bill Walsh, the investigator, carried Tina's bags into one of the conference rooms. She sat down across from them at the table and pointedly looked at her watch. "If I'm not out of here in half an hour I'll miss my plane," she said. "Where's Fred?"

"He's down the hall," Nat said.

"What's he done?"

"Maybe nothing except be a delivery man. Tina, let's talk about Vivian Carpenter's missing emerald ring."

Her eyes narrowed. "What about it?"

"Then you know about it?"

"Anyone who reads the papers knows about it, to say nothing of all the talk at the inquest."

"Then you know it's not the kind of ring that would be mistaken for another one. Here, let me read the description of it from the insurance company." Nat picked up a sheet of paper. " 'Colombian emerald, five-and-a-half carats, fine deep green with no visible inclusions, two fine emerald-cut diamonds, one-and-a-half carats each, on either side, mounted in platinum, value a quarter of a million dollars.' "

He laid down the paper and shook his head. "You can understand why the Carpenters wanted it back, can't you?"

"I don't know what you're talking about."

"A lot of people seem to think that ring was wrenched off Vivian's finger after she died, Tina. If true, that could get whoever has it now in big, big trouble. Why don't you think about that? Mr. Walsh will stay with you. I'm going in to talk to Fred."

He exchanged a glance with the investigator. Now Walsh could take the fatherly approach with Tina and, most important, he wouldn't leave her alone to go through her luggage. Nat had not missed the quick, nervous dart of Tina's eyes when he mentioned the ring. She thinks it's in her suitcase, he thought.

Fred Hendin looked up when Nat came into the room. "Is Tina here?" he asked quietly.

"Yes," Nat told him.

They had deliberately left Fred alone for nearly an hour. "Coffee?" Nat asked.

"Yes."

"Me too. It's been a long day."

The semblance of a smile passed over Fred Hendin's lips. "I guess you could say that."

Nat waited until the coffee was brought in, then leaned forward, man to man. "Fred, you're not the kind of guy who worries about fingerprints. My guess is that some of your prints are on that package that someone, and I emphasize *someone*, in a dark green Plymouth with the numbers 7 and 3 or 8 on his Massachusetts license plates, placed in the Carpenters' mailbox last night.''

Hendin's expression did not change.

"The way I look at it," Nat said, "someone you know might have had that ring. And you remembered seeing her wear it, or maybe you saw it on her dresser or in her jewelry box, and after the inquest and reading all the papers, you got worried. Maybe you didn't want that person to be tied to what may have been a crime, so you helped her out *by getting the ring out of her possession*. Help me out, Fred. Isn't that the way it was?''

When Hendin remained silent, Nat said, "Fred, if Tina had the ring, she perjured herself at the inquest. That means she goes to prison unless she cuts a deal, which is what she should do. Unless she was in on a plot to kill Vivian Carpenter, she's small potatoes. If you want to help her, start to cooperate, because if you do, Tina will have to follow your very good example.''

Fred Hendin's hands were folded. He seemed to be studying them. Nat knew what he must be thinking. Fred is an honest man. And proud. Every dollar he makes is earned honestly. Nat also reasoned that Fred knew enough about the law to be aware that, since Tina had said under oath she didn't know anything about an emerald ring, she could be in big trouble. That was why Nat was hinting that she could get out of trouble if she cooperated.

Nat also thought he had a pretty good idea of the way Tina thought. She would play every angle until she was backed into a corner. Hopefully they would accomplish that tonight. He knew that eventually they would track down Covey, but he didn't want to wait too long.

"I don't want Tina to get in trouble," Fred said,

finally breaking the silence. "Falling for a snake like Covey shouldn't get anyone into trouble."

It sure as hell got Vivian Carpenter into trouble, Nat thought.

Then Fred Hendin said, "I took the emerald ring from Tina's jewelry box last night."

The investigator, Bill Walsh, kept a sympathetic expression as Tina snapped, "This is like living in Nazi Germany."

"Sometimes we have to ask innocent people to help in our investigations," Walsh said soothingly. "Tina, you keep looking at your luggage. Is there anything I can get for you?"

"No. Listen, if Fred can't drive me to Logan, I have to hire a cab, and that's going to cost me a fortune."

"With this lousy weather, I'll bet your flight is delayed. Want me to check?" Walsh picked up the phone. "What airline and what's your departure time?"

Tina listened while he confirmed her reservation. When he hung up, he was smiling broadly. "At least an hour delay, Tina. We've got plenty of time."

A few minutes later, Nat rejoined them. "Tina," he said, "I'm going to read you the Miranda warning."

Obviously stunned and confused, Tina listened in disbelief, read and signed the paper Nat gave her and waived her right to a lawyer. "I don't need one. I haven't done anything. I'll talk to you."

"Tina, do you know the penalty for being an accessory to murder in this state?"

"Why should I care?"

"At the very least you accepted a valuable ring that may have been torn from a victim's finger."

"That's a lie."

"You had the ring. Fred saw it and returned it to the Carpenters."

"He *what?*" She rushed to the pile of luggage in the corner and grabbed the carry-on bag. In one quick motion she unzipped it and pulled out a book.

One of those fake jewelry boxes, Nat thought, watching as Tina opened it to reveal the hollowed-out interior. He saw the color drain from her face. "The miserable sneak," she muttered.

"Who, Tina?"

"Fred knows where I keep my jewelry," she snapped. "He must have taken . . ." She stopped.

"Taken what, Tina?"

After a long moment, she said, "The pearls and pin and watch and engagement ring he gave me."

"Is that all? Tina, if you don't cooperate we have you cold on perjury."

She stared at Nat for a long moment. Then she sat down and buried her face in her hands.

The stenographer took down Tina's story. After the tragic death of his wife, Scott Covey had turned to her for comfort, and they had fallen in love again. He had found the emerald in his wife's jewelry box and given it to Tina as a token of their future life. But when those ugly rumors started, they had agreed that it would look very bad to admit he had the ring. They also agreed that she should keep seeing Fred until everything blew over.

"Do you have plans to join Scott?" Nat asked.

She nodded. "We're truly very much in love. And when he needed comfort . . ."

"I know," Nat said. "He turned to you." He paused. "Just as a matter of curiosity: You visited him at his house late at night sometimes and parked your car in his garage, didn't you?"

"Fred always left early in the evening. Sometimes I'd pay Scott a visit."

Tina was crying now. Nat wasn't sure if it was because she was beginning to see the serious implications of the questions or because she hadn't gotten away.

"Where is Scott now?"

"On his way to Colorado. He'll meet me there at my brother's house."

"Do you expect to hear from him before then?"

"No. He thought it was better to wait. He said that the Carpenters were powerful enough to have his car phone bugged."

Nat and the assistant district attorneys soberly discussed Tina's testimony. "Sure, we've got enough for a grand jury, but if she sticks to that story about how Covey gave her the ring after he found it—and she may well believe that it is true—we've got nothing concrete, nothing more damaging than his lying about the ring having been lost," one assistant said. "After his wife died, it was Covey's ring to give away."

The cellular phone in Nat's pocket began to ring. It was Walter Orr. "So how much do you want to know about that boat?" He sounded triumphant.

Don't play games, Nat thought. Trying to keep the irritation out of his voice, he asked, "What can you tell me?"

"It's an inboard/outboard motor, about twenty, twenty-three feet. There's a guy sunning on the deck."

"Alone?" Nat asked.

"Yes. Looks like the remains of lunch beside him."

"Is there a name on the boat?"

The response was just what Nat had been hoping to hear.

"*Viv's Toy*," Orr told him.

101

The plane circled Logan Airport for ten minutes before finally landing. Adam rushed out of the plane, then raced along the corridor to the terminal. A long line of people was waiting at the car-rental desk. It took another ten minutes before he had secured the necessary papers and flagged down a courtesy van to the pickup area. He called Menley again to say that he was on his way.

She was distracted. "I'm holding a flashlight and trying to light candles," she told him. "We just lost the lights. No, it's all right. They went on again."

Finally he was inching his way through the massive traffic that led into the Sumner Tunnel. It was quarter of nine before he was on Route 3, the road that led directly to the Cape.

Menley sounded perfectly calm, Adam thought, trying to reassure himself. But should I phone Elaine and ask her and John to go over and stay with her until I get home?

No. He knew Menley would never forgive him if he did that.

But why do I have this gut-level sense that there's a problem? he asked himself.

It was the same queasy feeling he had had the day

of the accident. He had played golf that afternoon and reached home in time to pick up the phone when the policeman called.

He could still hear that restrained, sympathetic voice: "Mr. Nichols, I'm afraid I have bad news."

102

*A*fter Adam called from the airport, Menley went upstairs and checked on Hannah. The baby was restless, though she did not awaken. Teething or just the noise of the wind? Menley wondered as she smoothed the blankets and tucked them around her daughter. She could hear the mournful shriek of the wind wrapping around the house, sounding more and more like a voice crying, *"Rememmmmmmberrrr . . ."*

Of course, it was her imagination, the powers of suggestion at work, she told herself firmly.

Downstairs, she could hear a shutter flapping. Giving the baby's back a final pat, Menley hurried down to try to secure the loose shutter. It was on one of the windows in the library. She opened the window, and gusts of rain drenched her as she reached out and pulled both the shutters over the glass and fastened them together.

The driving must be terrible, she thought. Adam, be careful. Had she said that to him? She realized suddenly she had been so busy resenting his concern for her that she had forgotten to show concern for him.

She tried to settle down, but was too restless to watch television. Adam wouldn't be home until at least nine-thirty, another hour and a half away. She decided to try to arrange the books on the library shelves in some sort of order.

Carrie Bell had obviously dusted them since Menley had looked through them a few weeks ago. But the pages of many of the oldest ones were swollen and torn. One of the past owners of the house had obviously been interested in acquiring secondhand books. The penciled prices on the inside cover of many of them were as low as ten cents.

She thumbed through some of the books as she organized them. The sporadic reading helped her to ignore the weather. Finally it was nine o'clock and time to start dinner. The book she was holding had been published in 1911 and was a dry history of sailing ships, illustrated with sketches. She knew she had glanced at it a few days after they had arrived in the house. And then, just as she was about to close it, she saw the familiar sketch of Andrew and Mehitabel on the ship. The caption read, "A ship captain and wife in the early seventeenth century, by an unknown artist."

Menley felt a great weight fall from her. I did see that picture and subconsciously copied it, she thought. She laid the book open on her desk under the pictures she had taped to the wall. The lights flickered again, dimming for a moment. In the deep shadows of the room, she had the unsettling feeling that the sketch she had made of Andrew with his ravaged, grief-filled expression in this light somehow resembled Adam.

As Adam is going to look very soon, flashed through her mind.

Ridiculous, Menley thought, and went into the kitchen where she took the precaution of lighting all the candles in case the electricity failed for good.

103

Adam turned from Route 6 onto Route 137. Another seven miles, he told himself. Twenty minutes at the most. Provided you move it, he fumed at the driver several cars ahead who was traveling at a snail's pace. He didn't dare try to pass, though. There was moderate traffic coming in the other direction, and the roads were so wet he would probably cause a head-on collision.

Only another six miles, he said to himself a few minutes later, but his sense of urgency was steadily increasing. Now he was driving through whole sections that were in total darkness.

104

Menley switched on the radio, twisted the dial and found the Chatham station that played forties music. She raised an eyebrow in surprise as the Benny Goodman orchestra went into the opening bars of "Remember." A particularly appropriate song, she thought. She picked up a serrated knife and began to slice tomatoes for a salad. "But you forgot to remember," the vocalist warbled.

The whooshing sound of the wind was growing stronger again. *"Reeememmmmmmberrrrr."*

Menley shivered as she reached for the celery. Adam will be here soon, she reminded herself.

There was a sudden noise. What was that? Had a door blown open? Or a window? Something was wrong.

She snapped off the radio. The baby! Was she crying? Was that a cry or a muffled, gagging sound? Menley hurried to the counter, grabbed the monitor and held it to her ear. She heard another throttled gasp and then nothing. The baby was choking!

She rushed from the kitchen into the hall and toward the staircase. Her feet barely touched the stairs as she raced to the second floor, and a moment later she was at the doorway of the nursery. There was no sound coming from the crib. "Hannah, Hannah," she cried.

Hannah was lying on her stomach, her arms outstretched, her body motionless. Frantically, Menley leaned down, turning the baby as she picked her up. Then her eyes widened in horror.

The china head of the antique doll rested against her hand. The painted face stared back at her.

Menley tried to scream, but no sound came from her lips. And then from behind her, a voice whispered, "I'm sorry, Menley. It's all over."

She spun around. Scott Covey was standing beside the cradle, a gun in his hand.

The cradle. Hannah was in it. Hannah, stirring, beginning to whimper. Relief flooded through Menley, followed by a surge of terror. She felt suddenly light-headed, besieged by a sense of unreality. Scott Covey? Why? "What are you doing here?" she managed to ask through lips so dry she almost could not form the words. "I don't understand. How did you get in?"

Covey's expression was the same as it always had been: courteous, attentive. He was wearing a sweat suit and sneakers. But they were dry. Why wasn't he drenched? Menley wondered.

"It doesn't matter how I got in, Menley," he said pleasantly. "The problem is that it took me longer to get here than I expected, but since Adam's in New York it doesn't matter."

Adam. Had he been talking to Adam?

It was as though he could read her thoughts. "Elaine told me, Menley."

"Elaine? I don't understand." Her mind was racing. What is going on? This can't be happening. This is a nightmare! Scott Covey? Why? She and Adam had befriended him. She had urged Adam to defend him. Adam had saved him from a murder charge. And

Elaine? What did Scott have to do with Elaine? It all seemed so unreal.

But the gun in his hand was real.

Hannah whimpered louder, starting to wake up. Menley saw the annoyed look on Covey's face. He glanced down at the baby, and the hand with the gun moved.

"No!" she cried. Bending down, she grabbed Hannah from the cradle. Just as she pulled her close, the lights went out, and she ran from the room.

In the dark she rushed for the staircase. She had to focus. She knew every inch of the house. Scott didn't. If she could only get to the kitchen door before he found her. The ignition key was on the hook beside it. The station wagon was right outside. She only needed a minute. She ran down the sides of the steps, praying they wouldn't creak.

He wasn't behind her. He must have turned the other way; maybe he was looking for her in the other bedrooms. Please God, please God, just give me this one minute, she prayed.

A clap of thunder broke over the house, and Hannah began to scream.

The rush of the train, Bobby's cry, her own voice screaming.

Menley pushed the memory aside. She heard swift footsteps overhead. He was coming. Hugging Hannah tightly to her, she ran through the hall and into the kitchen. She raced across the room, wishing passionately she had not lit the candles. They were burning all too brightly now. Glancing over her shoulder, she saw Covey in the entrance from the hall. His expression was different now. His eyes were narrowed, his lips a knifelike slash.

Her fingers were closing over the car key when he caught her, pulling her roughly against him. "Menley, it's you, or it's you and the baby. Take your choice.

Put her back in the cradle and come with me, because if you don't put her back, Adam will lose both of you."

His voice was quiet, level, almost matter-of-fact. It would have been easier if he had been nervous, if there had been some hesitancy. Then she might be able to reason with him. Why was he doing this? She kept trying to understand. Yet clearly he meant what he said. She had to get him away from Hannah.

"I'll put her back," she promised desperately. "I'll go with you."

He picked up one of the candles. She felt the gun pressed against her back as she led the way up to the nursery and laid the frightened, crying baby in the crib.

"The cradle," he said. "Put her in the cradle. And put the doll back in the crib."

"Why?" Delay, she thought, stall for time. Keep him talking. Adam can't be far away now. *Adam, hurry. Please hurry.*

"Because you're crazy, Menley, that's why. Crazy and hallucinating and depressed. Everyone, even Adam, is going to be so grateful that you didn't take the baby with you when you committed suicide."

"No. No. I won't."

"Either put the baby in the cradle or bring her with you. It's your choice, Menley. Either way, we are going now."

She had to get him away from Hannah. Alone, if he was taking her away in a car, she might be able to jump out, might be able to make a run for it. Somehow she might still save herself, but not here, not with Hannah in danger. She would have to leave Hannah here.

Menley laid the baby down, bringing fresh wails from the frightened infant. "Sshhh . . ." She pushed the cradle to start it rocking and looked up. "I'll go with you," she said, willing herself to be calm. Then suddenly she had to bite back a shriek.

A section of the wall behind Scott Covey was opening. A musty, stale odor was drifting in from the space behind it. Covey beckoned to her. "This way, Menley."

105

As rain slashed against the windshield, Adam drove down the darkened main street of Chatham. He could not see more than a few feet ahead and forced himself not to speed. The road turned right. Now it ran along the ocean.

He passed the lighthouse. In five minutes he'd be home. Morris Island was just ahead. And then he came to the dip where Little Beach and Morris Island roads joined. It was flooded and the road was closed.

Without hesitating Adam drove through the barrier. As clearly as though she was in the car, he sensed that Menley was calling him.

106

The opening in the nursery wall wasn't more than a foot and a half wide, Menley realized, as Scott Covey nudged her through it.

"Go ahead, Menley," he said.

She heard a faint tap as the door closed behind her, and Hannah's cries became muffled. The candle's flickering light cast crazy shadows about the narrow space. Scott blew it out as he picked up a flashlight he had left lying on a pile of debris, its beam piercing the shadows of a small room piled with rotting clothes and broken furniture.

The musty odor was overpowering. It was the same smell she had noticed several times in Hannah's room and in the minister's cabinet downstairs. "You've been here before," she cried. "You've been in the baby's room other times."

"I've been here as little as possible, Menley," Covey told her. "There's a ladder in the corner. I'll follow you down it. Don't try anything."

"I won't," she said quickly, trying desperately to clear her head, to overcome this sense of unreality. He doesn't know Adam is coming, Menley thought. Maybe I can get him talking. Maybe distract him. Trip him. I'm stronger than he knows, she thought. I might be able to surprise him, get the gun away from him.

But could she use it? Yes. I don't want to die, she thought. I want to live and be with Adam and Hannah. I want the rest of my life. She felt anger surging through her.

She looked around her, taking in all that she could in the dim light. This place. It was what she had suspected. There *was* a hidden room in this house. More than just a room, in fact. Between the chimneys, the entire core of the house was storage space. Were these piles of rotting rags part of the cargo from the *Thankful*? she wondered.

Play for time, she told herself. Even though she knew Hannah must still be crying, she could not hear her. These walls were so thick that if she died in here, no one would ever find her.

If she died in here.

Was that Covey's plan? she asked herself.

"I'm not going to get out of here alive, am I?" she said.

"Aren't you?" He smiled. "What makes you think that?"

Menley felt a surge of pure hatred. Now he was toying with her.

But then he said, "Menley, I honestly am sorry about this. I'm doing what I have to do." His voice was completely sincere.

"Why? At least tell me *why*."

"You can believe this or not," he said. "I didn't want to kill Vivian. She was crazy about me, always giving me presents when she came to Florida, but never a dime after we were married. No shared bank account, no assets in my name, no cash. Anything I wanted, she'd buy me, but would you believe, I had to ask her for every nickel I spent?" He shook his head in disbelief.

"And then she wanted me to sign something renouncing any interest in her estate if the marriage didn't last at least ten years. She said that would prove I loved her, that she'd heard people in the beauty parlor whispering that I'd married her for her money."

"And so you killed her?"

"Yes. Reluctantly. I mean, she wasn't a bad person, but she was making a fool of me."

"But what has that got to do with *me?* I helped you. I felt sorry for you. I urged Adam to defend you."

"You can blame Adam for being here now."

"Adam! Does Adam know you're here?" Even as she asked, she knew that wasn't possible.

"We've got to get moving. Menley, I'll make it simple. Elaine has always been crazy about Adam. A couple of times over the years she thought he was falling for her, but it never worked out. Last year when she thought you two were breaking up, she was sure he'd turn to her. Then he went rushing back to you, and she gave up. After that, she decided it was useless. But when Adam phoned about renting that place in Eastham, and she found out how emotionally unstable you were, she hit on this plan."

"Are you telling me you're doing this for Elaine? Why, Scott? I don't understand."

"No, I'm doing it for me. Elaine recognized my boat in that aerial photo of this place. She realized I was alone on the boat at 3:15, and that blew my story about what had happened to Vivian. She was ready to use that information. So we made a deal. She'd be my star character witness. And I'd help her try to drive you crazy. Adam had told her about your flashbacks and depression, and she figured that this old house with its legends and hidden rooms—which she had learned about from some workmen—would be the perfect place to push you over the edge. She planned it all; I just helped her carry it out.

"She brought me here to the house, showed me around, explained what she wanted done. That was the day that crazy woman wandered in and followed us up here. She's just lucky her husband came along when I took her for a walk in the ocean."

Menley shivered. He might have been talking about a walk along the shore. That's what Phoebe was trying to remember, to warn me, she thought.

Keep him talking. Keep him talking.

"The ring. What about the emerald? Where is that?"

He smiled. "Tina. She's quite a hot little number. And giving her the ring was a stroke of genius. In case they ever do try to indict me, she's an accessory. She'll have to keep her mouth shut. Elaine and I would have made a good team. We think the same way. She's been in and out of here at night. I guess she's pulled some stuff that's gotten under your skin, like dubbing your son's voice from the tape and playing it with the sound of the train for you at night. It certainly worked. The word around Chatham is that you're close to a total breakdown."

Where was Adam? Menley thought frantically. Would she hear him when he came? Not in here. She saw Covey glance over at the ladder. "Come on, Menley. You know it all now."

He waved the gun. Trying to follow the beam of the flashlight, she picked her way across the rough, uneven flooring. She tripped as she reached the gaping hole where she could see the top rung of the ladder. Covey caught her before she fell.

"We don't want any marks on you," he said. "It was hard enough explaining the bruise on Vivian's finger."

The wood of the ladder was rough, and a splinter stabbed her palm. She felt with her feet for the rungs, descending carefully. Could she drop to the next level, somehow escape him? No. If she twisted an ankle, then she really would be helpless. Wait, she cautioned herself, wait.

She reached the area on the main floor. It was wider than that above; but there was debris scattered all about. Covey was right behind her. He stepped down from the final rung. "Take a look at this," he said, pointing the flashlight to what seemed to be a mound of rags. Then he kicked it with his foot. "There are bones under there. Elaine found them the day she showed me this place. Somebody's been buried in here for a long time. We talked about that being a good plan for you, Menley, to leave you here. But then if you just disappeared, Elaine was afraid Adam might spend the rest of his life hoping you'd come back."

She felt a moment of hope. He was not going to kill her in here. Outside, she might have a chance. As he shoved her ahead of him, she looked back at the bones. Phoebe had said Tobias Knight was in this house. Was that what she had meant?

"Over there." Holding the flashlight, Covey gestured toward an opening in the floor. She could smell dampness from a few feet below.

"Let yourself down slowly. There's no ladder." He waited until she had dropped through. Then he carefully let himself down beside her, closing the heavy trapdoor behind him, sealing the opening. "Stand over there."

Menley realized they were in a narrow storage area of the basement. Covey played the flashlight back and forth. A large yellow slicker was spread out on the ground where they had dropped through the hole, a pair of boots next to the slicker. That was why his clothing wasn't wet, she realized. He had come in this way.

With a swift movement, Covey picked up the

slicker, and rolled the boots in it and threw the bundle under his arm.

Menley sensed a change in him. Now he wanted to get it over with. He prodded her toward the wide basement door and pushed it up. "They'll think you went out this way," he said. "Makes you look a little crazier."

They'd think she left the baby alone and wandered out into a storm. Where was Covey's car? Maybe he was going to drive her somewhere. In the car she might have a chance to jump out or force him to crash. She turned toward the driveway, but he took her arm. "This way, Menley."

They were heading for the beach. He was going to drown her, she realized suddenly.

"Wait, Menley," he said. "Give me your sweater. In case your body never turns up, they'll at least know what happened."

The rain was pounding down, and the wind tore at her clothes. Her hair was drenched, falling forward in her face, covering her eyes. She tried to shake it back. Scott stopped, released her right hand. "Hold up your arm, Menley."

Numbly she obeyed. In a quick gesture, he ripped her sweater over her head and pulled it free, first of her left hand and then the right. Dropping the sweater on the ground, he grasped her arm and forced her down the path that led to the bluff and then to the sea. Tomorrow, with the torrents of rain, there wouldn't be a trace of his footsteps.

They'll find my sweater, Menley thought, and think I committed suicide. Would her body wash in? Vivian's had. Maybe they were counting on that. Adam. Adam, I need you.

The waves were slashing against the shore. The undertow would pull her down and out to sea, and she wouldn't have a chance. She stumbled as he hurried her down the steep path. Try as she might, she could not pull away from his viselike grip.

The full force of the storm struck them as they reached the place where only yesterday she had lounged on a blanket with Adam and Hannah. Now there was no beach, only the waves, breaking upon the land, eroding it, hungry to reclaim it.

"I'm really sorry, Menley," Scott Covey said. "But drowning isn't that bad. It only took Vivy a minute or so. Just relax. It'll be over soon."

He pushed her into the water and, crouching, held her under the angry surf.

107

*A*dam saw the flickering candlelight in the kitchen as he rushed into the house. Finding no one there, he grabbed a flashlight and raced up the stairs.

"Menley," he shouted as he ran into the nursery. "Menley!"

He shone the light around the room.

"Oh God," Adam cried as the beam reflected on the china face of the antique doll.

And then a whimper came from behind him. He turned and played the light around the room until it found the gently rocking cradle. Hannah was there! Thank God! he thought. Hannah was all right!

But Menley—

Adam turned and ran to their bedroom. It was empty. He raced down the stairs and went from room to room.

Menley was gone!

It wasn't like Menley to leave Hannah alone. She would never do that. But she wasn't in the house!

What had happened? Had she heard Bobby's voice again? He knew he shouldn't have let her watch that tape. Shouldn't have left her alone.

Outside! She must have gone outside! Frantically, Adam rushed to the front door and opened it. The rain drenched him immediately as he stepped outside and began calling to her. "Menley!" he cried. "Menley, where are you?"

He raced across the front lawn, headed toward the path to the beach. Slipping in the heavy, wet grass, he fell. The flashlight flew out of his hand and disappeared over the edge.

The beach! She couldn't have gone down there, he thought frantically. Still he had to look. She had to be somewhere.

"Menley," he called out again. "Menley, where are you?"

He reached the path and clambered and slid down it. Below him the surf was roaring, while all about him was darkness. And then a bright flash of lightning illuminated the angry ocean.

Suddenly he saw her, her body surfacing on the crest of a huge wave.

108

Menley had to will herself not to panic. She had held her breath until her lungs were bursting, forced her body to go limp when she was wild to struggle. She felt the water surging about them, Covey's strong hands holding her, pressing her down. And then he let her go. Quickly she turned her head, gulping air. Why had he released her? Did he think she was dead? Was he still there?

Then suddenly she understood. Adam! She heard Adam, calling out to her. Calling her name!

She started to swim just as a wave crashed over her. Momentarily stunned, she felt herself being pulled out by the powerful undertow.

Oh God, she thought, don't let me drown. Choking and gasping, she tried to tread water. The mountainous waves were everywhere, pulling her, sucking her down, tossing her forward. She forced herself to hold her breath when the water closed over her, to fight her way back up to the surface. Her only hope was to get into a cresting wave that would carry her back to land.

She swallowed more water, then flailed her arms and legs. Don't panic, she thought. Get into a wave.

She felt a surge building behind her, lifting her body up to the surface.

Now! she thought. Now! Swim! Fight! Don't let it pull you back.

Suddenly a bright flash of lightning illuminated everything around her—the sea, the bluff. Adam! There was Adam, sliding down the steep path toward her.

As the thunder crashed around her, she threw her body into the wave and rode it toward the shore, toward Adam.

He was only a few feet away from her as she felt the strong pull of the undertow drawing her back.

Then he was with her, his arm firmly around her, pulling her back to the shore.

109

*A*t eleven o'clock Amy and her father were saying good night to Elaine. The evening had been less than successful. Elaine had rehashed with Amy the importance of never taking anything without permission, and certainly never giving that object to another person. Her father had agreed, but she had gone on about it until even he had said, "I think we've milked this subject dry, Elaine."

They had been late eating dinner because the electricity failed for more than an hour, and the roast wasn't done. As they were finally finishing dessert, Elaine brought up Menley Nichols again.

"You must understand that Adam is very worried about Menley. She's in a state of serious depression, and seeing the tape of her little boy might upset her terribly, plus she's alone for two nights. That's a big worry for Adam."

"I don't think she's depressed," Amy said. "She was sad when she watched the tape, but we talked about it, and Mrs. Nichols said that you should be grateful when you've had the chance to love someone wonderful, even if you didn't have them very long. She told me that her mother always said she'd rather have been married to her father for twelve years than to someone else for seventy years."

Then Amy looked at her father and added, "I certainly agree with her." With some satisfaction she saw a flush come over his face. She was hurt and irritated at him for taking Elaine's part so vehemently about the tape. But then, I guess that's how it's going to be from now on, she thought.

Conversation throughout the entire meal had been strained. Plus Elaine seemed awfully nervous. Even Amy's father had noticed it. Finally he asked her if anything was wrong.

That was when Elaine dropped a bombshell. "John, I've been thinking," she said. "I believe we should delay the wedding for a while. I want it to be perfect for us, and that's just not going to be possible while Amy is clearly so unhappy."

You don't give a damn whether I'm happy or unhappy, Amy thought. I bet there's more to it than that. "Elaine, as you've said all summer, in another few weeks I'm going to be in college and starting my own adult life. You're marrying my father, not me. My only concern is my father's happiness, and that should be your concern as well."

Elaine's bombshell had come just as they were about to leave. Amy liked the dignified way her dad said, "I think this is something that you and I should talk about at another time, Elaine. I'll call you tomorrow."

When Elaine opened the front door, they saw a police car with its lights flashing pulling up in her driveway. "What can be wrong?" Elaine asked.

Amy sensed something odd about Elaine's voice. It sounded strained, as though she were frightened.

Nat Coogan got out of the squad car and paused for a moment, looking at Elaine Atkins as she stood in the doorway. He had just gotten home when the call came from the station. Scott Covey had gone to Morris Island and tried to murder Adam Nichols' wife. He had run away when Nichols showed up and had been caught at a roadblock on Route 6.

Now it was Nat Coogan's extreme pleasure to be the one to arrest Elaine Atkins. Ignoring the pelting rain, he went up the walk and stepped onto the porch. "Miss Atkins," he said. "I have a warrant for your arrest. I'll read you your rights, and then I'll have to ask you to please come along with me."

Amy and her father stared at Elaine as her face drained of all color. "That's ridiculous," she said, her voice shocked and angry.

Nat pointed to the driveway. "Scott Covey is in that car. We're just taking him in. He was so sure of himself, he told Menley Nichols the whole story of your interesting deal with him and all about how you wanted her out of the way so you could have Adam Nichols to yourself. You're just lucky that Covey didn't succeed in drowning her. This way you'll only have to face charges of attempted murder. But you will need a good lawyer, and I don't think you'd better count on Adam Nichols to defend you."

John Nelson gasped. "Elaine, what's going on? What's he talking about? Nat, surely you're—"

"Oh, shut up, John!" Elaine snapped. She looked at him with contempt.

There was a long silence while they stared at each other. Then Amy felt her father take her arm. "Come on, honey," he said, "we've been around here long enough. Let's go home."

110

When Menley awoke on Thursday morning, sunbeams were bouncing off the windowsill, darting over the wide-planked floor. Her mind filled with memories of last night and quickly skipped to the moment when she knew she was safe, when they reached the house, and Adam had called the police while she ran to Hannah.

After the police finally left and they were alone, they took turns holding each other and holding Hannah. Then, both too weary to even think about eating, they brought the cradle into their room, unable to leave Hannah alone in the nursery until the storage area was cleaned out and permanently sealed.

Menley looked around. Adam and Hannah were still sleeping. Her eyes moved from one to the other, marveling at the miracle of being with them, of knowing that she was strong and whole.

I can go on with my life, she thought. Mehitabel and Andrew never had a second chance.

The police had looked into the storage area last night, saying they would be back to photograph it for evidence in the trials. They had examined the skeleton also. The silver buckles resting among the foot bones bore the initials T.K. Tobias Knight.

The side of the skull was caved in, as if by a heavy blow. My guess is that Captain Freeman had surprised Tobias here, Menley mused, and learning, or guessing, the true reason for his late-night visits to the house, struck him down for fostering the lie that had destroyed Mehitabel. Then he left the body here with the stolen cargo. He must have surmised the truth of his wife's innocence. We know he was out of his mind with grief when he sailed into the storm.

Phoebe and I were right. Mehitabel was innocent. She died protesting that fact and longing for her baby. When I write her story I'm going to put Phoebe's name on it too. It was the story she wanted so much to tell.

She felt Adam's arm go around her.

He turned her toward him. "Did I mention last night that you're a terrific swimmer?" he asked. Then the light tone disappeared from his voice. "Men, when I think that I was so obtuse about everything and that you almost died because of me, I could kill myself."

She put her finger on his lips. "Don't ever say that. When you told me there was no train whistle in the tape of Bobby, I began to suspect that something was going on. But you didn't know what I had been hearing, so I can't blame you for thinking I was crazy."

Hannah began to stir. Menley reached down and picked her up, bringing her into the bed with them. "Quite a night, wasn't it, Toots?" she asked.

* * *

Nat Coogan phoned as they were finishing breakfast. "I hate to bother you people, but we're having a struggle keeping the media away. Would you consider talking to them after our people finish the investigation?"

"We'd better," Adam replied. "Tell them we need a little more time to ourselves, then we'll see them at two o'clock."

Moments later, however, the phone rang again—a television station wanting to set up an interview. That call was followed by others, so many that they finally disconnected the phone, plugging it in only long enough for Menley to call Jan Paley, the Spragues and Amy.

When she hung up from her last call, she was smiling. "Amy sounds like a different person," she said. "Her dad keeps telling her that he wished he had half her common sense. I told her I feel the same way. She knew all along that Elaine was a phony."

"A very dangerous phony," Adam said quietly.

"Amy wants to baby-sit for us tomorrow night—for free! Her dad's paying for the whole car."

"We'll take her up on it. How is Phoebe doing?"

"Henry told her that we were safe and he was proud of her for trying to warn us. He's sure that she might have understood a little of what he was saying." Menley paused. "I'm so sorry for them."

"I know." Adam put his arm around her.

"And Jan's coming over. She said she would bring lunch makings and offered to pick up the mail, so I took her up on it."

When the police arrived to photograph the hidden room, Adam and Menley took chairs and Hannah's carriage out to the bluff. The water was calm now, and inviting, with gentle waves breaking on a shore that was in surprisingly good shape, considering the severity of the storm the night before. Menley knew that from now on, if she dreamed about that night, the dream would always end with Adam's hand closing over hers.

She looked back at the house and up at the widow's walk. The metal on the chimney was gleaming, the sunbeams bouncing off it through the shifting shadows cast by occasional clouds. Did that really cause an optical illusion that day Amy thought she saw me? she wondered.

"What are you thinking?" Adam asked.

"I'm thinking that when I write Mehitabel's story, I'm going to say that she was a presence in the house, awaiting her innocence to be proven and her baby's return."

"And if she were still a presence here, would you want to live in this house?" Adam said teasingly.

"I almost wish she were," Menley said. "We are going to buy it, aren't we? Hannah will love growing up summers on the Cape the way you did. And I love this house. It's the first place where I've ever really felt a deep sense of home."

"Of course we're buying it."

At noon, a few minutes after the police photographers left, Jan arrived. Her silent embrace spoke volumes. "The only mail for you was a letter from Ireland." Menley ripped it open immediately. "It's from Phyllis," she said. "Oh look at this, she really has done some heavy research on the McCarthys."

There was a sheaf of genealogical records, birth and death certificates, copies of newspaper items, a few faded photographs.

"You dropped her note," Adam said. He picked it up and handed it to her.

It read:

Dear Menley,

I'm so excited. I wanted you to see this right away. I've traced your family back to the first Menley, and it's a wonderful story. She was raised from infancy by her father's cousins, the Longfords, in Connemara. There's no record of where she was born, but the date was recorded as 1705. At seventeen she married Squire Adrian McCarthy of Galway, and they had four children. Part of the foundation of their mansion can still be seen. It overlooks the ocean.

She must have been quite a beauty (see enclosed snapshot of her portrait), and I see a distinct family resemblance between you and her.

But, Menley, this is the best part, and it's something Hannah might want to keep in mind if she decides that she likes your name better than hers but doesn't want to be known as "young Menley" or "little Menley."

The reason for your unusual name is that when she was little, your ancestor could not pronounce her real name and called herself Menley.

The name she was given at birth was Remember . . .

Visit the
Simon & Schuster Web site:
www.SimonSays.com

and sign up for our
mystery e-mail updates!

Keep up on the latest
new releases, author appearances,
news, chats, special offers, and more!
We'll deliver the information
right to your inbox — if it's new,
you'll know about it.

SIMON & SCHUSTER
A VIACOM COMPANY
www.SimonSays.com

POCKET BOOKS   POCKET STAR BOOKS